CW00432120

A Late Awakening

Noel Stevenson

To Joseph.
Thank you for believing in me.

Trainspotter

Down the line things look different.
The countryside flickers by
And passengers have come and gone
So now this train is not the same.
Different places; different faces.

The moving scenery produces an illusion.
"All change" is the porter's call,
And so it seems to me, centre stage
As the sets move and the lighting flares and dims,
Reality is neither here ahead or left behind.

How many moments vie to make their claim?
Images enhanced or air-brushed out,
A muffled soundtrack playing somewhere still
Blurring in a tinnitus accompaniment:
". . . don't know where, don't know when . . ."

The traveller, the trainspotter,
Remembering still the days of steam
But moving on, all life a brief encounter
Glimpsed in swirl of steam and smoke,
Voices drowned in the engines whistle clank and
roar.

Did I meet you once before?
How familiar you seem tugging at my dreams.
Ah yes, I have it now. You were always there.
A gas-lit station,
Something in your eye.

Chapter 1

She was fifty-four when John died. An awkward age. Amanda was not inclined to believe the pinhead crap about sixty being the new forty, or whatever it was the old age defiers liked to pedal. She was in good shape, successful and more than well provided for. Things could be much worse. But there was no getting away from it: it was inconvenient.

She was on her third coffee of the day, mid-morning, showered but still not dressed. The elegant morning room dutifully received the morning sun. The vast manicured garden was a picture viewed through the wisteria festooned wall of sliding glass which had replaced the ancient Georgian French windows. The wisteria, however, remained.

A copy of Vogue lay discarded on the French marquetry coffee table, a gift to John from Amanda for his fortieth birthday, she remembered, absently brushing the polished patina with her likewise polished nails. She picked up the already microscopically examined magazine only to put it down again, opting instead to light her third cigarette.

Amanda hadn't smoked when John was alive. He'd persuaded her to stop before they were married, over twenty years before. John, the fitness fanatic, the health freak, ten years her junior, and here she was, his widow, vengeful in her high tar rebellion. She liked the irony and smiled to herself, an angry smile, the smile of someone who has been abandoned.

It would have to be said that the aforementioned elegance of the room was nothing if not enhanced by its occupant. There are certain women, so it is said, who improve with age. If the inevitable ebb tide had in recent years begun, the visible evidence would have been hard to find, and Amanda, lounging in her plain silk robe, unmade up and hair yet in some disarray, looked good. She knew this, of course, but it didn't help.

Amanda had no questions. She wasn't concerned about 'finding somebody' (or not), or how she would fill her diminishing days. But she was aware that they were diminishing, that she was on the downward slope. She was aware that she had lost her investment. Stocks can go down as well as up, and hers had gone completely. The life she had constructed with John was gone. She did not have her half intact. It wasn't like that, and she contemplated a new landscape where her familiar partner, her constant reference point was no longer to be seen. She was still the person she had been before: a successful writer, wealth, possessions, friends, and the accumulated experience and knowledge of fifty-six years. She *was* the same person she had been before. Except that she was not. Her investment had failed when John's heart had stopped. Her self-view and connection with the world about her had shifted. Everything had changed.

Over two years had passed. Measured in fathoms Amanda's grief would not have plumbed the depths. On the Richter scale it would not have been sufficiently violent to bring down buildings. But measured in longevity her grief was impressive.

There was a dislocation, disorientated as if the map of her life had vapourised leaving only tantalising flakes of burnt paper. Those who thought her hard, who were surprised by her cool acceptance of her husband's loss, did not see the private tremors, the aftershocks. They saw only her outward control, not the obsessive compulsive need to hold on which drove her, her commitments all kept, not a single appointment missed, her latest novel completed and submitted ahead of time, published reviewed and selling well. The passage of time, if it had not healed as it was meant to, had seen Amanda become accustomed to her situation. But nothing was the same.

The phone rang and Amanda spoke without bothering to look at the caller display.

'Hello Trish.'

'Hello Darling, this is your morning call!'

'Well it *is* morning and it *is* a call, so full marks.'

'Oh, tetchy tetchy! What are you up to, assuming you *are* up. Are you?'

'Well, let me see. I've just finished polishing the

silver and am about to run a duster over the porcelain figurines. I *was* going to wash them in warm soapy water but would you believe it, one of my marigolds has a tear in the thumb.'

'Alright alright I get the picture: dressing gown, cigs, coffee, without even any foundation on!'
Trish's mock horror forced a reluctant smile.

'Well I *have* had a shower, and anyway, it's Saturday.'

'So?'

'So it's the weekend and traditionally one lounges about at the weekend. That's what weekends are for darling. Anyway, I didn't want to get dressed yet,' she teased, lowering her voice to confide in a husky half whisper, 'Jesus will be here soon . . .'

Jesus was the unlikely (but not in Spain) name for Amanda's young Spanish gardener, who's employ made her the envy of her friends. In Spain it was pronounced '*Hay*sus', but not by Amanda et al, much as many did not see the logic in referring to Bombay as Mumbai or Burma as Myanmar. It was the particular prerogative of the British elite to believe that the English names for people and places were indeed what they were called, regardless of the native's own appellation. Amanda did not herself fall in with such facile snobbery, but in any case Jesus was always Jesus. His mention had the anticipated effect on Trish:

'Oh Amanda don't! Or rather *do*! Think of it, just what you need. Rather a nice take on 'Jesus loves you,' don't you think?'

Amanda was suddenly bored and felt guilty both for having encouraged the subject and for the resulting impatience in her voice: 'Anyway, what do you want Trish . . . sorry, I wasn't being . . . but I actually have to get a shift on now as I'm on the train to London at one for a book signing.'

'Oh no.' Trish whinged. 'I've arranged with Marcia to have lunch at Alfredo's and we were hoping you'd come.'

Amanda relented. Trish had been a brick since John's death, despite her sometimes irritating mother hen routine. She softened. 'Sorry darling, would have been nice but no can do. What about Monday?' And that was that. Monday it was and with a glance at her watch Amanda was hastily clattering her cup into the sink and heading up the stairs to get ready for her adoring public.

Having shaken off her morning sloth Amanda was brisk and business-like as she prepared for the day. Her book signing was at Waterstones on Oxford Rd, a routine event for her, but one which she was looking forward to not least because she anticipated having plenty time afterwards to browse the shops. Her weakness was clothes and particularly shoes. She avoided sales with the hoi polloi buzzing like honey bees around nectar bargains, preferring the most expensive stores, attended upon like royalty by courteous smiling minions. She invariably returned their courtesy it has to be said, whilst remaining suitably aloof. Amanda knew her place.

But first there was business. And she looked 'business' in her fitted cream suit, locking the front door to the comforting beep of the burglar alarm and turning to see Jesus, emerged from a thicket of blazing azaleas and rhododendrons like the lone emissary of a lost tribe. He was standing in the border, secateurs rather than blowpipe in hand and smiling broadly.

'Hola.'

'Hola yourself. Sorry Jesus have to dash.'

Jesus said nothing and raised his hand in a comical wave as Amanda strode to the car, aware of his eyes tracking her, as he waited for the inevitable bonus that a woman with a short skirt getting into a car is liable to bestow.

As she eased the Merc along the crunching gravel, Amanda thought about Jesus and Trish's lascivious remarks. It amazed as much as amused her. He was just a boy. She noted his always shy but always appraising and approving look. Continental men were always more honest about looking than their more constrained and indeed furtive British peers.

It was fine with her. It was hers by right, to have him look and desire her. Amanda had never misunderstood her effect on men, but viewed it with patient amusement, a somewhat superior neutrality which might easily have teetered on disdain but was rescued by the fact that she liked it.

Emerging blinking from the tube into bright sunshine Amanda felt a surge of quiet optimism, in her element as she strolled along Oxford Street drinking in her beloved London: Fortnum & Masons, Saville Road, the black cabs and hordes of shoppers and tourists, it all lifted her spirits.

The train journey in had been tedious and the initial cheer of the sunny West Sussex countryside had soon given way to maudlin thoughts pulling her back. Despite the length of time elapsed since John had died, his passing remained Amanda's constant reference. Life beyond love. It was complicated.

How she would have preferred to have been wracked with grief, to have sobbed and wailed, to have not coped, been overwhelmed, or (as she had noted was the modern response to every small mishap) devastated! She had lost her closest friend, companion, her partner with whom she shared the daily business of life.

She had drifted away to the hypnotic repetition of train sounds, swooning into a reverie where she and John were young and passionately in love. They had been adventurous. John had a penchant for 'looking.' Amanda had surprised herself at how readily she grew to enjoy accommodating her husband's voyeurism. She bought sexy things to wear, to parade . . . to take off. It turned her on. The fabled power of the stripper, brazen, in control.

It was an anomaly for someone like Amanda, cultured, refined. That in itself was for her an added frisson. To shed the constricting trappings of polite society. Nobody she knew could have guessed at what she did. The sharp sweet tang of forbidden fruit. It seemed a lifetime away: the wanted woman. How he had wanted, and how she had obliged. It *was* another life, and even as the memories arose and faded to the clack of wheels on track there was a curious dissociation, someone else in a movie she had seen; a stranger.

It was true, the passion of the early days had abated over the years, succumbing to the inevitable cooling that familiarity brings, ultimately bowing to the implacable law of diminishing returns. But it had been replaced by a different more precious kind of intimacy, close in their separateness.

This part of her, of him, their enduring love, had been scooped out of her with surgical brutality and buried with her husband. It was a kind of Sati, the Hindu woman self-immolated on her husband's funeral pyre. She endured an indefinable detachment, a constant tinnitus alienation, the construction and order of her world having shifted irrevocably. The strange altered place where she now found herself was not one where she fitted any more. Just one piece of the jigsaw was missing, but the whole thing was spoiled. Worse still, she was dogged with a vague sense of guilt.

'Is it a present?' Amanda smiled at the young woman shyly holding out a copy of her book for signing.

'Yes, it's for my boyfriend. He's called Mark.'

Amanda scribbled a dedication ending with a signature flourish. 'Have you a favourite?' she asked, always interested to know what her readers liked best, and sensing this young woman to be a serious reader.

'Oh I *love* Falling From Grace.' she said.

'My favourite too.' Amanda smiled warmly and the girl beamed and coloured.

'Oh! Thank you!' She scurried away tucking the book in her little rucksack as an elderly woman stepped up for her moment with the author.

Amanda enjoyed this part of the job. It mitigated the remote and in some ways lonely endeavours of the writer, and in these brief exchanges with people who read and loved her work she felt real and connected. It squared the circle. The things she thought and wrote about were shared and appreciated by others, and she felt humble and touched by their wish to meet her, nervously appreciative and in many instances paying her compliments. She was not alone.

It was getting on for four and the manager had indicated that Amanda might draw things to a close if she so wished. A lot of people had turned up in the first hour, queuing to see her, but now it was quieter and it wasn't good to be the much adored writer sitting amongst her diminished piles of unsold books with nobody paying any attention at all. She had picked up her bag and was rising to her feet when the inevitable tailender appeared, hurriedly striding across the carpet, making to pick up one of her books but then thinking better of it and retreating a step, momentarily embarrassed by his own over-eagerness:

'Oh . . . sorry I . . . have you finished for the day? I heard you were here and . . . well I'm rather a fan!'

She sat down again replacing her bag. 'No, that's fine. Did you want to take a book?'

'Well if it's not too much . . . yes, I would rather.'

The late arrival had momentarily thrown her. Seated again she relaxed and appraised him like a kindly headmistress from behind her desk, offering an encouraging smile to a nervous pupil. He was older than she was, sixty-something. A 'silver fox', well to do she thought judging by the tweed sports jacket, the posh accent. He had that unmistakable public school diffidence, which invariably hid a type of innate confidence who's hallmark was understatement. He wore a shirt and tie and evidently did not consult the weather in choosing what to wear. Amanda made a small bet with herself that his shoes, hidden from her by the table, would be expensive tan brogues.

She opened a book at the fly-leaf, and before she could make the usual enquiry, the information she sought was volunteered.

'It's a present for myself actually . . . Sebastian.'

It was said with a shy smile and smiling too she

wrote the dedication. 'To Sebastian, best wishes, Amanda Carling.'

She stood as she handed over the duly signed book. 'I hope you enjoy reading it.'

'Actually I've read it already. It's good.'

'Oh,' she replied, considering the compliment which in the choice of adjective was probably less enthusiastic than she was used to from her fans. She knew it was good. 'Thanks. Nice of you to say.' She was tired now, wanting to be away and unintentionally curt.

Sebastian picked it up. 'No I mean it really is . . . *really* . . . good! I think you're very . . . well anyway, thank you.' With which he hesitated as if about to say something else but then just smiled and when Amanda didn't reply he nodded rather formally, almost an abbreviated bow, and quickly turned to go.

Amanda sat down again to rummage in her bag for her mobile She was checking her messages, unaware that Sebastian had quietly retraced his steps. He waited politely for her to finish and look up, which at last she did and offered a slightly bemused: 'Oh. Hello again.'

'Do forgive me. Look, I hope this doesn't seem . . . well anyway, I'm going to the Royal Academy you see, for the Manet. I'm a member and you wouldn't have to . . . well . . . I know it's rather presumptuous but would you like to come along for a coffee, and they do very good food in the members lounge if you've missed lunch? The exhibition *is* wonderful, and I' d be *so* interested to talk to you.'

He had been so hesitant and unsure before but suddenly had found his voice and spoke with purpose, not to say intent, holding Amanda's eyes with a steady look which caused her to swerve at the last nano-second from her intended polite refusal, instead hearing herself say: 'Yes, that would be lovely!'

Chapter 2

'Amanda's got a *man.'*

'Has she? Have you?' Marcia asked looking first at Trish across the table, then at Amanda, next to her.

'No.' Amanda replied, matter of fact continuing with her lunch.

'She says she hasn't.' Marcia said, knife and fork poised aloft and looking quizzically at Trish again.

'Oh she *has*.'

Trish had phoned on Sunday and gleaned from Amanda that she hadn't in the end done the shops after her book-signing, but had a late lunch with Sebastian. Amanda's best efforts had failed to dent Trish's full throttle acceleration to the conclusion she was now offering to Marcia.

Amanda capitulated; it obviously wasn't going to go away:

'What Trish is referring to Marcia, is that I had a lunch with one of my readers. She's at it.'

'She says you're at it.' Marcia parroted, the two of them now into a familiar double-act, spurred on by the favourite topic of conversation. Trish liked men. She was elegant, sexy, chic, and a ready supplier of suggestive innuendo. Marcia was petite and disarmingly boyish, with her ultra short styled hair a shade of blond that was almost white. She was quick and direct to the point of bluntness, and had cultivated a persona which amused Amanda: T-shirt and jeans, androgynous themes, yet always expensive and immaculately turned out. It was a look that had caused Amanda to surmise that Marcia's sexual preferences might be less than exclusive, though Marcia herself had never provided any evidence that might support it.

Trish had recently grieved her fiftieth birthday. She looked good, and her liking for men was more than reciprocated. Marcia was almost a decade Trish's junior, and an interesting foil for her glamorous friends. Often, as now, Amanda adopted an air of fond maternal impatience with erring children. She carried her years lightly. Her sultry beauty was enhanced by her considered self-possession. She had that singular ability to be silent, and to convey with a look, like Rampling or Bacall.

'For goodness sake you two, he's a retired judge who's married with a disabled wife at home, and not the slightest inclination . . . and even if he did have, *I* have not!'

'Oh.' Marcia said, effectively a full stop.

But Trish couldn't resist a final sally.'So you won't be going to see him in his *chambers*?'

The joke, duly appreciated ended the ribbing, but Marcia was curious. 'What's he like Amanda. I've never met a judge before.'

'Oh he's lovely, really, a gentleman. Not at all like you might expect a judge to be. Quite posh I suppose, Eton & Oxford and all that, but very unassuming. *Very bright.*"

'Oh well,' Trish chipped in, 'Peas in a pod then. You went to Oxford didn't you?'

'Cambridge.'

'Same difference darling.'

'Yes but from Egham Grammar sweetie, distinctly down-market.'

'Oh but you're a professor!' Marcia was indignant and not prepared to see her clever accomplished friend do herself down. 'That's easily on a par with a judge in my book!'

The 'girls' were indeed rather proud of Amanda's high flying academic successes prior to becoming a full time writer. A rare Cambridge first in literature had seen her eventually with a professorship at London's University College. Trish and Marcia viewed her as the clever sister who'd done so well, but wasn't too proud to slum it with them and indulge in the tittle tattle of the day.

'*Was* darling; and anyway it's completely irrelevant. Nice man, nice wander around a gallery, end of story. Are we having another bottle?'

And it was back to the said tittle-tattle of the day. Trish and Marcia were outrageously unreserved. They were scathingly funny about their uninterested husbands lack of sexual endeavour, and offering desultory (and often hilarious) accounts of the perfunctory act when it did occur. For all three, their marriages had long since found sex becoming, like a good steak, rare rather than well done. Even Marcia, despite her relative youth was already reaping the inevitable familiarity premium.

Amanda had always contrived to join in the camaraderie whilst actually giving away very little about her own own marriage. Now she was free to be consultant and sympathiser in chief. She'd long sensed a serious function underlying the fun of women sending up their husbands. It facilitated catharsis, a humoresque coming to terms with loss and the dimming of the vital spark. It was the prerogative of all women, but especially bored well-to-do wives.

The trip to the Royal Academy with Sebastian *had* been enjoyable, much more than she let on. She'd learned that he did indeed have a wife, incapacitated by multiple sclerosis and requiring around the clock care at their home in rural Surrey. They had a "small pied a terre" in Mayfair. He'd coloured a little and smiled his assent when Amanda had playfully hazarded that he'd been educated at Eton and Oxford, causing her to rejoin with mock superiority: 'Egham Girls Grammar and Cambridge!' She was further amused, laughing when Sebastian revealed he'd attended Jesus College. His eyes twinkled when she shared the joke, that her gardener was a young Spaniard called Jesus, lasciviously adored by all her friends. Sebastian's mischievous follow-up wasn't lost:

'Then I shall look forward to meeting him. We Jesus fellows must stick together!'

Amanda found herself smiling more encouragingly than she would've intended, *she* now the one colouring a little at her own mildly flirtatious riposte. 'But of course, you must!'

That night Amanda retired early and read. At last when she could no longer keep her eyes open she deposited her book on the bedside cabinet, switched off the light and curled up to sleep. There was an owl loudly hooting very close by. She smiled in the darkness as she recalled lunch with the girls. But it was not the girls who occupied her thoughts, as she drifted off to sleep. It was Sebastian.

Chapter 3

Amanda was already working on an idea for her next novel. She was driven, needed to work. No sooner had she submitted her last manuscript than she was pondering her next. It was not a question of starting from scratch. She had over the years imagined the essence of several potential stories which might in due course form the basis of a novel, put by and stored away. Now she alighted on a particular twist to one of these, and the days slid by as she worked out a sequence, considered scenarios, layers and sub-plots, the characters who would populate them alongside her principal protagonists.

She knew essentially what it was to be, the big story, but *how* this would be achieved, the structure, the detail was another matter. She was capturing clouds and tethering them to a landscape constructed from a blurred picture in her mind, as compelling as it was evasive.

This was the artisan, the sculptor with mallet and chisel facing the block of marble which hid wonders inside already perceived and waiting to be cut free. She still used pen and note-pad, her waste paper bin in demand, regularly abandoning her study to wander around the garden jotting things down, smoking or distractedly dead-heading daffodils.

The May sunshine was exceptionally warm and the arrival of longer days had found Amanda waking early to a cacophony of birds, sunlight streaming in through the tiny gap above the curtains. It had been a fortnight since her book-signing and she had several times picked up Sebastian's card and considered phoning him. How she wished she had given *her* card to *him*, thus relieving her of any necessity to take the initiative and able to abdicate responsibility. Of course she could e-mail him, briefly, politely, thanking him for lunch and as it were hanging it out there for him to do with whatever he was inclined to . . . que sera sera. But that didn't feel quite right.

It was one of Jesus's days and he was annoyingly cheerful, whistling as he worked and remarking to Amanda (always "Mrs Carling") about various horticultural matters in which she had not the slightest interest. She escaped back into the house abandoning the sunshine. Once more she picked up Sebastian's card from the side in the kitchen, her eyes adjusting to the diminished light as she studied the number.

'Sebastian Hartley.' He answered the phone with just his name announced as a question, rising on the final syllable, welcoming and inviting a response.

Amanda relaxed.'Sebastian. It's Amanda Carling.'

'Amanda! How lovely to hear from you! We were just talking about you. Gwyneth has just finished your book.'

19

Amanda was thrown. Sebastian was evidently in the company of his wife and she found herself unusually at a loss.

'Oh. That's . . . well . . . I just thought I'd . . .' She actually dried up and the phone in her hand felt heavy and uncomfortable, needing to be put down.

Sebastian picked up on it and jumped in. 'I'm *so* glad you rang Amanda. Really I've been kicking myself that I didn't ask you for your number. Hang on a minute the reception's not too good here, I'll just go through to the drawing room (it's Amanda Carling darling).'

('Oh, what a coincidence. Tell her I loved the book.')

('Yes of course darling.) Hang on Amanda, I'll just be two ticks.'

There was a pause as Sebastian re-located and Amanda collected herself, having noted that the phone reception had from her end at least seemed perfect, and relieved to be able to continue the conversation in private.

'Ah, that's better. Well. This is a *lovely* surprise. I was just thinking about you earlier. Oh and Gwyneth said to tell you she loved your book.'

Amanda thought the first three words were said with the unmistakable tone of someone settling into an armchair, and intuited also that they referred to now being, as it were, able to talk. 'Oh, that's nice of her. Tell her thanks.'

'Yes I will, of course.'

There was another pause and a slight awkwardness, Amanda suddenly struggling for what to say. She hadn't phoned to talk about Sebastian's wife. Her sails had deflated at this unforeseen turn. Sebastian too had momentarily stalled but quickly gathered himself. 'Look Amanda I really did enjoy our afternoon. It's so rare nowadays for me to be able to enjoy an exhibition or a concert with someone. So much of the pleasure is in being able to share the experience, don't you think?'

Amanda was relieved. It was said with such unmistakable warmth. She was emboldened. 'Yes. I love Manet. And I very much enjoyed spending the time with you.'

It was stronger than she would have wanted it to be and having said it wavered, even as she did so feeling the rare sensation of a blush heating her cheek. 'I mean . . . what I meant is . . .'

'No, really no need. The same goes for me. Absolutely. Guilty on both counts!'

Another pause, but the awkwardness on both sides had slipped away, positions declared, and the way ahead cleared. Amanda smiled. 'In that case perhaps I ought to sentence you, due clemency in view of your guilty pleas of course.'

Sebastian wasn't to be outdone. 'No I'm afraid that would never do. *My* court, and *I* do the sentencing. How about dinner?'

Amanda froze. The question hung in the air. Everything had been leading to this, but in the end it felt sudden. Since John's death she had had no interest in 'dating,' and had stubbornly resisted her friends' attempts to tempt her. Her life had settled into a rhythm which was manageable, predictable, safe. She was resilient and self sufficient, and she momentarily perceived now, apprehension lurking in equal measure with excitement, that all this might change. A falling knife that she could catch or run from.

Sebastian began to fill the void with words. 'Of course the sentence can be suspended. Take a little time. Check your diary. Drop me an e-mail when you've had time to . . .'

'No. I mean yes. I'd like to have dinner with you. I'd like that very much.'

When Amanda replaced the phone she remained still for a very long minute, her hand covering her mouth. What had she done? What was she doing? She made her way through to the living room and standing by the inglenook ran her fingers over the cold steel of the stove, ashes still not cleaned out, unlit since John died. They had spent many winter nights together here, had talked, read, listened to music, or just watched the ever changing pictures painted in the fire, lost in their own thoughts. She picked up a photo of them together at Brighton. They were on the pier eating ice-creams and Amanda sported a fringed cowboy hat that John had won on the rifles at the fairground.

She felt a faint tremor in her hand as she put the

photo down and turned away, aware of the blood coursing through her veins, leaning against the mantlepiece to anchor herself. She drifted between the past and future, remembering with contentment the life she had had, but feeling her grip soften and relax as she allowed herself to begin to let go, awakened by the excitement of new beginnings.

Her face flushed, her body opening, so long closed, hunched inward against the world. How long did she stand, steadying herself lest she would faint?

A movie reel of random images played. Here, curtains drawn and lamplight, the stove casting it's flickering glow across her nearly naked body. John, watching her, but now it was Sebastian for whom she moved and turned and showed herself, Sebastian who swept her up in his arms to take her up to bed.

She shivered. Her whole body was delightfully vibrating. A sound outside caused her to start, and through the window she glanced Jesus working away, oblivious.

She was breathless and not entirely due to her swift ascent of the stairs. She knew exactly what to put on. *Those* shorts. The ones she had only ever worn at home. Lasciviously favoured by John for whom, she'd sometimes teased, she *might* put them on . . . if he was 'good.' Drawers and cupboards hung open, the contents spilled haphazard onto the bedroom floor as Amanda searched, impatient, aroused. She had them! Now a gossamer thin silk blouse tied up in a knot baring her midriff, her hard-tipped breasts pushing heavily through the translucent fabric leaving nothing unsaid. It was familiar territory. Impelled by her own delinquent recklessness she looked in the mirror to approve the effect, a trembling hand smoothing her hair behind an ear, a quick application of lipstick then hurrying impatiently down the stairs.

In the morning room Amanda lit a cigarette, paused, breathed, counted to twenty, like an actress in the wings before at last 'entering' to stroll barefoot on the lawn innocent as the darling buds of May. Her notepad was now nothing more than a theatrical prop.

Ostensibly absorbed in her work, she jotted down random miscellanea, trailing hither and thither like a latter day Isadora Duncan, equally undressed. The sound of digging had stopped. The sun was hot on her skin, but more than that her gardeners appreciative gaze burned into her, tracking her like a predator might track a gazelle grazing close by.

Her outwardly relaxed languorous state belied her shortness of breath, her tingling skin, the cloying wetness seeped between her legs as his eyes by tacit invitation swept over her. She looked up. She was close to him now and she tossed back her hair and smiled. 'Hola?' It was a little brisk, her look querulous, superior, her smile *not* one that extended the presumed invitation to look. She was once more 'Mrs Carling,' and Jesus was caught on the hop. If

Amanda felt guilty it was mitigated by her amusement and expunged by the visceral excitement coursing through her like a wraith. Nonplussed Jesus returned her greeting and with a shrug resumed his digging more vigorously than before, as Amanda turned and strolled back to the house.

Out of sight and she was running. Her pad released in the morning room like an injured bird fluttered gracelessly to the floor. A Chinese pot toppled from it's pedestal in the hall shattered on the marble tiles in her wake, and still she ran. Up the stairs, gasping for breath, unzipping as she went. On the half-landing, hobbled by her descending shorts she flung herself down on the carpet convulsing to release her foot, at last splayed, taking her relief, crying out loud again and again. It had been a long, long time.

Chapter 4

The warmth of the day had lingered into the evening, the air heavy and sultry. Amanda lay awake considering the sketch she had at last arrived at for the story she'd been mulling in recent weeks. The principal characters were drawn, and minor ones pivotal to the plot already imagined.

It had been a fruitful day. This was how it always was, an idea taking shape, growing organically like a culture on a petri dish, elusive and shapeless at first until a form would begin to emerge that she could capture and tame with her pen. It was an inflection point in her creative process, the point where the child of her imagination began to take it's first steps away from her. She could stand back and observe it, guiding, charting it's progress, observing it's idiosyncrasies, nurturing and helping it to thrive and find it's way. It was a relief, something tangible at last, a beginning that looked like a plan.

She put it down and tried to submit to her tiredness, waiting for the gentle waters of slumber to fold darkly over her. She was beginning to drift in the soft twilight meandering that is the prelude to sleep. But it was too warm and she broke to the surface once more, irritated, throwing back the duvet, heading for the bathroom to freshen her face.

She paused to look at herself in the mirror that covered one wall, appraising her body as a man might. There were no blemishes, no extra pounds. She turned this way and that looking for fault but happily finding none, well satisfied as she returned to bed and hoiked the duvet onto the floor to make do with a sheet.

As she lay on her side and began to drift off she thought of the phone call with Sebastian. She pictured him smiling as he imparted to her how much he enjoyed being with her, unequivocally, abandoning his innate reserve.

Then there was his wife, Gwyneth, who he'd left in another room unable to move, to be with him, unable to . . . Amanda not for the first time felt a twinge of guilt at the not entirely palatable sense of her own clandestine opportunism. Her scheme for something more than coffee and conversation was undeniably made easier by the limitations of the opposition. It was as she knew full well a mean unworthy thought. But she did not recant. Instead her thoughts turned to her own nakedness. She felt the pressure of the sheet stretched on her hip and let her hand slip down to her knee to trace with a gentle caress her thigh and shapely haunches, her perfect skin, flat belly. Her palm at last cupped and weighed her full breast, pleasingly more than a handful, her fingers trailing deliberately across the hard jutting nipple down and up again, before settling on the pillow under her cheek as her breathing began to deepen and find the rhythm of sleep. It was all good, and there for the taking . . . should she choose to give.

She woke with a start. The green digital display of her bedside clock told her it was twenty past two. Amanda was a heavy sleeper and often slept right through. Something had woken her, and she lay tense and alert straining for a sound. Then she heard it: the unmistakable sound of a drawer sliding open. Her heart rate exploded pounding in her ears as she froze, listening, her mind a blank. Think . . . *think*!

Now she could hear other sounds, rummaging, things being tipped carefully onto the floor. He was in her dressing room. With a Herculean effort she turned her head and perceived through the open door a moving beam of light. Don't move! He thinks you're asleep. He'll go. Stay calm. Her heart banged in her chest urging her to flight, but she knew that in the night time silence he would hear. The distance to the bedroom door was too great. He would see her, grab her, naked, exposed and alone. Never had she felt so alone. A film of cold sweat was beading on her skin. Stay still! Do nothing! The bedroom door stood ajar, a light on downstairs. Yes, he was trying not to wake her. He would take her jewellery and go. Yes. Wait. Do nothing. He'd soon be gone.

All this raced through Amanda's mind in a fevered jumble of thoughts ending with a straw of comfort which at last she seized upon, letting out her pent up breath in a long silent flow that to her horror picked up a low moan as she exhaled. It was hardly any sound at all, nothing, but amplified by the stillness of the night it seemed to fill the room, and the sounds from her dressing room abruptly stopped. She feigned sleep, trying to breath evenly, aware of his movement in the room. He was close. The torch shone on her closed eyelids. Breathe. Breathe. *Breathe*!

'You must think I'm fucking stupid.'

Amanda opened her eyes and turned her head to face the source of the voice, blinded by the light:

'Please . . . take the things . . . whatever you want. Don't hurt me.'

He laughed and turned away, crossed to the door and turned the light on, switching off the torch and putting it in his pocket as he returned to where she lay. She shrank away, the sheet pulled up under her chin. He wore a black balaclava with holes for the eyes and mouth like a terrorist. He laughed again, arms folded, amused at the terror his appearance brought about.

'I think you'll have to get a new burglar alarm dearie. That one isn't any good. Well it isn't now.'

His amusement was not infectious. Amanda's knuckles were white, gripping the sheet as if for life itself.

'Don't worry darlin', nobody's going to hurt you.' He paused, stroked his chin considering the situation. 'OK, as you're awake you may as well be of some use. I'll have those rings for starters.'

With haste bordering on enthusiasm Amanda pulled off her rings and handed them over, noticing with a shudder his latex gloves as she dropped them into his outstretched hand. She struggled with her wedding ring.

'Thought you'd have had that off by now, back on the market an' all that, nice woman like you.' The balaclava couldn't hide the leer in his voice and a tremor ran through her.

He knew about her, that she was widowed, alone. She felt sick.

'Wet it.'

She obeyed, licking her finger wet until her wedding ring pulled off over the knuckle to be surrendered for its weight in gold.

'And the watch.'

It was all so matter of fact, and Amanda quietly complied.

'Right. Up you get. You can show me round.'

She hesitated. 'I can't. I'm . . . you see I haven't got a . . . could you pass me my dressing gown?' She indicated with her eyes to where her dressing gown hung behind the door.

He paused, looked, took a couple of steps back and gestured with his arm. 'Be my guest.'

Amanda began to protest but his tone changed. 'Don't fuck me about. OUT! NOW!'

She tried to wrap the sheet around herself but he advanced, cursing, and violently wrenched it away.

She fell back on the bed with a scream, crying, contracting into a foetal curl, whimpering as she tried to cover herself with her hands, the word 'please' faltering through breathless sobs.

'Well well. Very nice. *Very* nice.' He stood over her perusing her nakedness. A minute ticked by. Her sobs quietened, eyes closed, her body still but for her uneven breathing punctuated by small convulsive aftershocks.

He repeated to himself, 'Yeah. *Fuck.* That's . . . really . . . *very* nice.'

Still her eyes were closed as if she would somehow hide within herself. But she heard the unmistakable snap of latex gloves peeled off. A silent hopeless prayer as she trembling awaited the inevitable, preparing not to fight, planning with withering despair her own submission. But at last he heaved a long sigh, leaned over her, and with incongruous gentleness smoothed back some strands of hair that had strayed over her face so that she flinched. He was talking quietly now, the moment passed, a decision reached.

'Alright. I'm going to get your dressing gown, and you're going to put it on. And then you can make us both a nice cup of tea.'

She heard him cross the room, felt the cool silk of her robe draped across her hips and opened her eyes. He'd retreated to the door where he leant, arms folded, watching, waiting. Catching her look he nodded toward her robe. She hesitated.

His voice was still quiet when he spoke again, but with an edge of impatience that under most circumstances would not have conveyed the menace it did now.

'Get up, and put it on.'

Already defeated, Amanda arose, naked, and meekly obeyed.

Downstairs she led the way to the kitchen. He'd followed behind carrying a large hold-all retrieved from her dressing room. He'd dropped it in the hall, and suddenly was there, up close behind her as she picked up the kettle. His hand reached around and closed over hers, guiding the kettle back to its base where he continued to clamp her.

'Do you always do what you're told, *Amanda*?'

The sneering proprietary pronunciation of her name chilled her. It was a sudden change. He was leaning heavily against her wedging her hard against the work-top and whispering in her ear, his breathing quickening in short staccato bursts, the smell of onions.

'Do ye? I bet you do! Are you a *good* girl . . . are ye . . . *Amanda . . . darlin?'* She felt sick but daren't move, petrified by his rapid mood changes, by the knife edge of the moment as he pushed harder against her, his voice hoarse, leery. 'Bet you miss it . . . eh? Course ye do!' He pinned her with his weight, breathing heavily now and moving his groin against her as his free hand snaked under her armpit to grab

32

her breast. She wept aloud crying like a child but no one to hear. He was oblivious, suddenly panting like a dog, tearing aside her dressing gown to grab her naked breast. He released her hand on the kettle to grip her chin and yank her face around to his, eyes ablaze, his mouth a spit-flecked hole in the balaclava seeking out hers as he squeezed her breast and ground himself against her.

She tried to twist her head away, voice small, pleading, distant, imploring between her sobs, 'Please . . . no!'

But his grip only tightened. Her breast was hurting, her face irresistibly pulled back around to his. He was too strong. She had ceased to exist. No escape. His fetid onion breath. Glazed eyes. Mouth hole pushing down onto hers. 'NO!' She jerked her head back but he grabbed her behind her neck, pulling her to him. 'BITCH!' He was too strong. He'd hurt her. Let him do it, kiss her . . . and the rest. Get it over. Then he would go! And yet she held, strained her head away, repelled beyond all rational considerations by the horror of the kiss.

Still she held but failing now, irresistibly drawn to him, his larvate face inches from hers, droplets of sweat beaded on the red protruding nose. He paused, held her there his vice-like grip ready to pull her in. '*Come on*!' he muttered through gritted teeth as if he'd have her even now be a willing party to her own rape. A fleeting instant, a micro second as their eyes met was all it took. He froze, startled. Her terror and loathing pierced the moment like a dagger. It was as if a switch had tripped. A tremor ran through him and abruptly his whole body slackened. His head dropped onto her shoulder, face buried in her hair, long deep tremulous breaths, his palm resting against her cheek, her tears small rivulets streaming over his hand, his other softly cradling her breast. A minute. Two. At last he disengaged, turned and walked away, paused, a long pause and picked up the hold-all.

'Right. I'll tell you what's going to happen. We're going to walk around the house, and you're going to tell me what's what, understand? Small valuable things, small enough to fit in here. Got it?'

He spoke in a brisk chatty way as if nothing had happened. He'd fished from a pocket another pair of latex gloves putting them on as he spoke. Amanda nodded quickly, eager now to be robbed. She hadn't moved except to cover her bruised breast. She still faced the window, staring out into the darkness, feeling his eyes still upon her, afeared that he might change again. How should she be? Nice may encourage, cool could anger him. Her body shook, ears pulsed.

'Hey?'

With a superhuman effort she turned, arms wrapped around herself and hunched as if against the cold. Her gaze was downcast upon the floor tiles. There was a tiny crack in the corner of one she hadn't noticed before. It must have been where she'd dropped an ashtray a couple of weeks ago.

When he spoke again his tone was conciliatory.

'Come on then.' She looked up, wary. Was he smiling beneath his mask? He indicated the cigarettes and lighter on the side.

'Hey. Come on. No harm done eh? Have a fag. Let's get at it. Light one for me.'

Chapter 5

When Jesus arrived he went to ring the bell as he always did, reporting for duty and to ask if there was anything particular Amanda wanted him to attend to. There rarely was. Amanda was completely happy to leave the running of the garden to the gardener, but the ritual persisted. Today he found a note pinned to the door, asking him to enter and find Amanda in the drawing room. He carefully extracted the drawing pin and looked again at the note, puzzled. With a shrug and a 'hmmm' to himself he entered and began a tour of the downstairs rooms (Amanda hadn't thought to indicate which one *was* the drawing room). He poked his head around each door in turn quietly enquiring as he did so: 'Meesis Carling?'

At the third attempt he found Amanda unexpectedly lying down on the couch covered with a duvet, the scene causing him some confusion such that he backed a couple of small steps toward the door. She appeared to be asleep. He fished out the note and read it again.

'Meesis Carling?' He whispered, perplexed.

Amanda awoke and hurriedly sat up so that Jesus could now see her wrists taped together and the rope that snaked from them over the back of the couch to the radiator to which she was tethered.

'Jesus! Thank god you're here!'

He had already sprung forward in alarm, exclaiming at length in Spanish, on his knees and taking hold of Amanda's bound hands as he tried to unwrap the duct tape.

'What has happened? Who did this? I will keel him! Oh Meesis Carling . . .' and off again into an angry Latino torrent, the gist of which was evidently continuing the theme of violence toward the perpetrator of this act.

Amanda could not suppress a beat up smile as she eased her hands away from Jesus's failing efforts and directed him to the kitchen to fetch some scissors.

Freed she rubbed her wrists whilst Jesus fussed around her, at last dispatching him to make coffee whilst she showered and dressed. She wanted time to think but was reluctant to send Jesus away. She was touched by his concern, and didn't want to be alone, even though the sun was streaming in and the terrors of the night long gone.

But the need to shower and dress, to rid herself of the unwanted touch, breath, the animal craving which had blazed at her from the holes in the balaclava brought it all instantly back. She shuddered and instead of going upstairs she tarried. She joined Jesus in the kitchen, showing him where things were, but effectively taking over whilst he stood by redundant but close, protective. She clattered about and chattered: must go to Waitrose, coffee's nearly finished, did he need to feed the lawns, would he like something to eat, all the time reassuring herself that he was there, that she was not alone. He was sombre, patient, waiting, but at last stepped forward interrupting her with a steady voice and unexpected authority, a large brown hand gently but firmly touching her arm.

'Meesis Carling, we have to call the police. I think we should call the police now. I think we should do that *right* now. Would you like me to do that for you Meesis Carling?'

Amanda smiled even as tears prickled her eyes, took a deep breath and placed her hand on his. 'Not yet Jesus. Soon. Thank you . . . thank you. I'll get dressed and let's have a coffee. Just . . .'

'What? What would you like me to do to help you?' He spoke so gently now, but his voice still firm and resolute.

A shadow passed over Amanda's face and there was a tremor in her voice. 'Just, will you stay here please? Don't leave me alone. Please?'

Jesus bowed, a small formal bow, with his hand pressed against his chest, and as he straightened Amanda saw to her surprise that his eyes ablaze with righteous anger, were also misted with tears.

'I am here Meesis Carling. You are safe now.'

After the assault in the kitchen they had gone into every room and Amanda had pointed out everything of value as she had been told to. The figurine's, the French clock, the Dutch clock, the Picasso drawing, the Turner watercolour. She had not held back, such that at points he'd doubted her truthfulness, looking askance at her as she guided him to yet another prize. It was her quid pro quo for not being raped, grateful for this small mercy.

The 'things' were her insurance. Like a child appeasing a violent parent she eagerly engaged her assailant's greed so that he would not return to his lust, the more deadly sin.

In the end he'd prepared to leave with an attempt to befriend her, talking about her insurance paying out, finding out if she was expecting any visitors the next day, and making her comfortable to await Jesus arriving in the morning. He'd taken her phone from her but let her write a note for Jesus, and when he'd tied and tethered her fetched the duvet from her bed.

He'd told her to swing her legs up onto the couch so that he could drape the duvet over her, and in doing so the folds of her robe had parted and he'd paused to look. Her legs were visible. The rope hadn't enough slack to enable her to reach down, and her struggles to cover up had made it so much worse. She was exposed. He'd stared, still holding the duvet. She'd glanced up at him, a pleading look but his eyes were fixed elsewhere, and she turned to cower foetal into the back of the couch. She prayed, lips silently moving like a child, as his long leering look lingered for an aching age on her bare buttocks, peering. All her efforts had been in vain

When he spoke it was a slow audible whisper, thinking aloud, a pause between each phrase. 'Oh yeah. Like I said. *Very nice*. Pity not to . . .' He could not see the colour drain from Amanda's face, her wrists involuntarily straining against her bindings as she looked impassively away awaiting her fate. How long had he hesitated before she at last with a start felt the duvet alight upon her, then heard his retreating footsteps departing abruptly without another word, the front door closing.

Showered and dressed Amanda felt more composed and able to contemplate doing what needed to be done. Beyond the initial traumatic discovery, Jesus was visibly awkward now, unaccustomed to being in the house or in Amanda's close company for any length of time. She reassured him that she was feeling better. He could get on in the garden. She would call the police and would call him if she needed him.

Suitably reassured that his employer would be alright by herself, Jesus was none the less evidently relieved to be released, happy that Mrs Carling was once more in charge, the correct order at last restored.

Alone now Amanda picked up the phone. Sebastian. It's Amanda."

'Amanda! How lovely . . .'

'Sebastian I've been burgled. He was here most of

the night. He tied me up. My gardener came half an hour ago. He cut me free. I . . . I . . .' Her voice trailed off.

'My dear child, I'm so sorry. Are you alright? I mean . . .'

'Yes yes, don't worry. A bit shaken, you know.'

'Yes, I'm sure. I'm glad you called me. I'll come over now. Have you called the police?'

'No. I'll do it now. I should have I know. It's just . . .'

'Amanda, did he assault you?'

'Yes. Not . . . you know. But . . . he started to . . . I was . . . but then he stopped. *Oh god Sebastian*!'

'Alright. I understand. Listen. It's over now. He's gone and he won't come back. It's over. I want you to give me your address and postcode. *I'll* phone the police, better if *I* speak to someone. They'll phone you then and send someone across. I'll try to get there before they do, but don't worry, they'll be very nice, nothing for you to worry about at all. Is the gardener still there?'

Settling down with her coffee to wait, Amanda thought about Sebastian. A weight had been lifted. It had seemed the obvious thing to do, the only thing. But this one action had instantly put their connection on a different footing. In her distress she had turned not to a close friend but to Sebastian, who was at that very moment preparing to speed across the home counties to be with her.

41

Her ruminations were interrupted by the phone. It made her jump, spilling coffee on the rug. She found herself speaking with a police inspector whilst dabbing at the spill with a tissue. It was all very calm and low key, reassuring and efficient. She wondered if it was always like this or whether she was receiving special treatment. Beyond establishing that she was alright and the bones of what had happened, the emphasis was for Amanda not to disturb things in any way and to wait for the CID to arrive. She was asked to put her dressing gown aside, and not to shower or bathe, which irked her having explained what had (and hadn't) happened. She was in a system with procedures which didn't assume anything, least of all that the victim was necessarily divulging the entire truth.

The police would be there within the hour. Amanda doubted that Sebastian would make it before that and was agitated. How to fill the time? Another cigarette. Her mind returned to the previous night, and hot fat tears spilled onto her cheeks, tiny salt rivers that dripped onto her hands in her lap, darkening the whiteness of her cigarette. Still she sat, marveling at the amounts of water her eyes could produce, blinking each pair of brimming tears to race away, hot then cold. It passed. The couch reminded her of Emin's 'Unmade Bed,' an S&M version but with the rope snaking over the back and littered with pieces of duct tape which had stuck to the duvet. She laughed and even as she did was teary-eyed again.

A sudden sound and she tensed, glanced around over her shoulder, on her feet now and at the window. Just Jesus in the garden hammering at something. There he was; just Jesus. A long sigh escaped her and she reached for the phone scrolling town to 'Trish', only to put it down and light another cigarette instead.

Back in the kitchen she paced, smoked. Where *were* they?! 'Don't bathe or take a shower.' Was he deaf?! She stubbed out her cigarette screwing it into sink and strode resolutely into the hall. Fuck them. Fuck them all!

As she pounded up the stairs Amanda shook her head as if to physically dislodge the image conjured by her rage. But it was not her masked attacker. Nor was it the policeman doing his job, advising her not to wash. It was not a vague figure of an unknown man, an anonymous scapegoat to bear the burden of her consuming anger. It was John.

Crunching gravel announced the first arrival, an unmarked car from which emerged two detectives, an older man and a woman in her early thirties. Amanda met them at the open front door. The woman introduced herself as DS Hannigan, and her colleague DC Gilbert. The smart brisk young woman was the senior officer, and her overweight constable trailed in her wake, his look of permanent mild amusement conveying his subverted disappointment at having been left behind. 'Uniform' would arrive soon. Forensics too, to check fingerprints and for any DNA evidence etc etc. It was going to be a busy morning.

They sat in the morning room and DS Hannigan recorded the interview on her phone, making an occasional note in her notebook. Amanda recounted what had happened from going to bed and being awakened, through to being freed by Jesus. DC Gilbert's eyes wandered aimlessly around the room, and when it came to the part about being tied up on the couch he seized the opportunity:

'Was that er . . ? Would you mind if I . . ?' he pointed toward the door.

'Of course not,' Amanda smiled, 'Straight across and it's the door to the right.'

He shuffled off and DS Hannigan listened to the account of the note on the door and Jesus arriving and freeing Amanda.

'He knew things about me: my name, he knew about John, my husband, that he had died.'

'Yes. They (some of them) do their homework. It wasn't a random burglary.'

Amanda lit a cigarette, thinking about this. She'd known, of course, it was obvious, but hearing it said, and wondering now how much more he knew she shivered. DS Hannigan put down her notepad and pen.

'Mrs Carling I have to ask you. I know you've said not, but sometimes people for various reasons don't want to say it. But I have to ask you, and please tell me. Other than grabbing your breast and trying to kiss you, did this man touch you in any other way. Did he . . .'

'You mean did he rape me? No he didn't. If he had done I would say. I thought he was going to, twice . . . no, three times I thought he was going to.' Up to now Amanda had been composed but now her voice faltered. 'I don't know why he didn't. He was so . . . I don't know. In the kitchen he seemed to completely lose control then . . . I don't know. He just didn't.'

DS Hannigan remained silent, sensing more to come. There was the sound of another car arriving and DC Gilbert's voice from the hall.

'That'll be uniform. I'l sort them.'

DS Hannigan waited, and Amanda gathered her thoughts. 'You see, the thing is, and this may sound strange, I think he wanted me to . . .'

'Yes? What did he want? Tell me.'

Amanda let out a sigh and looked straight at the young officer. 'He wanted me to want him.'

A well-timed hand reached out and rested on Amanda's. 'That's not so strange. They do. You'd be surprised how many times I've heard that said. The poor deluded . . . but most of them go on and do it anyway. But not this one?'

She was persistent, but Amanda didn't mind, glad of the touch, the tentative bond, the comradely comment. She knew now why DC Gilbert had made himself scarce, but whether or not it was part of their routine, she was still glad of it.

'No. No honestly. I'd say. I hope he rots in hell.'

'He will.'

They sat in silence. Voices in the hall, DC Gilbert's and two others. DS Hannigan spoke first.

'He hurt you didn't he?'

'Yes. My breast. He was rough. It's sore, you know, bruised.'

'I'd like some photos if you wouldn't mind Mrs Carling. I know it's probably the last thing you want right now, but if we *do* turn up something that leads us to him . . . well it would be evidence in court of the severity of the assault. Could make a difference. It would be a female colleague of course.'

Amanda thought for a second. 'If you do? Do you think you will?'

The young policewoman was candid. 'It was clearly a professional job. We'll dust the worktop and kettle for prints when he had no gloves on, but other than that I think we may struggle.'

'Yes. Look, I'd rather not if you don't mind. What if I take some photos. I can send them to you?'

'Ok. Fine. Do that.'

DS Hannigan was nothing if not thorough. Could Amanda give a description of the man - clothes, height, eyes, weight, build, hands, hair. Was there anything distinguishing about him - his accent, anything at all, any clues from his conversation in all the time they's been together?

She queried various practical things: the sabotaged alarm, what was taken etc etc. She asked Amanda to show her around the house, continuing to clarify things as they went.

Forensics arrived and Amanda was relieved to be left to her own devices. DS Hannigan ran a brief conference with the police team before forensics set to work whilst Amanda took herself back to the morning room with a coffee, thankful that DS Hannigan had declined on behalf of her team. She lit a cigarette and waited for Sebastian to arrive.

'Amanda! Amanda! Where on earth are you? Oh here you are. Are you alright? For god's sake darling what on earth's going on, the place is crawling with police!'

It was Trish. Amanda had completely forgotten. They were to lunch out today and Trish was to to pick her up.

'Oh god you're not alright are you? What's happened?'

Trish alighted like a bird in the other armchair. She was perched on the very edge and craning her head forward, not quite within reaching out distance for Amanda's second comforting touch of the day. Amanda sank back in her own chair her palm pressed against her forehead.

'Damn I completely forgot Trish. It went *completely* out of my head, what with . . . I've been burgled.'

'What? When? Why didn't you ring me? Honestly Amanda! Has much been taken? Hang on I'd better ring Marcia before she sets off. Marcia, it's Trish, it's off for today darling. Amanda's been burgled. Yes, yes, I'm with her now, and a whole squad of boys in blue. No I don't thing so (do you want her to come over?) no she's shaking her head. Yes I'll tell her. Yes I *will*. Bye . . . bye. Marcia sends her love, and *call* her.'

Trish put her phone back in her bag and slumped back watching Amanda lighting yet another cigarette.

'You look terrible. What happened?'

'He broke in in the night. Woke me up.'

'Oh my god. You poor thing. He didn't . . . I mean . . . he didn't . . .'

'No, just . . . well you know, it was scary and he was a bit rough, grabbed me and . . . well you know, not . . . but I . . . he wanted . . . anyway, he didn't in the end, just made me point out valuable stuff. Look I . . . ' She tailed off.

There was a stunned silence. Trish's voice when she spoke was a whisper. 'I'm so sorry.' She gathered herself. 'Look, it's alright now. Everything's alright now. Don't say anymore. Oh God Amanda, you should have *rung me*.'

'I couldn't. He tied me up.'

The full gravity of what had happened was slowly unfolding for Trish. It was the only time that Amanda had ever seen her lost for words, except for one spat out in whispered rage.

'Bastard!'

'Judge Hartley is here to see you Mrs Carling.' DS Hannigan had appeared in the doorway with Sebastian who hesitated seeing Amanda in conversation with Trish. Amanda registered the quizzical look from Trish as she rose and Sebastian demurred.

'Please, don't let me interrupt, I can . . .'

'Sebastian, come in do, so nice of you to come.' Amanda was unusually unsure of the correct etiquette to greet him as he approached. She left it to him to reach out and gently rest his hands on her arms, no awkwardness and thus maintaining a polite distance whilst he held her.

'Amanda. How are you?'

'Oh, fine. Really. Sebastian this is my friend Trish.'

Trish arose and offered her hand. 'Hello, nice to meet you. And she isn't.'

Sebastian raised his eyebrows and turned again to Amanda, holding her with his eyes as he replied to Trish.

'No, I rather think you're right.'

'Oh stop it both of you. Sit down Sebastian and I'll make us a coffee.'

'I'll do it,' said Trish already making her way to the kitchen. 'I know where everything is.'

Sebastian knew DS Hannigan, and had spoken with her when he arrived. He was able to shed some light on the police findings so far. It was a professional job, and as such they would not have expected the interference with Amanda that took place. The man would have checked out the house in advance, and Amanda's circumstances too, easy to do given her well known public persona. He'd expertly disabled the alarm and forced the side door to the garage at the opposite end of the house from Amanda's bedroom. The chances of finding him were minimal unless forensics turned something up.

And that was that. The police were certain that he would not return, which Amanda was anxious to be reassured about, even though it was obvious to her anyway. He'd taken such valuable items and was clear away, making it ridiculous to envisage him putting both his success and resulting (soon to be) substantial bank balance in jeopardy.

Trish had returned with a cafetiere and only two cups, discreetly making her excuses. She would ring later, and stiff drinks and dinner at her house was on offer, not to mention a bed. Left alone Amanda and Sebastian finished their coffee in silence after his update. It was a comfortable silence. Amanda was grateful that Sebastian wasn't pressing her to tell all, to fill in the gaps, to go over it all again. He knew from the little she'd said that she had suffered. DS Hannigan also had intimated as much. She'd said more than she would have to someone who was not a high court judge, but had none the less respected Amanda's privacy, referring only to the burglar having given her a 'hard time'. Along with what Amanda had told him on the phone this was enough for Sebastian to have a pretty good idea.

'Thank you for coming Sebastian.' Amanda said at last, holding his eyes with a steady gaze. "I don't know why I rang you. I mean I hardly . . . well anyway, it seemed the right thing to do, and I just did. I'm glad I did.'

For a second time that day Amanda felt a hand on hers, and once again as if a tap had been turned, her eyes misted over.

'Amanda I understand. Really. Sometimes we just know what we must do.' That was all he said. There was such economy in his words, but the sentiment was crystal clear.

Amanda's heart leapt and she felt a deep down tremor. 'Yes.'

The moment was broken by a tap on the door. It was DS Hannigan.

'May I . . ?'

She joined them and Sebastian began to excuse himself until Amanda insisted he stay.

'That's us finished. Forensics are just packing up their stuff and we'll be away. Nothing so far I'm afraid. There's just a chance the lab may turn something up, but don't hold your breath. How are you feeling?'

The question elicited a wry smile. Amanda liked this young police woman, efficient and on the ball, but not sealed off in a bubble of officialdom.

'Oh I'm OK. A bit shaken I suppose, but I'll survive. You don't think there's any chance that he might come back?'

'Not a chance I'd say. Really. Don't worry. But you've had a shock. Is there anywhere you could go for a day or two? You'll need a joiner and a locksmith first off. This guy's both and unusually prompt.' She was jotting down a name and number and gave it to Amanda. 'He'll drop what he's doing for emergency repairs. I'd get that done today. Otherwise, it may be worth investing in a new alarm. Posh modern ones can't be so easily sabotaged. If you don't mind the extra expense you could get one that alerts the local police. Only trouble with those is that you end up making brews for coppers who turn out when you've forgotten your passcode! Still, after what you've been through it might appeal.'

'Good idea. It does. And I'm fine here. Really. Just so long as I can get the door fixed. Thanks for everything.'

She rose to go. 'Here's my card. E-mail me a list of everything he took, and if there's anything, anything at all you think of or remember about him, let me know. I'll let *you* know if we come up with anything. But as I said, don't hold your breath.'

Jesus left shortly after the police having stayed on longer than his normal Wednesday half-day. Sebastian phoned the joiner, who, true to his reputation said he'd be round late afternoon to do the job.

'How about a drink?' Amanda said at last. 'I need a large one, and I'm sure one won't put you over the limit?'

'Absolutely. Whisky for me., but not too stiff. Listen Amanda. DS Hannigan's right. You've had a terrible ordeal from what I understand. Gwyneth and I discussed it before I came here, and we'd like to invite you to stay with us for a couple of days, unless you have friends or family around who you may prefer to be with, Trish perhaps?'

Amanda handed him his drink. 'Cheers.' They clinked glasses and the astringent burn of a particularly peaty malt felt good as Amanda took one then two deep quaffs. 'Come on,' she smiled, leading the way outside to sit in the sun on the patio.

'Do I take that as a no then?' Sebastian said after they had settled with their drinks.

A jet trail bisected the cloudless sky, the distant boring heightening the stillness. A blue tit appeared on the feeder, pecked twice at the nuts and was gone.

'Oh it's very kind of you, and Gwyneth too. And I'd love to meet her. She sounds so nice. But really I'm fine. Perhaps another time? I can have dinner with Trish, and I feel sort of as if I have to brass it out here tonight. Do you understand?' Sebastian nodded and murmured his assent. 'I *will* be a bit nervous, but it's the thing about getting back on the horse straight away.' She took another sip, perused her drink a moment then downed it in one. 'I've a feeling that if I don't do it and take myself off somewhere else it'll be so much more difficult to come back.'

'Of course.' Sebastian said. 'You must do what feels right for *you*. And *I* mustn't be selfish.'

He uttered the last sentence with an impish grin which made Amanda laugh. The Talisker vapours had already found their way to her head, causing her (or at least that's what she told herself afterwards) to impulsively lean across and give Sebastian a little more than a peck on the cheek.

'Your very sweet. I'm so glad we met.'

Chapter 6

Sebastian had left exhorting Amanda to ring him any time day or night if she felt the need, whilst reassuring her that there was nothing to worry about. His offer still stood should Amanda change her mind in a day or two. That this was not entirely logical was left hanging. The suggestion intrigued her. She was in no doubt now that her own clandestine desires were reciprocated. But there were easier ways of moving this forward than bringing her home to, as it were, 'meet the wife.'

The joiner had been and gone by four. Amanda had dug out her insurance documents and made the necessary call. She put things that were scattered around back in drawers and cupboards whilst the joiner was fixing the door. As his van drew away she was suddenly overcome with tiredness.

It was a relief to have the house to herself. She decided not to take up Trish's offer and wandered outside to take a turn around the lawn. It was warm and not a breath of air stirred the rhododendrons or the pale new leaf of the tall silver birch, but in the shade the grass felt cool under her slow deliberate tread. Talking to the 'normal' people, Jesus, the police, Trish, Sebastian, even the joiner, had helped to retrieve some sense of perspective. The sunshine and clear skies helped.

Her emotional snowstorm had settled, like one of those hollow Xmas paper weights where it snows when tipped upside down. She went inside and carefully locked up, suddenly exhausted and craving sleep.

She slept soundly and was awakened by the phone at six. It was Trish. Amanda excused herself from the dinner invitation, too tired and not really in the mood. She was happy enough with plan B, however, for Trish and Marcia to call round in an hour or so for a blether and a glass or two of wine. She'd felt the awkwardness when Sebastian had turned up earlier. Only minutes before she'd told Trish that she was unable to phone her. But she clearly *had* found the time to ring someone else. So there was a small fence to mend, and it *would* be nice to have a little time with her friends now.

They arrived at seven thirty. Marcia drove. She hardly drank as a rule, and was the go-to person for chauffeuring when the need arose. It was apparent from a glance at Trish, emerging from the car with a bottle of Chablis in one hand and Bordeaux in the other, that tonight was a case in point.

Marcia, not usually the demonstrative sort wrapped her arms around Amanda. It was a quick, tight hug. She didn't say anything, just held her for a brief moment, then normal service was resumed.

'Where is he then?'

'Oh bloody hell! Come in, sit down. What sort of a day have *you* had? *Isn't* coal expensive at the moment?' Amanda was leading the way through to the lounge, singsonging her reply sarcastically as she went. Glasses and nibbles were already on the table with some non-alcoholic elderflower drink on ice for Marcia, and having been forewarned that Trish would be bearing gifts.

Marcia and Trish flopped into the cavernous sofa and Trish kicked off her shoes. They helped themselves to food as Amanda uncorked and poured. The elephant in the room remained hid for now at least.

'Well, this is very nice, really. Thanks for coming. Cheers.'

'So he's gone has he?' Marcia's 'innocent' voice was bait, and Amanda was determined not to rise to it.

'Oh. Sebastian? Yes, he went ages ago. What have you done to your hair? It's darker isn't it?"

It was Trish's turn. 'Now Marcia I really don't blame Amanda for ringing her *new* friend for help and support rather than either one of her *best* friends. Sometimes you just *need* a strong man around.'

'Of course.' Marcia agreed. 'I don't blame her at all. Do the police think there's going to be any chance of catching the burglar Amanda?'

Amanda was glad to move on. 'No, not really. They as good as said that they were going through the motions. They reckon he was a professional except for . . . well . . .'

'Quite.' Trish filled in. 'It makes my blood boil. Bloody men! There's no justice!'

This caused Marcia to perk up:

'Except that there was, wasn't there, well today anyway?'

Trish was baffled. 'What?'

'A Justice. There was a Justice. But he went . . . *ages ago*!'

The two tipped into giggles and Amanda shook her head. 'Pathetic.'

Trish ventured in a sensible voice. 'No, joking aside, Sebastian seems really nice, and he was the obvious one to call. I bet you had five star treatment from the boys in blue with connections like that. And he *is* charming and *very* good looking. I'm not at all surprised you fancy him Amanda. A catch I would say!'

Amanda was reeled in despite her best intentions issuing a weak denial. 'I don't *fancy* him.' Honestly! Look, he's a married man with a severely incapacitated wife at home.'

Trish and Marcia's heads momentarily swiveled to look at one another and Amanda immediately realised her mistake as Marcia pronounced in her 'innocent' voice once more:

'Well darling you know what they say: a friend in need . . .'

'Oh for god's sake!' Amanda cut her off, irritated

now not least because Marcia had adroitly
alighted on a thought that had also occurred to her,
and it touched a nerve. She reached for a cigarette,
careful not to catch Marcia's eye, and guiltily self-
conscious that Marcia at least would probably have
picked up on the real reason for her discomfiture.

Marcia relented. 'Sorry, we shouldn't . . . it must
have been really awful. How on earth did the swine
get in without the alarm going off? You do set it at
night Amanda *don't you*?'

They turned at last to the traumatic events of the
night before, and Amanda forgave the bad jokes.
She knew that it was their way of dealing with
things, a diversionary tack around the houses. They
obviously wanted to know what had happened, and
she was touched by their sensitivity and restraint.
Her intention had indeed been to demur, as she had
with Sebastian, but in the event, and in keeping with
the 'best laid plans . . .' she did not. They were
women, her peers, and this made a difference.

It began logically enough, with Marcia's question
about the alarm, then another about what had been
taken. Slowly then things shifted to less firm
ground. How had the burglar known so well what to
take? Amanda explained how she had shown him,
told him what were the most valuable things, what
he *should* take.

They listened quietly as she talked of her fear, her
need for him to be distracted, to be satisfied with
having her possessions and not her. A trade-off. But

describing the incongruity of pressing all her most precious possessions onto her abuser led Amanda irresistibly back into the fear itself. So raw the wound, so easily re-opened, the darkness suddenly and inescapably before her, drawing her on where she had not wished to go. She felt herself entering a dimly lit featureless corridor where she could only go forward. Her demeanour changed as her friends looked on not knowing what to say, and so not saying at all. Words seeped from her unbidden, and she seemed to swoon, remembering, distant now, quietly agitated, pulling on a loose thread in her cuff that unravelled the fabric as she spoke.

Trish and Marcia listened aghast as Amanda took them back and forth through the dark hours of her ordeal, at times pausing for what seemed like a long time, lighting a cigarette, speaking haltingly, falling into a monotone, squeezing the words out as she stared into space.

She who was so good with words was struggling now to find the right ones, words that could impossibly convey how it had been. The uneven delivery, the stops the starts the gaps told as much of the story as the elusive words Amanda searched for in vain. When at last she finished she reached for a cigarette, smiling a pained exhausted smile. 'So you see, it was really very easy to give everything away.'

She lit up and inhaled deeply, and for the first time looked at her friends, both now shocked and struggling for what to say. Amanda on the other hand was steadier. She had unpacked it. Faced it. It was not going to be the monster in the cupboard. It hadn't gone away, but a first important step had been taken. Her friends shared her burden which was a few straws less for her to bear,. They knew her pain, more manageable now that it had been brought out into the light.

After Amanda's account of her ordeal the mood had dipped. Words failed. A pale half-hearted effort or two to revive the usual banter fell dismally flat. The two friends had departed relatively early, moist eyed and with much hugging, Amanda ironically finding herself comforting *them* rather than the other way around. She was purposeful now, busied herself tidying up, and headed upstairs to bed.

She slept immediately, but awoke around midnight, experiencing the sinking feeling which quickly became a self-fulfilling prophesy that she probably wouldn't get back to sleep again. Rather than oppressed by what had happened she was buoyed by the love and support she'd experienced. She thought about Sebastian, about DS Hannigan, cool and professional but managing to be supportive and caring despite Amanda's trauma being for her an unremarkable routine event. She had empathy. And then there were her kind, kind friends. The good people greatly outnumbered the bad.

The security light went on. It lit up a thin strip above the curtain rail diluting the darkness of the room which returned seemingly darker than before when the light went off again. Amanda tensed and let out a long breath telling herself to relax, to go back to sleep. It flicked on again. She was straining her ears for a sound. Off then immediately on again, and a film of sweat was beginning to form on her forehead. Still she didn't move, her eyes fixed on the strip of light willing it to go, though experiencing no relief when it did, returning her to total darkness.

A chaos of jumbled thoughts assailed her. They vied for supremacy: hooded maniac or fox? If I turn on the light he'll see it. Lie still. Listen. Do something before it's too late. Don't be stupid, it's nothing. Get a grip!

The light flicked on again and Amanda thought she heard a noise. What was it? Was it a noise at all? There was no alarm. He could be in the house now. The light had gone off again. Now she was willing it to go on, but it did not. That was it, proof, he was already in the house, downstairs, going through her things. No, he had returned for her, not for her things. She remembered his parting remark. He had wanted her. Of course. They were all wrong. He was here. Amanda's heart was sped up and pounding in her ears.

She eased out of bed and made her way on tip toes to the bedroom door, only realising as she reached out in the darkness that her dressing gown had been taken by the police. Damn! It was pitch black. She began to hyper-ventilate. The security light was still off. So he *was* in the house. She recoiled from the door as if it might burst open any second. Two, three hurried backward steps; her heel collided hard against the bed and she stifled a cry.

She felt her way around the it to the wall, then to the left seeking the door to her dressing room, gasping as she tilted a picture almost knocking it off. There were no windows in her dressing room. She could put the light on in there, get dressed. More than anything she needed to be dressed. Dressed she had a chance. Dressed she could talk to him, reason with him.

At last in her dressing room Amanda put on the light and momentarily steadied herself her hand remaining against the wall by the light switch, her eyes adjusting to the brightness. She hurriedly dressed. What now? Still no sound. She didn't have long. She pictured him, confident, taking his time, making himself at home, even pouring a drink; but he would come, and this time he would not be denied. She looked for a weapon picked up a shoe and put it down again. The built in wardrobe was crammed with clothes. Of course! All she had to do was to climb in there, down behind her long dresses to the far end, he would never think to look. He'd think she'd gone away as everyone had advised her to!

It was a very long fitted wardrobe with four sliding doors. Amanda opened the first, turned off the light, and crawled into it as far as she could go, pushing impossibly as in a nightmare through endless fabric, and over mountains of jumbled shoes. At last she sat with her knees drawn up, sweating, foetal. She didn't clear a space impervious to the discomfort. She waited.

Only then did it occur to her that her car was outside for all the world to see. The doors were locked from the inside, the keys in a china dish on the chest by the door. She heard his voice again: 'Do you think I'm fucking stupid?' She would be dragged out. He would be laughing. She remembered how he had laughed. She began to shake.

How long she had been there Amanda could not tell. Sensory deprivation can play tricks. It seemed a long time. She may even have slept. There are many recorded instances of people having slept in terrifying circumstances, the body needing to switch off, choosing inertia when neither flight nor fight is possible. But it did seem a long time, and there had been no sign, no light no sound, nothing to indicate anything out of the ordinary.

At last Amanda edged open the wardrobe door next to her. A few inches at first, straining her ears. Nothing. She slid it open and climbed gingerly out, stiffly standing with the light still off. She found the door, opened it an inch. Nothing. Darkness. Silence. She turned on the dressing room light and leaving the door only slightly ajar so she was able to see, made her way to the bedroom door which she opened, stepping out quietly onto the landing. All was still. For several long minutes she remained. Nothing.

At last with a deep sigh Amanda turned on the light and went downstairs to the kitchen. She picked up the card that was still there on the side and dialed the number. It rang and rang but she waited:

'Sebastian. It's Amanda.'

'Amanda . . . are you alright?'

'Yes, yes I'm OK. Sebastian I'm so sorry to ring so late. I've been so frightened. And you said . . .'

'It's alright. You were right to phone me. I meant what I said. Now, just take your time. Has anything happened? He hasn't . . .'

'No of course not, except that . . . oh I feel such a fool! I've been hiding in my wardrobe for the last god knows how long! I was fine but then woke up and the security light was on. It kept going off and on and I panicked. It was probably a fox. I think I'm losing it.'

'No I don't think you're losing it. It's a normal reaction. You're probably suffering from delayed shock. Amanda you've been through a terrible ordeal. Anyone would have a reaction to what you've endured. Your'e alone and it's the middle of the night. I don't think you should be alone for a day or two. Look, why don't you throw a few things in a bag whilst I drive over and pick you up?'

It was what Amanda had wanted to hear, calm now but shocked by her own extreme reaction and no longer trusting herself to be alone. At the same time she felt pathetic, and now that the offer had been made was embarrassed by her weakness. She imagined waking up in the morning and being introduced to Gwyneth. What would she think?

'No honestly Sebastian, I'm fine, really. It wouldn't be fair on you, or Gwyneth. I've probably woken her up already. What must she think of me?!'

It wasn't convincing, and he wasn't convinced. 'Listen Amanda Gwyneth *wants* you to come. She had a similar experience years ago. She immediately said when I told her what happened that you shouldn't be on your own. And you haven't awakened her. Her night time medication knocks her out. And *I* most certainly want you to come, if you would like to. There's nothing I would like better.'

Amanda sighed, smiled, made no attempt to hide the pleasure in her voice as she willingly capitulated. 'Ok. If you really want me to. I *would* like to come. Thanks. But I'll need to bring my car, so don't worry about coming over. Just give me the address and post code for the sat-nav . . .'

As she drove through the stillness of the night Amanda's doubts and fears dissolved. Country smells wafted over her from the open window and she breathed them in, her hair lifted by the breeze which blew away her cares. Bach's preludes and fugues rippled from the hi-fi. She felt the contrapuntal synchronicity, the mathematical perfection of the composition, and imagined a similar purpose and meaning mapping her own actions and connections now, as she followed the path cut by her headlights into the darkness ahead. She was alive. She had stepped onto her husband's funeral pyre, but had survived the flames. There were more chapters in Amanda Carling's book of life, chapters not yet written, chapters she would not herself write, but would be written for her. All she had to do was to turn the page. Like a phoenix from the ashes she was rising, lifted on the wings of hope.

Chapter 7

The sound of rain gusting against the window heralded a break in the weather, and Amanda took her cue to turn over with a satisfied 'humph.' A rainy day was permission to sleep in. It was probably a remnant of childhood, long school summer holidays when to get up meant to go out to play, weather permitting, and if it did not there was the warm musty comfort of bed. But sleep was already a dispersing mist slowly shredding into broken wisps to reveal the landscape of the day.

She opened her eyes and closed them again as the events of the last couple of days lazily took shape in her mind, like icons appearing one by one on a slow computer screen. But her waking drowse pushed back, just the rain, gusting against the window in great sloshes as she drifted back asleep.

It had been an unremarkable arrival at the Hartley residence. The ivy-clad Georgian country house was exactly what Amanda had expected. Sebastian had kissed her on the cheek and carried her bag into the house. After showing her to her room and a brief tour they'd drunk camomile tea in the kitchen, speaking quietly as people often do at that time of night in deference to the lateness of the hour. There were the practicalities: where things were in the kitchen cupboards, tea, coffee, crockery, to help herself if she couldn't sleep. Sebastian outlined the morning routine for Gwyneth and her carers. Amanda wouldn't hear anything of this in her room tucked away on the second floor at the back of the house. She should rest. He'd bring her coffee at ten-thirty. Sebastian's bedroom was on the first floor, and Gwyneth occupied a ground floor purpose-built extension which they had added three years before.

To Amanda's great joy Sebastian had asked her did she ride, and was duly gratified by her enthusiasm. Riding had been her childhood obsession, still doing so whenever she could. He'd show her the stables after brunch and introduce her to 'the boys.'

All was well with the world. Amanda could not explain it. She felt alive. She would like Gwyneth, she knew, and she did not think about the rights and wrongs of her imminent affair with Sebastian, evidently seen as a fait accompli by Marcia and Trish, and now by Amanda too. What would be would be. She luxuriated in her bed. There could be no negative thought. No drop of rain could fall on her parade.

She'd dozed off again and was awakened by a soft knocking on her door. 'Come in.' She was already starting to sit up, a little nervous now, the morning after, and uncharacteristically shy. Sebastian entered with a tray on which were a small cafetiere, milk and sugar, and a china mug with a blue and green oriental pattern in swirling Paisley motifs edged in gold.

'I forgot to ask you how you take it, so I brought the lot.' Sebastian said very quietly, placing the tray on the bedside cabinet and beginning to retreat back toward the door.

'Sebastian.' Amanda reached out a hand to him and he stepped forward and took it, sitting down on the edge of the bed. 'Sebastian thank you so much. I can't tell you how glad I am to be here.'

He squeezed her hand and held it in both of his.

'Me too. I . . . well I think it's right for you to be here. Amanda I . . .oh listen to me your coffee will be cold! Take your time and come down when your ready. Gwyneth is very much looking forward to meeting you.'

'Me too.'

Left with her coffee Amanda mused, deep in thought. This time she hadn't felt uncomfortable at the mention of Gwyneth, and on the contrary meant it when she said that she was also looking forward to meeting her. What Sebastian had said, that it was 'right,' rung true for her, and she no longer harboured feelings of guilt or opposition to the wife, despite believing no less that she was moving ever closer to intimacy with the husband. The thought led her to think of her friends and their salacious predictions. She reached for her phone. 'Trish, it's Amanda.'

'Oh, hello darling. You must be telepathic, I was just about to ring. How was your night? Did you sleep alright?'

Amanda summarised the tale ending with her flight to Sebastian's.

'Oh. That's . . . it must have been really awful . . .' Trish was computing the new turn of events with unusual slowness. She was quick to recover: 'I *knew* you shouldn't have stayed there by yourself. Honestly! I was really worried, we *both* were. Marcia went all quiet on the way home. Has she phoned you yet?'

'No, not yet, unless she tried the landline. I'll phone her in a bit. She's no need to worry *and you neither*. I'm fine, really. Actually I felt much better just talking to you both about it. Thanks.'

'Oh Amanda it must have been so *dreadfu*l. We were really . . . I mean I just can't imagine it. Anyway, it's all over. When do you think you'll be home? I might come across and stay for a day or two."

'Yes, do. That would be really nice. I don't know. I'll stay here for a day or two anyway and see how it goes. I haven't met Gwyneth yet, so Ill just have to . . . well you know, *see how it goes*!'

There was a pause, and when Trish spoke again it was with her sensible maternal voice: 'Yes. Well. Be careful Amanda.'

Showered and dressed Amanda was unable to find Sebastian and wandered from the kitchen into a the living room. A tall bay window overlooked the garden at the front of the house. It was a comfortable lived in room with a large book case and a sprawling three piece suite, luxuriously old and its best days behind. She guessed that here was where Sebastian relaxed, pictured him in one of the cavernous armchairs engrossed in a book or listening to classical music. Who would it be? Beethoven perhaps. There was an ancient sideboard with two framed photographs, one an old family gathering, the other a young woman, perhaps mid-thirties. Amanda picked it up. She was in riding gear, her hat under one arm. She was laughing at something as she swept her wavy auburn hair back from her face with her free hand that held her riding crop. Amanda froze. It was her. The woman was her twin. The likeness was uncanny.

There was a sound and she turned to see Sebastian in the doorway. 'Oh, I couldn't find you.' She put the photo down as Sebastian approached her smiling his apology.

'Sorry Amanda I'd just nipped out. I see you've found Gwyneth though!' He picked up the photo and they both looked at it.

'Yes. . . . it's amazing . . . I mean she looks . . .well she looks just like me!'

'Yes. She was very beautiful.'

Amanda coloured slightly but side-stepped the oblique compliment: 'I'm sure she is still; older like all of us, but surely she hasn't changed *that* much?'

Sebastian replaced the photograph and took Amanda's elbow guiding her gently toward the open door: 'Come on. I'll introduce you. But listen, this damned illness takes everything Amanda. It's not just a matter of frailty and simpering ill health. And then there's the treatment, drugs, steroids amongst other things. They have a bloating effect, and the lack of any activity, the weight gain . . .well you'll see. But the photo is of another person Amanda. Five or six years ago she would have been recognisable. Not now.'

They' crossed the hall and entered the enormous dining room on the south west side of the house. It comfortably accommodated a full size grand piano as well as a magnificent ornate table with twelve chairs. At one time there would have been large windows to three sides. To the front and rear they remained, but facing them now, in the side of the house was a modern door, about half as wide again as a normal one, and set in a large square framework of glass. The effect was jarring and unbalanced the room. They passed through the door into a very short corridor constructed entirely of glass and tubular steel, just three or four steps. Amanda found herself in what might best be described as a very modern studio flat in the open plan minimalist style often associated with Scandinavian design.

'Oh there you are! I do hope you had a good sleep my dear. What a dreadful time you've had of it!'

Gwyneth was sitting in a large and complicated looking wheelchair in which (Amanda guessed) she probably spent most of her waking hours. Amanda had expected there to be a carer or two in evidence, and it was with relief that she was greeted with a scene of relative normality, put at her ease by Gwyneth's warm welcoming smile.

'Darling this is . . . well you know who it is! Amanda let me introduce you to Gwyneth.'

Amanda reached out to take Gwyneth's barely extended hand, feeling the lack of any grip and the soft puffiness of the skin. 'Hello Gwyneth. It's lovely to meet you, and I'm so grateful to you both for taking me in like this. I feel rather stupid I have to say.'

'Nonsense! After what you've been through!? I'm not at all surprised you've had a reaction. Anyway, forget about that now, and it's *we* who are grateful to *you.* We've read all your books. What a pleasure to have you captive so that we can make you talk about them! Do sit down darling, you're making me nervous.'

Sebastian remained standing as Amanda grinning did as she was bid. 'Well I thought I'd make us all some tea. You'll have plenty to talk about. Gwyneth is a writer too Amanda. She used to publish under her maiden name, Swift.' He smiled mischievously at Amanda's look of pleasure and surprise, her hand flying up to her mouth.

'Goodness! That's amazing! Gwyneth Swift! I've read your work. Weren't you short listed for the Orange? I loved that one: The Pearl Divers wasn't it?'

You're very kind Amanda but I think you're confusing me with *you*. It was *long* listed actually and I have to say I was very happy with that.1994. Yours was the next year, and you should have won. A travesty. It was by far the best.'

'Well I agree entirely, of course!' Amanda replied preening, eliciting an impish grin.

On his return with the tea Sebastian made his excuses, evidently pleased to see his wife and Amanda animated and enjoying each other's company.

It was lunchtime when he reappeared, and introduced Jean and Becky, Gwyneth's carers. They were to give Gwyneth her lunch and attend to her 'personal care.' Amanda was whisked away to eat lunch with Sebastian.

'It's a pity Gwyneth couldn't eat with us. I really like her Sebastian.'

'Yes, you're right of course, it's a damn shame.' An assortment of cheeses and crusty bread had awaited them in the kitchen and Sebastian spoke in between mouthfuls. 'The thing is we tried to keep things normal for a long time, but in the end you just have to accept how it is. And the girls are so good. It's just so much less stress for Gwyneth to get everything done in the most practical way with minimal fuss.'

Amanda considered this. 'Yes I suppose so. It must be hard for you too I'm sure. It *was* a bit of a shock, after seeing the photo. But then I forgot all about it.

We had such an interesting talk. I mean, I wasn't avoiding it or anything.'

'No, you're right. She wouldn't have minded in the slightest talking about her illness. But what's the point? She was probably glad you didn't . . . I mean glad to talk to you as another writer about things which are important to you both. It's easy for an illness like this to take over. But life has to go on, such as it is.' There was sadness in the last few words despite his apparent efforts to strike an upbeat tone.

Amanda thought about this. She thought again about the photo in the living room, and all the things that Gwyneth could not do, imagined her ticking them off one by one as her illness had progressed. Goodbye, goodbye, goodbye . . .

'Yes, it's obvious when you put it like that. Your illness isn't who you are. And she's such an interesting woman. But then it all comes crashing back into focus when we have to leave her to have things done while we have our lunch.'

Sebastian poured tea. 'That's perceptive of you Amanda. It wasn't always like this of course. There have been times when Gwyneth's illness has obscured everything. She's became very depressed. She still does from time to time. But there comes a point. It's not going to get better, always worse.' Now he was almost musing to himself and Amanda felt his sadness. 'Either you accept it and live as best you can, or you suffer and wait. Gwyneth's a fighter, but such small victories, keeping going, little day to day pleasures. She *tries* to stay positive, but it's always there, no illusions about where it will end. Que sera sera. That's how it is.' There was resignation in his final remark, the hollowness of loss already and more to come.

They continued in silence having reached an end to this particular conversation and lost in their own thoughts. Amanda thought about Gwyneth's physical presence. There was no getting away from it. Her appearance was gross, hugely overweight and bloated, and nowhere was this more apparent than in her face which had swollen up to engulf her once fine features. She thought of Simone de Beauvoir's 'Woman Destroyed,' but even as she did realised that this was not such a woman. She had been able by the power of her personality and intelligence to so entertain and engage Amanda that her illness and it's awful expression were temporarily eclipsed. Amanda already knew she liked Gwyneth. She admired her too, her strength and humour in adversity. And yet she had registered Sebastian's words about depression, and intuited even now a deeper darker current, something perhaps Sebastian did not see, or would not say, but *something*.

'Come on,' he said at last, rising. 'Let me introduce you to the boys!'

'The boys' were geldings, Hector, a chestnut with a

white star and socks, and Achilles, jet black with a white blaze that missed one eye giving him a mechante look which Sebastian assured Amanda belied his genial if somewhat wayward headstrong nature. The rain had eased to a fine drizzle the sky was brightening.

'I think we've had the worst of it. What about a hack?' Sebastian said. 'You could take Hector. Have you ridden a hunter before? He's lively enough but very responsive.'

'Oh yes. But I haven't brought my things.'

'Oh that's no problem. Gwyneth's will fit you I'm sure, and she'd be very glad for you to put them to use.'

When Amanda returned to the stables in Gwyneth's riding gear Sebastian was already changed and throwing a saddle onto Hector who was shuffling around excited, Achilles stamping and whinnying in the next stall. When he saw her he froze. For a long second he looked. He abandoned the saddle and approached her, bewildered. He reached out, held her at arms length and continued to look at her. Amanda thought he was going to cry, then that he was going to kiss her. She knew his mind and heard her own voice, distant, pleading, 'Sebastian . . .'

It was a gentle kiss, a soft sweet pressure which Amanda craned upward to receive, so prolonging for a second what would have been a little less, and thus was infinitely more. He drew away, smiled, half apologetically, struggling, searching unsuccessfully for words. Amanda came to his assistance, her voice catching, little more than a whisper: 'Come on, lets go.'

The rain returned midway through their ride, but they carried on and returned drenched. The horses steamed as they tended to them. Sebastian was in good spirits, energised by the ride, attentive to the horses and no less so to Amanda. He was easier around her, some of the reserve gone as they worked together. He helped her as she struggled with the cinch on the girth then turned to her, close, gently pushing back her wet hair that was plastered against her face. His hands rested on her shoulders. 'There. I can see you now!'

'Mmmm . . . said one drowned rat to another. But *who* pray do you see?'

It had just slipped out, a light-hearted remark, but 'many a true word . . . ' caused her to backtrack. 'Oh. I didn't mean . . . I mean I don't think . . .'

Sebastian's forefinger pressed against her lips: 'Shhhhh. It's alright. Really. It's alright.'

She sighed, looking deep into his eyes. 'Yes. It is isn't it?' She was waiting for him to take her in his arms and kiss her, but he just brushed her cheek lightly with the back of his hand, looking at her, a long thoughtful look

'Come on!' He twirled her about and slapped her wet rump hard, eliciting a squeal of delighted protest as she fell back into him so that he held her and whispered in her ear. 'Let's get you out of those wet things.'

She craned her head back, their faces close now, her look earnest, breath uneven, giving the lie to her feigned propriety. 'I think you may be getting a little way ahead of yourself young man!' This time she would not be denied.

Chapter 8

The rain persisted. Sebastian had some work to attend to. He continued as a locum judge and needed to look through some paperwork. Amanda had promised Gwyneth that she would read to her from one of her earlier novels. Gwyneth had assured her she'd entirely forgotten it, claiming this as one of the few benefits of age.

Showered and changed she sat on her bed. What a wonderful morning. The feeling of renewal continued to lift her. Gwyneth was lovely, and although Amanda could not entirely escape a lurking twinge of guilt at what was happening between her and Sebastian, she wasn't troubled by it. What would be would be. Passion can find it's own rationale, and excuses flower with very little effort. Amanda was not asking too many questions.

Like being asleep, you only know that you have been when you awaken. The long aching months, almost three years, angry and alone. She had inwardly blamed her dead husband, railing silently against his departure. She had blamed herself without knowing why. She'd punished herself, exiled within her own closed off life. Undeserving. Unloved. And now? There was life! She whispered a message, a prayer. 'Sorry John. So sorry. I've missed you. Be happy for me now?' It was a small outpouring of enormous consequence. At last she had laid to rest the past, and knew in her heart that John would indeed be happy for her, would wish her to live and be happy.

Momentous events were afoot. The flirtation in the stable had changed everything Not for the first time Amanda had felt the stirring power of awakening desire long since forgot, the kiss shivering through her whole body. It was outrageously new. Even thinking of it now she again began to feel aroused.

Downstairs all was quiet. Amanda scanned the bookcase looking for her own book, the one pipped for the Orange that Gwyneth had asked her to read. The books were neatly in alphabetical order, and she was gratified to see that all her novels were there. She tapped on the door and entered to find Gwyneth propped up in bed in the corner of the room beaming at her.

'Ah, there you are! How was your ride? Hector's quite a handful isn't he?'

'Oh Gwyneth I can't tell you . . . it was amazing! Honestly I've never ridden a horse like him. It was as if he's on springs, but really easy to manage once I got the hang of him. You must miss it so much.' She added the last bit conscious of her earlier conversation with Sebastian over lunch, and resolved not to tip-toe around.

'Absolutely dear. I used to so love to ride. I kept it up as long as I could, probably longer than I really should have; but then I nearly came off four - no *five* years ago and decided that was it. The rot had set in anyway and I couldn't even walk too well by then. Anyway, I'm so glad you're able to step into the breach! Sebastian rides him sometime but I think Hector's really a lady's man.'

Amanda pulled up a chair. 'How long have we got? I mean the carers . . ?'

'Oh they won't be back till teatime now, then they'll get me back into the chair for the evening. It breaks the day up and they're a real laugh the pair of them. I mean we could get by on fewer visits, and it *is* a bit tedious being hoisted about. But I look forward to seeing the girls and having a brew, not to mention getting to the bloody bathroom! You found the book then?'

'Yes. I'm actually quite looking forward to reading it, well sort of anyway. I think I've probably forgotten it just as much as you have. I hope I like it!' She grasped the hand that slid weakly toward her across the bed clothes, returning Gwyneth smile that warmed her like the sun appearing from behind a cloud.

'Well it's so kind of you Amanda, really. I can just about manage my Kindle but it's a real luxury being read to. Sebastian sometimes reads to me, but we always have done that, even when I was well. Poetry more often than not, big soppy dates that we are!'

'Oh that's lovely! Who are your favourite poets?'

And so it went on, a good deal of time passing in this way before Amanda at last opened the book and began to read.

They barely registered the phone ringing, answered elsewhere. Sebastian appeared shortly after. There was a problem. The call had been from his sister Sophie in Scotland. Their aging mother had been admitted to hospital in Edinburgh. She'd suffered a stroke. Sebastian was going to have to fly up there.

Amanda immediately said she would return home, obviously. There was no need for Sebastian and Gwyneth to have any concerns on her account. But neither would not hear of it. She had only just arrived and had barely unpacked. Sebastian may well be back the following day or the next. He would let them know later on when he knew where things were up to.

She felt awkward none the less. This was an unexpected turn of events. She demurred. 'Your so kind, but please, don't even think about me, I'm fine now, really, and should be on my way. Can I help you with the flight and tickets while you get ready?'

'Would you Amanda? That would be very helpful. You can use Gwyneth's I-pad and here's a pen to jot them down. Oh. Let's see. Use this old envelope.' He was uncharacteristically distracted and disappeared in a flurry without waiting for a reply or pressing her further to stay.

'Oh dear.' Gwyneth pronounced solemnly. '*That's* not so good. Ninety-four if my memory serves. Go ahead Amanda you'll be so much quicker than me.' She gestured to where the I-pad lay beside her: 'Shufflingoff, lower case, all one word!'

Amanda laughed as she took it. 'Oh god sorry, I shouldn't be laughing! Gatwick I suppose . . . do you think?'

'Oh yes, absolutely. Check the trains into London too. Guildford's favourite, and he can get the Gatwick Express. That'll be easily the quickest. You could drop him at the station, just so long as you promise to come straight back here!'

Amanda smiled but didn't commit, busy with the task and quickly jotting things down. Gwyneth was right, there were plenty trains, and the times and a choice of flights lined up nicely. She was in high efficiency mode, booked and paid for the tickets for both, acquiring the necessary details from Gwyneth and ignoring her constant interjections to fetch her purse and credit cards from her bag. 'That's it, tickets bought!'

Gwyneth scolded but Amanda wouldn't be moved. 'Honestly, it's the least I can do, after all Sebastian's done for me.'

'Well in that case you absolutely *must* bring yourself back here my dear so we can at least look after you for a few days, or I shall be very cross indeed! And you know Sebastian will be very upset if his dashing off makes you feel you have to go too.'

Amanda   sighed   and   returned   Gwyneth's

mischievous disconsolate look. 'You're a very bad woman.'

'I know. Off you go then and get him sorted.'

She nearly collided with Sebastian in the hall as he hurried down the stairs bag in hand.

'4-15 from Guildford, Gatwick Express, and 7-30 flight . . . all sorted! I've forwarded everything to your mobile.'

'Thank you so much Amanda. That's wonderful! I'll ring for a taxi.'

'No time for that, jump in my car and I'll drive you.'

The traffic was light and Sebastian appeared calmer now he was at last underway. 'I'm so Glad you're going to stay on Amanda. Gwyneth said she'd persuaded you.'

'Did she indeed?!'

'Well see how you feel. Have a rest, take Hector out, get to know Gwyneth. I'm so glad that the two of you hit it off. Oh and there's dry riding clobber in the wardrobe in my bedroom if you do decide to ride.'

They arrived at the station in good time and Sebastian insisted Amanda drop him off rather than park. She complied though complained. 'Oh, that's too bad. I was rather looking forward to a Trevor Howard/Celia Johnson moment!'

She pulled into the drop-off area, and switched off the engine. They kissed. In all the rush neither had thought about the unexpected sudden separation, and it was a poignant moment. Sebastian took her hand. 'I think this is going to be something more than a 'brief encounter' Amanda, don't you?' He cradled her cheek in his hand and she held it there. The train was due. Her eyes were suddenly misting, her voice a cracked whisper. 'Go on then darling. You don't want to miss it.' Sebastian got out and grabbed his bag from the back seat; a look, a half smile, nod, and he was gone.

Back at the house Amanda was agitated. She went up to her bedroom and stretched out on the bed with her laptop seeking to distract herself with work, but gave up and went out to the stables. Both horses had their heads poking out, and Hector snickered and blew as Amanda approached. 'Sorry boy, just a social visit I'm afraid.'

She entered the box, backing Hector off before her, his tail swishing and prancing on the spot. Achilles had also withdrawn into his box and was looking through the rail in a 'what about me' way. She found a grooming brush and ran it in long sweeps over Hector's neck and withers. The smell of horses and hay was calming and Hector settled as she brushed, turning his head to nuzzle her appreciatively. She continued to brush, lost in the rhythm and the physical effort, humming quietly to herself. 'What do *you* think Hector?' she confided. 'Complicated or what?' She stood back and surveyed the shining chestnut coat then moved around to do the other side. When she'd finished she made her way back into the house.

The agitation had resolved itself. It had been a tender leave-taking. She'd called him 'darling' so easily. How could that be on such brief acquaintance? How strangely normal, how at home she felt there with her soon to be lover and his wife. What was it about Gwyneth that so drew her, made everything alright? And then there was the photograph. On returning to the house Amanda had gone to look at it again, struck once more by what she saw: herself as she had been that morning in Gwyneth's riding clothes; a doppelgänger, she knew, as did all three of them.

She'd promised to return later to continue her reading, and met Jean coming out with an armful of laundry. 'Are you finished? I was just coming through to see.'

'Ah.' Jean hesitated. She was a Geordie and had been very welcoming to Amanda, but now put her off. 'It may not be a good idea right now petal. She's taken a bit of a dip. It's what she calls the 'black dog'.'

'Ah. As in Churchill?'

'Aye so I'm told. She was really bad a while back. Better now, but just recently it's started again. Just the odd day right enough, but this is what happens, right out of the blue. To be honest pet I don't think you'd get much out of her.'

'Oh no. That bad? It must be awful for her. Will you tell her I was asking?'

'Aye. Course a' will. She'll probably be right as rain tomorrow. That's what it's like. Have you heard from Judge Hartley? Dead sorry to hear about his mother.' They were walking through to the kitchen where Jean dropped the laundry inside the door of the utility room and picked up the kettle.

'No not yet. He'll have only just got there I should think. It's not the best time for me to be visiting really. I'll see what he says. Maybe best if I come back when things are a bit more settled.'

Jean was waving a mug at her

'Go on then, coffee please. Black no sugar.'

'Oh that's a shame. She'll be better tomorrow . . . well probably. That's usually the run of it. But a' see what you mean.' She was in perpetual motion multi-tasking about the kitchen and making Amanda feel even more a spare part.

'Listen, a' hope you didn't think a' was rude backaways . . . gawping and all that. A' mean a' was a bit thrown a' must say. We'd always thought the photo in the living room was Gwyneth!'

'It was. I mean it *is*.'

'Really!? No!? But it's . . . no! Really? But . . .' She'd stopped what she was doing and stared in disbelief.

Suddenly Amanda found herself feeling irked. She glanced at her watch. 'Oh dear, is that the time? Sorry Jean I need to make a call. I'll skip coffee. See you later.'

She'd come to a decision. She'd return home the

following day after hopefully seeing Gwyneth in the morning to say goodbye. With Sebastian gone it was awkward to say the very least, and he'd surely be in Scotland for a few days, or longer still. It'd been a good to come here and an unexpected joy to meet Gwyneth, but it was time to go.

She found clean riding gear where Sebastian had said, and made her way to the stables relieved to have made up her mind: an early evening ride followed by a hot bath and late dinner, and tomorrow home.

She heard the whistling before she turned the corner into the yard, and there came face to face with a man in miniature. He couldn't have been much over five foot, wiry and weatherbeaten with a cloth cap and scruffy navy overalls. He carried two buckets of water which looked much larger than normal because of his own diminutive stature. He stopped dead as if he'd seen a ghost, not thinking to put down the heavy buckets.

'Jesus Mary and Joseph! Missis . .?'

Amanda realised this must be Seamus, the stable 'boy' and general retainer who had looked after the grounds and the horses for the Hartleys since time immemorial. She tried to keep a creeping weary tone out of her voice as she replied. 'I'm Amanda. Just staying for a day or two. You must be Seamus?'

Bethinking himself he put the buckets down and hastily stepped forward proffering his hand. 'Well I never. Very pleased to meet you Amanda. Quite a turn you gave me. Sure the wife'll not believe it so she won't.'

Amanda smiled and felt sorry for her curt response to the poor man's bemused mistake.

'Oh don't worry, I've seen the photo too. But this is definitely me!'

'Come on then me darlin' and we'll get ye sorted. I'm taking it that it's ould Hector you'll be wanting?'

He set about preparing Hector, talking all the while, evidently wanting to reassure himself that Amanda could manage the lively gelding. Seamus was was obviously a man of cautious disposition, and careful to whom he entrusted his much loved charges. He was, however, innately courteous and discreet.

'Well would you listen to that?! That boy in there's not too happy. Maybe I should give him a wee run out too if you wouldn't mind a scruffy ould fellah trailing along with ye?'

It was true that Achilles *was* stomping about, whinnying and snorting, and Amanda was glad of the offer of company. She'd immediately taken to Seamus. It was decided. With both horses ready in the yard Amanda mounted easily, despite Hector skittering around. She noted Seamus's approving smile. She then watched to see how this tiny man would seat himself on his enormous mount. She found herself hoping that she hadn't made a mistake in agreeing to the company, fearing that he might hold her up or dawdle along on a glorified pony trek.

How in fact Seamus made the transition from standing by the horse to being atop it Amanda would not in truth have been able to say. One second he was not on the horse, and the next he was, spurring Achilles forward onto the grass to leap the fence into the paddock. He cantered Achilles in a full circle to hold, the horse dancing excitedly on the spot. Seamus was grinning from ear to ear as he waited for Amanda. She laughed and kicked on, trotting Hector sedately through the open gate.

Bathed and dined, Amanda was enjoying being ensconced in what she'd decided was Sebastian's armchair. She'd poured herself a cognac and was contented, eyes closed listening to Chopin. At last came the expected call. It was good news. The 'old girl' was stable and doing well. Sebastian's sister had sped her into hospital where she'd had a scan and within the short window available was able to have an injection to disperse the bleed. It appeared to have been a success in limiting the effects of the stroke. All was looking positive, and it was expected that she would be returning to convalesce at Sophie's home in Linlithgow within the next few days. Sebastian was staying at the Balmoral in the city to be on hand, but hoped to be returning home within the next forty eight hours if things remained on track.

'So I'll see you quite soon. Can't wait. What about you, how's it been?'

'Oh fine, really, except that Gwyneth apparently had a dip this afternoon and Jean thought it'd be best for me to leave her be for now while she got a nights sleep and picked up a bit.'

There was a pause. 'Oh. That's not so good. There've been one or two of these lately. I thought you being around might . . . oh well. She'll probably be fine in the morning, so don't worry.'

'Yes, that's what Jean said. But I've decided I'll go home tomorrow Sebastian, after I've seen Gwyneth if she's up to it. It's just not good timing really is it? Please don't tell Gwyneth. I'll tell her in the morning.'

Another pause. 'Oh. Right.'

'In any case, I think I'd rather be with you in town just now. Things being as they are . . . you and I. You know I really like Gwyneth, but that makes it *more* difficult, under her roof as it were.'

It was economical enough but said it all, and Sebastian's sigh was both accepting of his short term disappointment and appreciative of the promise conveyed. 'Of course. Yes yes I understand. You know Gwyneth wouldn't . . . but anyway you're quite right. I think we need to talk Amanda. Let's spend some time in town, that would be lovely. So what have you been doing.'

'Oh, well, I met a *man*, and he took me for a *ride*!'

Sebastian laughed, 'Oh! Did he indeed? Well he'll

be looking for new employment when I get home!'

Amanda recounted her meeting with Seamus and learned, not to her surprise, that he had been a professional jump jockey in his youth, and had what Sebastian described as a 'veritably symbiotic' relationship with horses.

'Yes, I noticed! It's amazing. He doesn't seem to *do* anything. Do you think it's telepathy? And there I was before he got on hoping he wouldn't hold me up!'

Sebastian laughed, but the short silence that followed was awkward. 'Look, how about 'I'll call you, soon as I'm clear. Have you anything . . . can we . . .'

'Nothing that won't wait. Just as soon as you're free. And me too, by the way.'

'What?'

'Can't wait.'

Packed and ready to go Amanda made her way through to see Gwyneth, having learned from Becky that she was breakfasted and on good form. Rain had set in during the night and was beating against the connecting glass tube. Gwyneth's welcoming smile was radiant.

'Amanda.! How lovely to see you. So sorry abut yesterday my darling. It's just what happens sometimes I'm afraid.'

She was seated in her chair and Amanda squeezed her hand flopped at the edge of the tray in front of her. She settled on the adjacent sofa, 'Oh I was fine. I had a nice relaxing afternoon and an evening ride out with Seamus.'

Gwyneth laughed, 'Oh, a minor force of nature that one!'

They talked about the situation with Sebastian and his mother. He'd spoken to Gwyneth earlier and was possibly going to return the next day, if not the day after.

'Yes, so I thought I'd get away this morning Gwyneth. It's *not* good timing really, and well . . . but it's been lovely to meet you. I've *so* enjoyed talking to you.' She'd found herself reaching again to take Gwyneth's hand, suddenly feeling cowardly running off to have a tryst with Sebastian elsewhere, and seeing the look of disappointment Gwyneth was unable to disguise.

There was a long uncomfortable pause.

'So, would you like me to read . . .'

'It's alright Amanda. Really. It's alright. *I don't mind.'*

Amanda found herself filling up with tears, knowing only too well what was being referred to, and that it was *not* the fact that she was departing early. She tried to speak but couldn't find the words. Gwyneth's hand squeezed hers, hardly any pressure at all, but Amanda knew it was probably all the strength she could muster.

'Sebastian is a good man Amanda. *All these years!* But he must *live*. And you, *you* . . . be kind to yourself, to him. I'm happy for you. Do you understand?'

Amanda's tears brimmed over unchecked, her reply a whisper 'Yes. Yes. I do.'

'Go now then. Be happy my dear. Come back another time. Will you do that? Do I ask too much?'

Amanda's voice was stronger now. 'Yes. Of course I will. My dear friend. I'm so glad we met. Thank you.'

They embraced and she was gone.

Chapter 9

There was no let up in the rain over the next couple of days. Amanda hunkered down at home, glad to be back to work. With the initial groundwork already done she was drafting an opening chapter. In her mind the story was taking shape, but it remained fluid for now.

Like a painter making a preparatory sketch she had to put down words on paper to make it real. It would go through many changes, but it was always an exciting Rubicon to cross, breathing life into imaginary people and weaving the threads of their story. In time the characters themselves would begin to take matters into their own hands, such that she the author would become a participant in her own creation. But that was some way off and for now she was the sole arbiter of the new reality put down on the empty page, the artisan proceeding with discipline in her craft.

She was aided and abetted by the rain and the news from Sebastian that his mother had had a further minor stroke and his return would be delayed a few more days at least. So she was free from distractions. And there was something else, a new freedom, gone the stultifying emptiness that had been her lot since John died. Colour had returned to her life, washing away the sepia 'same old same old' that had stolen like a thief into her eye.

It wasn't until the evening of the third day that Amanda phone to let Trish know she was back. She knew that it would be impossible to put Trish off her plan to stay once Trish knew she was back, and this indeed turned out to be the case. She appeared the following day with her bag and an enormous bouquet.

By this time Amanda was 'in the groove.' The story was slowly unfolding and felt authentic, the characters already beginning to grow and assert themselves.

Now she would begin to loosen the rein and write more freely until the scene was fully set and the defining event had taken place. She would then pause and pass her opening chapters to Melanie, her trusted friend and agent for an honest opinion. She had long since been aware that her own could only be trusted so far. You *can* see the wood for the trees when living in the forest, but harder to visualise the forest itself.

She'd impressed on Trish that she'd be working and to bring a book to read. They knew each other well enough to be able to ignore one another. The warm sunshine of the previous week returned, and the temperature continued to rise. Trish was the perfect house guest. She spent long stretches of time reading on the terrace and sunning herself in designer shades and the tiniest bikini, which had prompted Amanda to comment simultaneously admiring and admonishing.

'You do look amazing darling! But I hope you're going to make a small contribution to the gardening costs for all the work Jesus is *not* going to be getting done!'

Trish glanced up from her book adjusting her shades to look over the top, smiled appreciatively and blew her a kiss. Trish had that winning combination of being lithe and leggy, but with what her male acquaintances universally concurred to be 'great tits.' Unlike some women of a certain age Trish *did* look better with her clothes off and knew it. Amanda's comment was well received. 'Why don't you join me for a bit darling? Bring your work stuff out here and get some sun on that lovely body.'

'Don't think so sweetie. The poor gardener has enough to contend with. And in any case, as his employer I do rather prefer it that he looks me in the eye, which is not dear heart where he looks at you!'

Preoccupied with her writing, Amanda was appreciative of Trish's unobtrusiveness. She was uncharacteristically quiet, obviously making an effort not to intrude. There was always dinner and long evenings for Trish to glean snippets about Sebastian and Gwyneth and the embryonic romance. Amanda didn't mind, glad to be able to confide. Trish was encouraging and supportive, despite her cautionary 'be careful' on the phone. On the contrary, she was at one point unmistakably teary, taking Amanda's hand and earnestly encouraging.

'Go for it darling. You look *so* well, it's amazing. I'm *so* happy for you!'

Marcia came over for lunch, and she too was very positive. Amanda had not told either about the photo, and avoided the obvious speculation that this would have caused. It remained a small irritant, the grain of sand in the oyster which even as it became hidden in the pearl could not be expelled. The idea that she was as it were an identical replacement for Gwyneth hovered uncomfortably in the back of her mind, whilst simultaneously fascinating her.

Lunch over they'd retired to the morning room. Jesus was walking the mower up and down the lawn outside. Marcia was sated on her update such as it was, and mulled it as they all three absently watched Jesus going back and forth. She was fascinated at what, Amanda knew, she misconstrued as the audacity of it all : Amanda setting out to seduce her man at home with his unsuspecting wife. 'Honestly Amanda,' she said at last, 'I never thought you had it in you! Well . . . as it were!'

Lewd giggles from Trish induced a brief comedic pause. 'I mean surely she must suspect . . . Gwyneth. I mean look at you, you're gorgeous, and if she's, well . . . do you think she . . .'

'She knows. And she *doesn't* mind.' Amanda hadn't mentioned this to Trish, or meant to do so now. She was surprised to hear herself capitulating so easily under Marcia's never less than forensic interest, anticipating the inevitable question.

'Oh.' Marcia was temporarily halted in her tracks assimilating this new and unexpectedly candid information.

'Are you sure?' Trish said in disbelief.

Amanda had immediately regretted her indiscretion but resigned now confirmed that indeed she knew this to be the case.

'She told me it's alright, she doesn't mind, that she wants Sebastian to be happy,' she summarised.

'Oh.' It was Trish's turn for the monosyllabic response.

Amanda lit a cigarette, momentarily gratified at least by her friends' apparent discomfiture. Marcia offered her own summary.

'Well, if she said what you said she said, she obviously means what you said you think she means . . . if you see what I mean."

'What did she just say?' Amanda was looking quizzically at Trish.

'No idea. But she's right. That's . . .' she paused, gazing into space, a look of bewilderment, 'Christ she must really love him,' she said, quietly, almost to herself. Once again Trish seemed to be teetering on the verge of tears and Amanda caught Marcia's quizzical look.

'Yes.' Amanda mused. She was registering the deeper truth within Trish's telling insight, and found herself curiously strengthened by it rather than upset. She was aware of both her friends looking at her now with new interest, temporarily silenced. Amanda's cigarette ash had grown precariously long before she noticed it and too late moved too quickly, spilling it on the rug as she reached for the ashtray to stub it out. She was calm now, turned inward, and when she spoke again it was to herself. 'Yes. I think she does. And yes, I think it is . . . alright.'

The news from Sebastian was good. His mother was much improved and miraculously had no significant longer term effects. She had returned home with Sophie, and Sebastian had flown home earlier in the week. Gwyneth was well and no more dips. It was Thursday afternoon when he phoned to talk about their weekend in London. 'So all told I reckon I can get away at last. All's well here. I told Gwyneth I may pop up to town for a few nights. So how are you fixed? We could stay at the apartment, or a hotel if you'd prefer?'

'Oh. I'd love to. I've been . . . well I've been looking forward to it. Hotel please if you wouldn't mind. Somewhere, somewhere new where neither of us has been before. Is that alright?'

'Yes of course. You're right. Let's do that.'

It was arranged. Trish had lingered much longer than Amanda had anticipated, giving no indication about when she would return home. She had continued to be quiet. Amanda had been immersed in her work, and had at last sent something to Melanie. Trish had cooked and they were having dinner.

'I spoke to Sebastian earlier. We're going to spend the weekend in London. I'm off up there tomorrow!'

Trish's fork was suspended between plate and mouth. For a few moments she appeared bewildered, then with some apparent effort she put it down and managed to contrive a smile.

'Oh. That's . . . that's lovely. I suppose I'd better . . . sorry, I just need to . . .' She stood up suddenly so that her chair scraped backwards, wobbled and fell with a clatter as she rushed out, Amanda calling after her as she fled upstairs. She followed and paused on the landing. All was quiet. A minute or two slid passed and at last Amanda tapped on the bedroom door.

'Trish? Trish darling, what is it?'

'I'll be down in a minute. Sorry. Just give me a minute.'

When Trish appeared in the kitchen Amanda hugged her. 'What's the matter? I've put the dinner in the oven. Come on. Here's one I made earlier.' She handed her a large Remy and led her through to the living room, Trish meekly doing as she was told.

They sipped their drinks. Trish stared vacantly out into the garden, reaching for a cigarette when Amanda lit one. Trish hadn't smoked in years, but Amanda gave her one none-the-less, now doubly concerned. The cigarette and brandy seemed to steady her, and at last she blurted out. 'He's got another woman . . . Richard. He's moving out.'

The story thus began was quickly told. Richard had told Trish that he'd been having an affair, and of his intention to move out. He was going to do so over the coming weekend. He wasn't moving in with the 'other woman,' and had rented a small flat in the London. He couldn't continue the deception but couldn't give her up and had to 'see it through'. He didn't know what he wanted longer term, but would 'fully understand' if Trish wanted to separate and even divorce, though he would not say that this was what *he* wanted.

'What a bastard!' Amanda said, never one to mince words, which earned her a mirthless smile.

'Yeah. Total fucking bastard!'

Engrossed in her own stuff Amanda had not read the signs. 'I'll put Sebastian off. He'll understand. And don't worry about staying here. You can stay as long as you want. Oh Trish I'm so sorry!'

'No you bloody well will not! But if I *could* stay, just till he's cleared off?' Her words dried up, just as her tears once more brimmed. Amanda put their drinks on the table and held her until it passed, rubbing her back like a baby as she cried. She fetched the bottle over and refreshed their drinks.

'Do you know who she is?'

'Yes. Well sort of. She was at my fiftieth, one of the group from Richard's work, the ones who arrived in a taxi late and quite drunk.'

Amanda remembered. It was fancy dress and they'd arrived by taxi, five of them doing the conga into the house and breathing life into what had been up to then a rather sedate gathering.

'Oh. It wasn't . . ?'

'Little miss 'life is a cabaret' eat your heart out Lisa Minnelli. Yes, you got it in one. How *did* you do that?'

'Oh God!' Amanda groaned.

The young woman in question was, even as Sally Bowles, under-dressed. She had, as the evening progressed, enjoyed without any hint of inhibition the approbation and concerted attention of every single (and married) man there. It was all treated as a bit of a joke. She was half the age of most of the guests. The conversation amongst the women *after* the event, though grudgingly forced to acknowledge the girl's undeniable attributes, focussed on the pathetic salivating men, and consigned the object of their attentions to oblivion with the classic:

'But she's a tart!' Amanda repeated it once more.

'Yes. I know that darling. And what do you think a man in his mid-fifties, a dirty old fucking scumbag bastard with his brains in his dick wants more than anything else?'

She was crying again. Amanda produced a box of tissues. Tears wiped and nose blown Trish now laughed, an angry bitter laugh. 'The thing is, I've been waiting the last few days for him to tell me it's all off and beg my forgiveness! I mean, nothing was settled before I came here. He just told me, as if he was doing something noble and right. Ha! I thought

105

with me gone and when he'd had time to think about it he'd . . .what a fucking fool I am! Ready to forgive him, try to give him a better time, even wear some of that tarty lingerie they all seem to like. He e-mailed me yesterday. Said he was going. Needs some 'space'. Some fucking SPACE!'

She spat the last words with such venom that Amanda flinched. 'I'll phone Sebastian.'

'No. I mean it Amanda. You go. I'll be fine.'

She took Trish's hand: 'Alright. If you're sure. Thanks. Come on. We need to eat.'

Amanda took a while to get to sleep, despite the eventual lateness of the hour and the amount of alcohol imbibed. She was glad that Trish was insistent on her not cancelling her trip. She *was* excited about it, though Trish's situation weighed upon her nonetheless. Lots of people had flings, but for dull reliable Richard to essentially be looking to off-load his witty and very attractive wife for a younger model shocked and angered her.

She recalled only too well the party and the way the men had been, but had difficulty squaring those poor sad lusting souls emboldened by too much drink with her friend's husband of twenty-five years lusting his way out of their marriage stone cold sober. She thought with distaste of Richard and the girl together, then pivoted to how it would be with her and Sebastian.

She was nervous. John was much younger than

her and they had always been adventurous lovers. Now *she* was going to be the younger one. How would *that* be? Her mind drifted back to their parting at the station, to the stables wet after their ride, and she she slid at last into a deep sleep. The barren years were over. All would be well.

Chapter 10

Arriving in London never failed to cheer Amanda. The smells and sounds of Kings Cross, the immediate increase of tempo. The cosmopolitan mix of people moving with energy and purpose. She strode along the platform with a confident swing, long strides as far as permitted by her tight ivory skirt, discreetly short and chosen with care to show her at her best. Her bag trundled along behind her like a well trained dog. She knew Sebastian would be waiting, watching somewhere among the sea of people, and this was her entrance. She wore a jade silk blouse, and a teardrop silver pendant hung low in the V of the casually inviting open neck.

It was a very long time since Amanda had felt the thrill of so deliberately dressing to be seen, but neither the lack of practice or the years weighed on her performance. She caught the eye of a young man staring at her, returned his smile, and he offered a tiny comical wave. It reminded her of Stan Laurel and she couldn't suppress a grin as she neared the barrier.

Retrieving her ticket she looked around and almost walked into Sebastian. He was half hidden amongst others waiting there, and stepped forward to greet her. Now she was in his arms and the kiss was long and tender.

'I think I might have something in my eye,' she purred, and craned up for a second. He held her close and Amanda could feel her heart beating overtime as she sunk into him. She hadn't expected such an intimate hello and sensed that Sebastian too had been taken by surprise. She drew back hardly at all then impulsively gave him another peck on the lips and whispered. 'I can't wait.'

The hotel was an Italian family run business in Mayfair. They were just in time for lunch. Up in their room, having unpacked and stowed their bags, Sebastian was suddenly hesitant, his usual easy command overtaken by shyness. This put Amanda more at ease, contrarily emboldened by Sebastian's unsureness. For the second time that day she acted on an impulse.

'Would you mind if I quickly changed?'

'No, of course not. Should I . . .?' He glanced toward the door and back at Amanda, already re-opening her wardrobe and glancing over her shoulder with a smile, teasing him with his own words.

'No. Of course not!'

Thus invited Sebastian sat down and watched Amanda change. She'd taken as much care about her choice of lingerie as her clothes, and now undressed slowly and purposefully, *before* looking to decide what to put on. She took her time, turning this way and that to extract and replace various possibilities.

At last she turned waving the chosen dress. 'What do you . . . oh Sebastian!'

The desired effect had been easily achieved. As he took her almost naked body in his arms the dress falling to the floor. As if awakening from a long sleep, Amanda once again felt a man's hands caress her body, long slow caresses, searching as they kissed, fanning her already raging fire. She forgot herself, forgot everything, her body seeking too and finding *him* out, shamelessly pushing against his hardened cock, offering, imploring. 'Yes! Yes.! Yes!'

It was a relief to Amanda to have gone too bed with Sebastian so early in their time together. It was not simply that she was out of practice; some things, like riding a bike, don't require repeated rehearsal. It was an 'age thing.'

She contemplated this as she thought about their lunchtime sex over a solitary coffee later that same afternoon. They'd both had things to do before people disappeared for the weekend. Amanda had called to see her agent to review with her the opening chapters to her new novel. Melanie had responded very positively, and she was buoyed by this. She had an hour to kill before meeting Sebastian at the Shard for a teatime cocktail with a view.

Yes, it *was* an 'age thing'. It struck her that the brash passion of seduction, could be supplanted by a nervous self-awareness, ironically not unlike a teenagers first hesitant attempts. There was a pleasing circular symmetry to this. She was glad she'd pushed it aside and rushed in. She'd taken a chance, thrown caution to the wind and it had paid off.

He was less sure of himself beyond his initial emboldened swoop. His hesitance had reined her in a little, and ultimately the denouement had been too quick. But it was a good first effort, and she was, if not satisfied, content. Sebastian was tender and caring, and it had been lovely to talk and laugh together naked in his arms. They were grateful to share this easy intimacy, an intimacy that neither (they'd both confessed) had thought to ever know again.

They were tourists, on holiday, taking in the sights as they took in each other. The Shard was spectacular. They competed to name landmarks. Amanda easily won. Arm in arm they arrived at Covent Garden for the pre-show dinner. Sebastian had acquired scarce tickets for the Royal Ballet's performance of The Rites of Spring. The significance wasn't lost, nor was the irony, and Amanda had laughed when he showed her the tickets. An adaptation of Elgar's Enigma Variations was also to be performed, which promised to be interesting. Both were in high spirits, an aperitif on top of the recently quaffed cocktails ensuring good cheer, as well as the anticipation of the treat to come.

There was so much to talk about. The arts of

course, but the arts being the expression of life itself there were inevitable branch lines as Amanda began to know her lover's political and social world. The elephant in the room was by tacit agreement not going to be discussed, at least just yet.

Their tastes coincided in many things, and there were spirited disagreements where they differed. Unsurprisingly Sebastian was a man of conservative views. He was after all a high court judge, a pillar of the establishment and dispenser of justice. But he was a long way from being an ideologue, and like Amanda looked to find his way inside things, to tease out the strands of an issue in order to better form and convey a view, interested in hers whether or not they concurred. He weighed things. Amanda could see how he would be good in his chosen profession, entrusted with the scales of justice. She divined that he was a man of compassion and liberalism, sentimental even. But also that there was at his core a strict morality, and wondered where this was anchored.

'Penny for them?'
Amanda lay on her side close against Sebastian who'd been studying the ceiling but now turned his gaze to her. They had made love and both were tired but unwilling to relinquish to sleep their beautiful day, their first alone together.

'Oh I was just thinking. . . . well I was thinking two things really: first what a wonderful day, and then - oh it's going to sound silly really, but I was wishing I could have made you . . . well it was all too quick again. Sorry, I'm out of practice!'

Amanda kissed him. 'Yes Judge Hartley you were right. It *is* silly. It was *lovely*, and we've all the time in the world to practice. *You expect too much too soon*. All in good time. We're just getting to know one another. It was *lovely* and we should be happy.'

He smiled sheepishly and took her in his arms. 'You're right. I know. I couldn't have hoped for more. My cup runneth over!'

They slept a deep contented sleep till morning. Amanda woke first. She lay quietly, the hum of the traffic barely audible. She had meant what she said, despite again feeling slightly cheated having been once more raised to a high pitch of excitement without the longed for coup de grace, too quick, indeed too gentle. John would have brought her off with his fingers but she didn't yet feel able to suggest that to 'Judge Hartley.'

No sooner had dissatisfaction entered her mind than she admonished the thought. That this was happening at all was a miracle. The sun had arisen in her life setting it ablaze with colour after so long when a monochrome tedium had dogged her days. There would, she knew, be many more joyful days and nights for the two of them, and the nights would get better. Sebastian awakened and even as he kissed her tenderly his cock stirred and pressed rigid against her belly, causing her to purr like a

113

contented cat. Oh she of little faith!

The weekend flew by. A trip to the Courtald, a concert at the Wigmore Hall, walking arm in arm on Hampstead Heath and ferreting through the bricabrac in the Hampstead antique shops. They talked easily. They communed in easy silences. The unexpected joy of synchronicity made them more than once stop and look at each other, reflecting on their luck. They couldn't quite believe it.

As the moment grew closer for them to part Amanda began to feel that long forgotten pang of parting, the 'sweet sorrow' that told her how good it had been.

Sunday afternoon. They'd checked out of the hotel and left their bags there. The warm sunshine was holding for another day at least. Sebastian had taken Amanda to lunch at a French restaurant he knew in one of the small streets adjacent to Regents Park. It had a small garden at the back with a few tables outside in the summer months.

After lunch they walked in the in the park. The afternoon sun filtered through traceries of beech, illuminating the newly unfurled leaves, translucent tender green. Amanda donned her sunglasses and they fed the ducks with a roll she'd saved from lunch for that purpose, breaking it into tiny crumbs to eke it out amongst the scrabbling paddling mallards. They found a bench to sit on by the pond. A small brass plate dedicated the seat to Edward Crichton, someone who had in life liked to walk and sit in the park. Amanda thought about the son or daughter or perhaps wife coming to sit here sometimes to remember.

'Its been wonderful. Amanda I can't tell you how much I've enjoyed this weekend.'

She linked his arm and snuggled her head into his shoulder. 'Yes. Me too.' She waited, sensing what was to come.

'Maybe next time we come here you'd like to stay at the flat?'

'Mmmm. That would be nice.'

There was a pause, heavy with intent, and at last Sebastian broached the subject that was in both their minds. 'Amanda you mustn't feel . . . about Gwyneth, about you and I, somehow - I don't know quite how to say it so that it doesn't sound wrong: *she doesn't mind*. It's not that it's happened before. It hasn't. She's always said I should feel free and all that sort of thing, but I never have . . . had an affair or whatever way you want to put it. But now . . . she really *likes* you darling.'

He was wading into deeper water and beginning to flounder. She sat up and looked him in the eye. There was pain there, and her hand reached up to tenderly touch his cheek. 'Does she know you're with me now?'

'Yes. Of course. I couldn't possibly lie to her, and I won't lie to you. *She doesn't mind*.'

Sebastian seemed at a loss. Amanda felt her heart squeezed. She saw an honest man, a man of integrity, wanting to do the right thing. He was reaching out to her, but in the only way he knew by telling her the truth, honouring her with his trust. There was a subtext, hardly even implied, but Sebastian knew that Amanda could infer it none the less. 'I know. She told me.'

Sebastian nodded. He didn't appear surprised. 'Oh. I thought she might.'

The ducks had dispersed. A young couple strolled by smoking, and the unmistakable smell of cannabis wafted across. Neither remarked. It was Sebastian who broke the silence at last.

'I don't really know what to say. She (Gwyneth), she feels a connection with you. She thinks you could be friends. She doesn't . . . she doesn't . . .oh god I'm saying it again! You know Amanda you can come to see us, spend time with us at home, as well as here. If you *want* to.'

He was like a car running out of petrol, stuttering, cutting out, spluttering back to life, then grinding to a halt. Amanda found herself unexpectedly annoyed. 'So I can be *your* lover and *Gwyneth's* friend?'

'Well it's not quite how I would have put it.' He said quietly, a sad wry smile, and Amanda regretted her sharpness.

'It's not that I'm. . . .oh I don't know. It just seems so . . . odd! You'll have to let me think about it. I'll ring you.'

She hadn't meant it to come out as it did, and straight away saw the bereft expression in

116

Sebastian's eyes, crestfallen, unsure of her exact meaning, and managing only a polite, 'Yes. Of course . . . of course.'

She took his hand and squeezed it hard. 'And anyway, I'll look forward to the apartment. *Soon*!'

He brightened a little and they kissed, a little longer than was quite respectable on a bench n a public park, and she laughed when in a minor panic he bethought himself, broke away and looked guiltily about. He smiled so warmly then, just the ghost of uncertainty lingering in his eye.

Amanda made a small detour via Fortnum and Masons on the way to the station and purchased a large bag of treats for dinner. She was in good spirits and looking forward to seeing Trish, determined to ply her with food and drink and cheer her up. It was almost impossible for Amanda in her radiant state to empathise fully with her friend, mired in travails. She *would* bring her some of her own good cheer, if only in the soothing claret of some very expensive vintage wine. She'd expected to be returning late evening, so it would be a surprise.

On the train Amanda reflected on her good fortune. She was sorry for having been to her mind, prissy about the whole Gwyneth thing. Hadn't she herself already said to Gwyneth that she would visit? So why had she given Sebastian a hard time? She saw his face, so sad when she responded the way she did, evidently fearing for a moment that

117

he'd blown it and pushed her away. What was it? She thought about the photo. Somehow it had unsettled her. She resolved to phone him when she got home and put things right.

Arriving home Amanda deposited the shopping on the side in the kitchen. There was no sign of Trish and she went upstairs to shower and change. On the landing she heard Trish's voice, but not as she had ever heard it before, or saying anything intelligible. She was unmistakably in the throes of passion, and now Amanda also registered a lower voice accompanying Trish's high-pitched rhythmic squeals with his own offering of gasps and grunts.

The bedroom door was ajar, and Amanda had no hesitation in (entirely needlessly) tip-toeing across to peer shamelessly at her friend having sex. She was curious, but now also becoming suddenly excited as she rested her cheek against the back of her hand placed on the door frame, hardly daring to breath, a tremor running through her whole body as she took in the scene.

Trish gripped the high Victorian bed-head, her arms and back extended in a long shallow arc like a yoga position. Jesus was fucking her hard from behind, her tits swinging heavily with every thrust. Amanda gazed mesmerised. Such was the violence of the act that the whole bed creaked and shook. She flinched at the physical collisions but felt herself inwardly urging them on like she would a horse over jumps. The vocal crescendo was building to a climax, a compulsive rhythmic explosion surrendered to the primitive urge to mate.

Amanda was transfixed. So compelling was it that she forgot herself, no longer conscious of being the voyeur, but drawn in, involved, unable to resist. Her breath came in short gasps, her gaze locked on Jesus as he bucked and groaned, her own hips involuntarily synchronized with him. They orgasmed together with a deafening outcry, less pleasure than pain, more tooth and claw than making love. Amanda took a sharp intake of breath when Jesus thrust his last and held, his muscular buttocks quivering with his final spasms deep in Trish. Amanda alone was not sated, left hanging like a halal beast half-bled, taut and unrelieved.

Jesus was still, his head bowed, hands resting on Trish's hips like a priest at an alter, a Caravaggio painting uniting the profane with the sublime. It was all quiet now but for the lovers' heavy breathing. Trish had collapsed her head down into the pillows, and was still, but for a hardly perceptible movement of her hips, her cunt still filled with Jesus's cock savouring the last moments of union.

Still Amanda looked, transfixed, until the sudden stillness alerted her to the hitherto forgotten possibility of discovery, and in a momentary panic she stepped hastily back from the door. The creaking floorboard *must* have been heard, and she froze, listening, but no sound came from within. Back in her own room Amanda hastily undressed and lay naked on the bed, instantly masturbating, immersed in the images of what she had just seen. At last, her knuckle jammed into her mouth to prevent her crying out, the other hand pushing, pushing, pushing, fingertips pushing desperately against her clitoris and still in perfect synchronicity with what had gone before, she came.

She lay breathing heavily in a state of shocked relief. Such an orgasm! She was shocked at it's power, but also to discover stirring within herself such untutored lust. She knew that the unbridled passion she had witnessed could never be hers with Sebastian. She had missed it. A small cloud momentarily flitted across her mental sky. It was only a milli-second, but she chided herself for such a 'glass half empty' thought, when her glass was so very full, her life renewed.

She jumped up and ran the shower. Before stepping in, however, she slipped on her bath robe and quietly stepped out onto the landing. All was still and Trish's bedroom door ajar just as it had been.

'Helloooo. . . I'm home! Just going to have a quick shower.' She hollered, audibly closing her bedroom door as Trish's voice attempted a casual 'Righto!'

She smiled at the thought of the panic that this would have caused. Tact was going to be called for and Amanda was good at that, though she and Trish were close and shared many personal confidences. She would see how it unfolded.

Under the power of the cleansing jets Amanda's mind wandered back to her disappointed thoughts. They appeared spoilt and petty now, and she banished them from her, what point in wanting that which you can never have? But even as she pushed them away, the images of what she had just seen returned to momentarily claim her, just as the wanting, aroused from a long forgetful sleep scurried away a little bit ashamed, to find a place to hide.

Trish had made coffee, and gave Amanda a big hug, holding on like a child to the comfort of a mother's embrace. Amanda had noticed immediately the red hollow eyes of someone who hasn't slept and has been drinking too much.

'Not so good eh?' Amanda produced a tissue from her pocket and Trish dabbed at her eyes.

'Been better.'

'Come on.'

They took their drinks through to the drawing room and sat down on the couch.

'How did *you* get on anyway? Silly question really. I can see just by looking at you!'

Amanda smiled. 'Oh, it was lovely.' It was sensitively far less than she felt. 'So. No last minute change of heart then?'

'No. No change. Not that I'd have the bastard back anyway! He's clearing off today. That's that.'

She sounded completely beaten, despite her

bravado. 'God I need drink. You'll have one won't you?'

It sounded like an invitation to a wake, and Trish was off without waiting for a reply to fetch the necessary. She placed a two thirds empty whisky bottle and two glasses on the table.

'I'll get you another tomorrow.'

They clinked glasses and drank. Amanda lit a cigarette, and frowned at Trish reaching over to help herself to one. Trish pulled a face and lit up. She'd already downed most of her very large drink, and Amanda suspected she was topping up rather than starting again.

'Trust you to find a man just as I'm cut foot loose and fancy free. Who am I going to go clubbing with?!'

'Oh Trish.! Look, it might not be . . . . things can *change* . . .' She was neither convinced nor convincing and decided against saying anymore.

Trish poured another and cradled it lovingly, puffing away on her cigarette. She looked askance at Amanda as she enquired. 'How come you didn't pop your head round the door?'

'What?'

'When you came in. Usually you'd tap on the door and pop your head in.'

Amanda looked skyward and shrugged. 'Oh I was . . . I mean I had my bag and . . .'

'And you didn't look through the door and see me in bed with Jesus?'

Amanda took a deep breath. 'Well, not exactly darling. Not *then*. Actually, I'd arrived about ten minutes earlier and . . .'

Amanda had never before seen Trish blush. 'Oh my god! You didn't I mean . . . when we were . . .'

'Fraid so darling. I just caught the end, as it were. I couldn't . . . well I *heard* you and *saw* the door ajar, so I . . .'

'Oh no! Oh god! It was just . . . I was just . . . *oh my god*!' At which point she crumbled into hysterical giggles.

The story was much as Amanda might have imagined. It had begun on Saturday. Trish had risen late, and when duly revived with several coffees had, as Amanda also guessed, sampled the hair of the dog. She was in her usual place on the sun lounger, in her usual state of undress with a large G&T. Jesus had unexpectedly arrived, apparently needing something from the shed for a job at home. Trish was in need of comfort. Jesus gave it.

'But honestly Trish, he's my *gardener* for God's sake! And he can't be a day over twenty-five!'

'I know. I'm *sorreee!* It wasn't . . . well it just *happened*. Sorry. And anyway, it was amazing. *Every time*!'

Amanda, by this time on her third large whiskey still tried to maintain her 'severe' look. 'Well it's not on. Alright *you're* going through stuff, but *he* knows full well. He's a little tinker!'

The choice of words was not wasted on Trish who

was relaxing into her on-going binge.

'No. Sorry Amanda, I absolutely have to correct you. Little he is not!'

By the time they went to bed it was too late to call Sebastian. Amanda wanted to more than anything, and her hand hovered over the phone, but she drew it away. She was quite drunk and realised with a hot rush of affection that she did not trust herself *not* to say something, to declare, to pronounce the three fateful words which alone could express how she felt. She'd ring in the morning.

Chapter 11

It was raining and Trish emerged late wearing her shades and scanning the garden nervously. Amanda fared better, up and about and breakfasted by ten, supported by the statutory dose of paracetamol and working on her novel. Trish was returning home and had packed her bag before coming downstairs for a reviving coffee. Amanda took a break to join her.

'There's no need to rush off darling, honestly, if you don't feel up to it.' Despite her generosity she was relieved when Trish demurred.

'That's really sweet of you but no, time to bite the bullet. No sense putting it off. You won't say anything to Jesus will you? It would feel sort of worse if *he* knew *you* knew, if you see what I mean.'

Amanda smiled. 'Don't worry, I won't. I take it you won't be inviting him round for dinner then?'

'Oh don't! I have a dreadful head. Is he . . ?'

'Working in the greenhouse and strangely keeping his head down!'

With Trish gone Amanda tried Sebastian's mobile again, only to find it once more going to voicemail. She'd already left a message. She immersed herself in her work and the rest of the morning flew by. It was one-thirty when she glanced at her watch. She broke off for lunch and tried Sebastian again. It went to voicemail, and she decided to dial the landline. She put the kettle on and leant against the worktop. But before she could dial the phone in her hand rang. She smiled seeing the number on the display:

'Hello you, I was beginning to think I hadn't pleased you.' She purred into the phone, thrown and embarrassed then to hear not Sebastian's but Gwyneth's voice.

'Amanda? Amanda dear, I'm so sorry. Something's happened. I'd have rang you sooner only it's been very difficult here and Seamus has just found your number on Sebastian's phone . . .'

Amanda froze, an icy fist clutching her innards.

'Gwyneth. What's happened? Where *is* Sebastian? Is he alright?'

There was a pause, a muffled noise, and she realised Gwyneth was crying. 'Oh dear girl! There's been an accident. Achilles must have refused and Sebastian was thrown - this morning. Seamus found him. He'd landed on a drystone wall, on his back . . . snapped. Oh Amanda, he's dead.'

Amanda tried to speak but no words came. Far away down a long long tunnel Gwyneth's voice was saying her name, drowned out by the buzzing vibrating through her head as she swayed, dropped the phone clutching blindly at the worktop as she lost consciousness and fell to the floor.

It could not have been long. The tiles were hard against her face. Her hand reached automatically to her throbbing temple as she sat up. Only then did she remember. She began to cry, sitting on the floor, her knees pulled up to her chin. A constant tone came from the phone on the floor nearby, like a heart monitor after the patient has breathed his last. And Amanda wept. Rain beat against the kitchen window driven by a rising gusting wind. Still she wept. And when at last the clouds began to clear, Amanda was weeping still.

Shock is a hard comforter. It numbs, freezes, road signs saying 'temporary diversion' to make you skirt the car crash up ahead. Small things can distract, become magnified through the lens of loss. For Amanda it was her small betrayal of Sebastian when she had compared their sedate love-making to the turbulent passion she'd witnessed the previous day. It buzzed around her mind like a troublesome mosquito, and she held onto her feeling of guilt as an unlikely comfort blanket keeping her a step away from the enormity of the loss itself.

She had climbed into bed, suddenly shivering with cold. She beat herself with her own shallowness, a sin she never would be able to expiate, a stain on her soul that would always be there. She saw Sebastian's face, gentle and full of goodness, in the stable, at the station, in the park. It couldn't be. *How* could it be? Had he been troubled by her failure to phone, riding out to clear his head, remembering her hesitance during their last conversation? Last. The word hung in the air like a pall.

There was no god, no transcendent power of good. Her husband taken young, and now her chance of autumnal happiness snatched so cruelly away, her lover soon to be lowered into the earth, or consumed in the fire. Oh the fire . . . let it be the fire. Let him not be cast alone and cold into the dark dank earth!

She should do something. Ring Gwyneth. Go there. Yes, she should go there. What else could she do? She should offer to help the living who's grief she shared; 'a trouble shared.' But no relief there, only the hardening set of reality as the burning molten pain cooled to hard unyielding steel. But even as she told herself to move, a wave of darkness rolled over her, a thickened murk in which to hide. She slept.

There were two other cars parked at the house next to Sebastian's Mercedes. Amanda suddenly regretted not having rung ahead. She hesitated. The front door opened and a woman appeared, saying her goodbyes to someone hidden by the half open door. She looked at Amanda and smiled, prompting the door to open wider. The other person was revealed to be an elderly man who also offered a polite smile before concluding their goodbyes. He waited as the woman left, giving Amanda a curious look. Amanda made her way up the front steps.

'Hello, I'm a friend of Sebastian and Gwyneth, Amanda Carling. Gwyneth rang me.'

'Oh yes, how do you do, Richard Forsyth. Friend

of the family. Do come in.'

They shook hands and he led Amanda through. 'Would you like a cup of tea? Dreadful business. Rather calls for a cup of tea. In the best tradition don't you think?'

In the kitchen Richard, went about the business of making tea quietly. Amanda was glad that he didn't press small talk upon her. What was there to say? She wondered whether he was a judge or QC, imagined him in robes. He had that sort of bearing, dignified, the same quiet assurance as Sebastian. He seated himself adjacent to her at the table and poured, continuing as he did so as if there had been no gap in the conversation. 'Yes. Dreadful business. That was the doctor. Coincidence really, GP calling round today. A routine house call. Gwyneth's actually coping quite well, considering. Anyway. There you are.'

They sipped their tea quietly, each with their own thoughts. The grandfather clock in the hall chimed and Richard started, disturbed from his reverie, turning to Amanda. 'I'm so sorry my dear, I'm not being a very good . . . I'll just let Gwyneth know you're here should I?'

'Where's Sebastian?'

Richard was almost to his feet but sat down again. 'Ah. Yes. He's . . . they have to do a post mortem. Accident, nobody around etc etc. They took him away about an hour ago.'

Amanda felt herself tense and a small involuntary

cry escaped her. Images of the cold mortuary slab, her dead lover's broken body to be cut by the mortician's cool loveless knife. The blood had drained from her face and Richard placed his hand on hers, his kindness not expressed in easy words of comfort. She responded to the supporting touch, determined that she would not crumple, fighting back her tears. If Gwyneth could cope then she could too. 'Yes. Sorry I . . . I'm fine, really. It's just . . . well you know.'

'Yes, of course.' He squeezed her hand and gave it a little shake. 'I'll not be long.'

Gwyneth was propped up in bed, from which Amanda deduced that it must be the afternoon. She hugged her and they held each other. Amanda sat, dabbed a tissue at her eyes. Gwyneth was doing the same; noses blown, now silence once more. Richard had padded off, and the two women were alone.

'Thanks for phoning. Sorry I . . . it was the shock. I . . .'

'You hurt your eye.'

Amanda automatically touched the magnificent black eye she'd forgotten all about, instantly comprehending the look from the departing GP, and appreciating that Richard had discreetly given no indication at all.

'Yes. The kitchen floor. Pathetic really . . . she convulsed suddenly overwhelmed but this time held fast and steadied herself, even managing a mirthless smile. 'I have no right. I hardly . . . I said I'd phone him and then couldn't because my friend was upset and . . . we'd . . . he'd wanted me to come here and I'd said I'd need to think because . . . because I wasn't sure about . . . it all seemed so . . . oh I'm so sorry. I shouldn't . . .' the words tumbled out and trailed away, Amanda wretchedly ashamed now, rambling her self indulgent grief tears streaming, a 'hill of beans' compared to what she knew Gwyneth must endure,

'Shhhhhh. Of course you were unsure. But he was happy Amanda. He wasn't worried. He went for a ride out in such good spirits. He believed in you. *I* believe in you. I meant what I said. Do you remember?'

Amanda nodded.

Gwyneth continued quietly. 'It's the end for me now. It was already. But I wanted him to be happy. He *was* happy. At least there was that. He was *so* happy. It was thanks to you.' She spoke very quietly. Her words were resolute, her expression calm. Her tone was heavy with the weight of finality.

Amanda nodded. She was becalmed. The frail vessel of hope that she had boarded with Sebastian now bobbed directionless shipping water on a vast windless ocean beneath endless grey skies. It was scant consolation that she had made him so briefly happy. It was alright for him . . . alright for John . . . and even Gwyneth too, already anticipating her own demise. In that moment Amanda envied her. Her generous words did not comfort Amanda, and like a small child she cried out inside. 'What about me!?'

Did Gwyneth read her thoughts? 'It's harder for you my dear. I know that. More than for me. I can go, but you must stay. And I know you loved him. You have been robbed. I at least had time, a lifetime. You must be strong. I will help you.'

Amanda marvelled at this woman, her own desolation trumped by such nobility of spirit, her selfless compassion. She raised her eyes overflowing again to meet Gwyneth's steadfast gaze. 'I didn't tell him. I nearly said, but then . . . I didn't!'

Gwyneth smiled and reached forward so that Amanda could take her hand, like a mother comforting a child. 'My dear child. He knew. You must know that. He knew.'

The night was long and sleep elusive. Her offer to help had been mercifully refused and Amanda had not stayed long. Richard was on top of things, and Sophie was flying down the following day as soon as she had arranged extra support for her mother.

She lay awake. Robbed. The word played on Amanda's mind. Yes. Robbed. She was a serial victim of robbery. There was no solace. No comforting knowledge glimpsed on the periphery of her vision to tell Amanda that time would heal. Time, the paler rider, her grinning nemesis.

Unlike Pandora's mythical box, hope too had

escaped. When she thought of Sebastian she cried. When she thought of herself, her life now, she sank into a void, a dark vacuum abhorred by nature, no trace there of the fecund joy that had gentled her forward in a new lease of being. Like a small cloud her memories were shredding in the harsh sun, the wispy vagueness of a dream which melts away as waking consciousness gains sway.

She'd resisted taking a pill, as if it was some kind of minor betrayal, not prepared to face her grief. But in the end she capitulated. She slept a chemical sleep, woke early, stalked around the downstairs rooms in her dressing gown; coffee and cigarettes.

What had seemed the endless spring of tears was dried up, and bitter despair unleashed it's dry excoriating wind. She sat where she'd sat so often in the morning room and lit another cigarette, looked at it, marveled at how little comfort it gave and yet was *such* a crutch! Slow suicide was attractive, self destruction without the stigma and so oblique as to dispense with the need for courage.

It was not one of Jesus's working days. That was one good thing. Trish, so recently gone was unlikely to call by, and Amanda could ignore the phone. She would be alone to nurse her grief and contemplate mortality; only she then changed it to 'futility' and found to her surprise that there was yet a small residue of tears to wet the sardonic smile that this thought brought with it.

The door bell rang. Fuck! She looked at her

watch. It was eleven. Who was this calling unannounced! Probably the gas man or a Jehovah's Witness. She stayed put and it rang again, longer, more insistent. Her mobile rang. It was Trish. She answered the door.

Trish had brought yet another large bouquet. Amanda had forgotten her promise to replace the whisky which peeped from a glittery bag next to the flowers on the ground. Trish was in the process of texting as Amanda opened the door.

'Sorry darling did I get you . . . oh my god.! What's happened?'

Amanda had again forgotten about her shiner.

'Oh. I fell. Sebastian's dead.'

What happens when tragic news is imparted to someone already immersed in their own troubles, who happens to have brought a gift of a bottle of fine malt whisky? The outcome was not so difficult to predict. Though Amanda did make a token gesture of resistance, the fact was she didn't care.

Soon they were both drunk. Amanda was inconsolable. Nothing Trish could say could help. For Trish things were different. The passage of the days had helped. She had the advantage of having been wronged. Righteous anger ameliorated the impact of her loss.

Trish new Amanda very well. She knew what Amanda had been through since her husband's death, and that her relationship with Sebastian was

134

not a fling. Amanda didn't do flings. But it had been less than a month. Trish's mistake was to see the brevity of the past that Amanda had lost, rather than the future that had been taken away. An easy mistake to make. But it meant that she could look to conscript Amanda into her very small group of two women in need of distraction, if not in due course the renewed pursuit of the many-splendored thing.

The bottle finished Trish located the unfinished one from the other day. Amanda was not used to drinking this much. She was becoming angry and obstreperous, railing against the world. Trish had decided they needed a break, a posh holiday in the sun. She'd do it on the joint credit card, her 'bastard husband' could pay. Amanda's only contribution to the holiday discussion was to echo 'Bastard . . . fucking bastard!' At which she got up and made her way unsteadily off into the garden with her cigarettes, comfortably numb, whilst Trish searched on her I-pad for last minute holiday deals, spurred on by what she took to be Amanda's tacit consent.

It was the evening after the afternoon before. Thumping head and parched, Amanda put off moving from her bed until lying there was so unbearable that moving was only a little harder, with the anticipated reward of painkillers and water. No pain no gain.

Dosed and slaked she gingerly emerged. Trish was thankfully nowhere to be found, though her car was still outside. A note informed Amanda that she'd got a taxi home. It also to her horror invited Amanda to check her e-mails 'Et viva l'Espagne!' She put the kettle on and lit a cigarette.

It was twilight and Amanda sauntered around the garden, the only sound the 'pike, pike' of a blackbird settling to roost, a lone spent jet-trail fluffing out pink in a faded pastel sky.

She had slept heavily and returning back indoors checked her phone messages. Nothing. The coffee was good. Her headache was becoming less overwhelming. She knew she should eat but made no move to do so. The receding of the thumping in her head only made room for her grief to say hello again: don't forget, you're lover's dead, just to to remind you . . . *Amanda.*

Things she should do formed an orderly queue and were one by one dismissed: phone Gwyneth, check e-mails, make a sandwich, shower. She took a sleeping pill and headed back to bed.

The sun streamed through the open curtains, but it was hunger more than the punishing light that drove Amanda from her bed far earlier than she would normally rise.

By the time Jesus arrived she'd breakfasted and showered. She moved as in a dream, observed her limbs obeying her. Her hand grasping the kettle, her foot pushing down on the pedal of the waste bin, her body propelled from one room to another by the movement of her legs. She greeted him at the front door having already been staring at her computer screen for half an hour with not a word written. So much for her intention to seek refuge in her work. Once again she was caught out by the reaction to her black eye, now turning various shades of yellow and purple though having lost much of the swelling.

'Oh . . . yes. I slipped getting out of the bath and head butted the sink.'

'Oh no! But I 'ave some *harnica*. `Always I have *harnica*, een the shed. Wait, I will bring.'

Before Amanda could explain that it had been done forty-eight hours ago he was off and returned with a small tube of cream. She tried again

'Honestly Jesus it isn't . . .'

'Please. Meesis Carling. Harnica ees perfect fora thees theeng. I show you.' Jesus wasn't to be put off and Amanda gave in, closing her eyes and tilting her head back whilst Jesus very gently applied the cream around her eye. He rolled his 'r's in the manner of many continentals, and she was thinking about the lovely way he pronounced 'harrrrnica' as she submitted to his touch. He cradled the back of her head in his left hand, the palm of his right resting on her jawbone as he spread the cream with the tip of his forefinger. She could feel his breath on her face. She was a small child in nursery with something in her eye, the teacher kneeling, unusually close and kindly, making everything alright.

'Ees done.' He said, very quietly. Amanda's eyes flickered open. Cold reality crushed down upon her. I was *not* alright, and now the momentary relaxation in employer/employee relations was over.

'Thank you Jesus. You're very kind. You can get on now.' She heard her own voice weak and inadequate. Jesus stepped back, looked at her concerned a long moment, nodded and was gone.

Chapter 12

It was a dull breezy day. The funeral took place at the small village church of Turton, an ancient square-towered building with a well-kept graveyard, containing many equally ancient illegible gravestones. A massive yew tree spread above the lychgate.

The church was packed, posh people out in force. Gwyneth was in her wheelchair at the front next to the coffin, helped by a tall angular woman who Amanda correctly guessed was Sebastian's sister, Sophie. She had declined Gwyneth's offer to sit with her at the front and took her place at the very back of the church.

Amanda had decided in the end that she *would* attend the funeral. She had struggled with it all, unable to face going to see the body in the chapel of rest, and grimly wanting to close the door completely on the whole episode.

She'd debated with herself. After all, she *had* only known Sebastian for a month, the briefest dalliance. She had tried to redefine it as such, to distance herself, abject in her futility like Peter in the Garden of Gethsemane. There had been only minimal contact with Gwyneth in the intervening days, Gwyneth for her part evidently respecting Amanda's retreat.

But her efforts to hide from herself were less successful. Heavy with sadness and a dark sense of foreboding, defeated she had retrieved her widow's funeral attire from the cellophane protector in the back of her wardrobe. She'd made her own way to the church at the appointed time, already decided that she would make her escape straight after. She would write to Gwyneth, and that would be that.

The service was traditional, Amanda grateful for the measured tone, no highly charged emotional reminiscences about the deceased. She was soon surprised to find herself hearing the dialogue responses of an interminably long Catholic requiem mass. The music was non-conformist, however, Jerusalem passably sung, and Faure's Pie Jesu beautifully by a King's Chapel choirboy at the very end of the service as the congregation stood.

They remained standing as the coffin was shouldered by six men to carry Sebastian to his grave. She recognised Richard as one of the bearers. Sophie pushed Gwyneth along after, the pews emptying front to back in an orderly pattern to process after them down the aisle. When Gwyneth drew alongside Amanda's pew she signaled to Sophie to pause and tried to reach out her hand. Amanda took it in hers, stepping out to walk behind the coffin, her plans to escape evaporating into the incense laden air, relieved and resigned all at the same time. She would do what she must.

The short cropped grassy path through the ancient graveyard was narrow, and Amanda dropped behind Sophie. All thoughts of escape were gone, now enjoined with widow and sister, and having uncomfortably gazzumped the ranks of black clad family and friends in the pecking order of the bereaved.

There had been a half smile from Sophie and a nod. Sebastian would not have said anything. Gwyneth perhaps? At the graveside she shivered though it was not cold. From a child Amanda had been horrified by burial. To lie 'a cold obstruction in the earth.' The coffin lowered as the priest muttered his standard text, her lover so sweet and gentle swallowed by the ground, never again to say her name. She shuddered tottered and emitted a small gasp, rescued by a steadying arm link tight inside hers. It was Sophie, eyes still fixed on the gaping hole, she clamped Amanda unceremoniously, as the ceremony drew to a close.

Sophie was handed a small pot of dry sieved soil which she held for Gwyneth who summoned all her strength to throw a handful into the grave. Sophie next then Amanda, composed now, easier for having something to do, this small ritual task. Like throwing salt over your shoulder she thought, and at that instant she caught the familiar glance of the tiny Seamus, his hard-weathered face streaked with tears. 'Good luck, good luck' said his leprechaun voice in her head. Too small to have been a coffin bearer she suddenly thought. A cacophony of rooks broke from a nearby copse, and Amanda thought of her father holding her small hand and pointing to a busy rookery, telling her that rooks mate for life.

'Amanda. *Amanda*!' Gwyneth's voice brought her back, and she saw that people were starting to move way. 'Time to go.'

At the house all was chatty and convivial as is so often the case, the brief brush with unpleasant mortality packed away with the coffin in the grave. If there was any curiosity about the mysterious stranger in their midst it was not apparent. This was polite society. Gwyneth introduced Amanda as 'Amanda Carling the writer,' which neatly implied the primary connection with herself rather than with Sebastian. It also allowed for some familiar ground as people inevitably were interested, especially those who were fans. Everyone appeared to have an alcoholic drink in their hand, and the conversation flowed with the liquid sunshine.

People were wanting to offer their condolences to Gwyneth, and Amanda drifted away. She gazed vacantly out the window. There was a squirrel on the bird-table stealing nuts. There was something wrong with it's eye, blistered and red. She wondered if squirrels could contract myxomatosis.

'You had a moment.' It was Sophie. She pressed a drink into Amanda's hand, smiling not unkindly and ignoring Amanda's '. . . oh I really shouldn't.' Sophie was an imposing figure, straight backed and almost gaunt, magnificent cheek bones and ice grey eyes, beautiful if not for the severity of her look.

But Amanda wasn't imposed upon. She really *needed* a drink. She took a sip. Brandy. For people who have had moments. 'Yes, I did rather. Thank you for the helping hand.'

She dodged the implicit invitation to reflect on her 'moment,'and Sophie moved smoothly on. 'Gwyneth is very fond of you. She was so glad you were able to come. Terrible for her, for me too. Sebastian and I are . . . *were* very close, but for Gwyneth it's the final nail, if you'd excuse the indelicacy of the metaphor.'

'I like metaphors. What do you think she'll do?'
It was an obvious consideration. Alone in the annex of a very large uninhabited house with stables and horses, hoisted from bed to chair and back again. Suddenly the absence of Sebastian lent an incongruity to it all, which Amanda had not actually thought of until then.

Sophie laughed. 'Oh I don't think Gwyneth will end her days anywhere but here. It's virtually the family seat! More help I should think, and perhaps a 'companion' if she'd entertain one, though I very much doubt that she would. It's tragic.'

The mirth of the initial exclamation shrivelled, and for a fleeting second Amanda glimpsed Sophie's grief peeping through her stoic business-like demeanour. They sipped their drinks, and Amanda felt she liked this woman; a little brusque perhaps, but with the same innate gentility and compassion as Sebastian.

'I'm so sorry Sophie. I . . . liked Sebastian very much.'

There was another pause as Sophie looked long and thoughtfully at Amanda, causing her to look away, unusually for her uncomfortable in a social situation. At last Sophie seemed to reach her conclusion, and touched Amanda lightly on the arm. 'Yes. Thank you so much for coming.' It had so much more meaning than that which the brief words carried, and none of it was lost on Amanda. They understood one another. It was a relief.

'How's your mother?' Amanda turned the conversation to safer ground.

'Oh health-wise she's remarkably well considering, but Sebastian's death has knocked her very badly. If she'd had her way she would have made the trip down here, but it would have been just stupidly risky.'

'Yes, I'm sure. It must be immensely hard for her.'

'Indeed. But she's made of stern stuff. And 'every cloud.' It was so lovely for us to have been able to spend time with Sebastian when he came up. And he seemed so very happy. Happier than I've seen him since before Gwyneth became ill.' She paused to take a sip of her drink, looking directly at Amanda all the while over the rim of her glass.

'Ever since he retired Sebastian always seemed to

have work to do, either court or consultancy, and I'm eternally *dreadfully* busy. It's really been a matter of never the twain for a while despite the usual best intentions.'

'Yes, it always tends to be that way. Are you involved in the law too or . . .'

'Yes. Different law mind - better overall I'd say but Sebastian would never agree! I'm a Sheriff. Same as a judge, only better!' Sophie's eyes twinkled with mischief, at the same time suddenly misting with tears. Amanda imagined Sophie and Sebastian sparring on the merits of English and Scottish law. It brought him so alive to her and it was all too much, tears flooding her own cheeks.

Sophie had her firmly by the elbow now and was steering her toward the door: 'Come with me my dear, we both need a cigarette.'

Fed and watered and at last tiring of the small talk, people began to drift away. The departure of the first seemed to trigger a chain reaction, and the herd one by one trotted off in a gathering exodus. This particular pasture was exhausted, time to move on.

The carers having changed from their funeral attire to set about their work discomfited and dislodged the last few. Seamus and his wife Concepta remained along with Richard, all pitching in to help with the clear up, and Amanda welcomed the activity, tired of the chatter and glad that it was over.

When order had been restored they sat down in the kitchen to drink tea. It seemed that they were all talked out, and they sat in sombre silence. They were quietly remembering why they were there, thoughts returning to Sebastian, the one who was not. Seamus and Concepta left immediately after tea and Richard took his cue from them.

Amanda had been prevaricating, weighing the possibility that had foolishly allowed herself to drink an amount that would certainly have put her over the limit. She knew she would be welcome to stay, but desperately wanted to be home and alone with her private grief.

It was decision time, the door having closed on the last three to depart, and Sophie returned from seeing them out. She cleared away the tea things, telling Amanda as she did so that she was very welcome to stay, that Gwyneth had asked her to say that.

'Oh, no, thank you. It's very nice of you to offer, but I think I'd rather get home.'

'Of course. I'll book a taxi. My treat! You can pick up the car tomorrow or the next day. Tomorrow if you can as I'll still be here and it'd be nice to see you before I fly home. If you come on the train I'll fetch you from the station.'

And that was that. It had clearly not been up for discussion. Sophie was not someone to argue with, and certainly not where the argument was about being 'probably alright' to drive after two very large brandies. Amanda acquiesced. The prospect of meeting Sophie again in any case gave her a lift. She liked her and this was evidently reciprocated.

They learned from Jean that Gwyneth was exhausted and had fallen asleep. Sophie would pass on Amanda's thanks and goodbyes. When the taxi arrived Sophie saw her to the car and paid the driver. Then without hesitation she hugged Amanda to her and kissed her hair: 'Courage mon brave.' She whispered in her ear. Amanda welled up as they faced one another, unable to see clearly. She knew that Sophie was studying her in that way of hers, but owned her distress, her rueful smile now liberating her tears, as Sophie squeezed her arm, turned and was gone.

Home at last Amanda was glad of the quiet of the house. She changed and put the kettle on, but then abandoned it to pour another large cognac. She'd been drinking much more in the past week, and at times of the day that she knew would rightly be considered dubious. She didn't care. The anesthesia helped. Under the influence her despair translated into a sardonic anger which railed against life's lottery dispensation of love and loss. 'The lord giveth . . .' but if there was one he was a total shit.

She'd glimpsed redemption. Before she had resigned herself to being alone, even embraced it, her bitterness and anger at losing John re-forged into a survival strategy which had served her well. She had carried it with her, like a toughened glass carapace which she inhabited like a stuffed animal in it's case, so life-like. She *had* survived, albeit a step removed from the world, maintaining a safe distance, keeping herself intact. But she let down her guard. Love. A tantalising mirage of an oasis shimmering in her desert, slipping through her fingers like sand as she reached down to scoop the reviving waters. Gone. All gone. She poured another drink.

She awoke early with the sun streaming in through unclosed curtains like a torturer's spotlight. Head pounding the very act of thinking required a supreme effort, and rendered little in the way of comfort. Her car was miles away and she had to return to pick it up. She would have to *talk*! *Why* had she agreed to leave it there? Damn them! Why must she go there . . . *be* there? What did they *want* from her? She would just pick up the car and leave making her excuses without going in. Better still she would send Jesus for it, give him a note to explain: flattened by a virus, taken to her bed.

Showered and fortified with coffee and cigarettes the mountain began to seem less daunting. She sat outside on the terrace. It was chilly despite the sun, and Amanda pulled her robe tighter around her, cradled her mug, puffing away. There a heavy dew on the grass and a song thrush was patrolling in short busts of high speed walking in search of

148

worms. It had a brood in the ivy thicket on the house wall. Three voracious chicks which Jesus had shown her, holding back the ivy for Amanda to photograph their gaping yellow beaks. She was going to show Sebastian. Not now. She needed a drink. No, she needed to get dressed and underway.

Sophie was on the platform to greet her. Faded jeans and an old T-shirt made her look younger. How slim she was but ramrod straight and poised, an unyielding elegance which might attract and rebuff in equal measure the less fair sex. This was what went through Amanda's mind as she saw her from the train window, wondering if she had a lover, envisioning an arrangement as passionate as it was controlled, a sporadic coming together rather than a shared life.

Stepping from the train to see Sophie's warm smile light up Amanda was glad she'd come. They embraced without awkwardness despite such slight acquaintance.

'How's Gwyneth?' Sophie drove Sebastian's enormous Mercedes with nonchalant ease, and Amanda settled back in the leather upholstery.

'Indeed. How *is* Gwyneth?' She replied, raising her eyebrows and a little roll of the eyes. 'Hard to tell Amanda. I've known Gwyneth for a very long time, but she's deep, hard to fathom. She appears to be 'coping' very well. Too well, which frightens me a little. Sebastian was everything to her, that much I *do* know.'

'It's going to be very strange for her, alone in that big house. Do you really think she'll keep it on?'

'Why not? She's a very wealthy woman. I doubt if she envisages being around too long anyway, so there doesn't seem much point in down-sizing with all that stress and difficulty.'

Amanda mulled this and the enormity of Sebastian's death for Gwyneth, helpless and immobile. Who would read to her now? Her own grief paled into insignificance weighed against Gwyneth's dreadful loss.

The hedgerows flew by. There was a farmer with his dogs shepherding a flock of sheep on the lower slopes of a nearby hill, and some crows flew up from a flattened bloody carcass on the road as they approached. Life goes on. How many of the people at the funeral would be thinking about poor dead Sebastian now? She wished she had never met him, that her ordered life had been allowed to remain as it was, quietly 'doing her time' in the shadows, creating fictional diversion for her readers, rewarded with their money and adulation for doing so. She felt the familiar prickle of anger toward the recently departed and was ashamed.

'You'll stay for lunch I hope?' The sun caught the keys dangling from Sophie's hand as she skipped up the steps to the front door.

'Yes. Thanks. That'd be nice.' She meant it. Now that she was arrived her previous resentment at having to as it were return to the scene had evaporated.

'Good, I'll see to it. It's just about organised already. Why don't you go on through?'

Gwyneth was as usual sitting in her chair, and exclaimed her delight as Amanda entered. They hugged. 'You look truly dreadful my dear. Sit, sit.'

She did as bade. 'What about you How are *you?* Silly question I know.'

Gwyneth smiled, only the hollow heaviness of her eyes giving away her true state of mind. 'Oh I'm very sad. Very *very* sad. But you know. They won't bring me a bottle and the drugs make me sleep so . . .'

They sat quietly. Amanda noticed her own book on the coffee table and Gwyneth caught her gaze:

'We didn't get very far.'

'No.'

Silence again. A small bird flew against the window with a soft thud and fluttered away. It caused Amanda to look that way and she continued to look out into the garden where a light breeze was ruffling the tops of the columbine. She was aware of Gwyneth looking at her, and intuited that she was preparing to say something.

'My dear, I want to ask you something.'

'Yes?' She waited.

'You don't have to give me your answer now. Sophie's been on at me to pay someone to be what they used to call a 'companion.' I told her no. Oh I could afford to pay handsomely, and finding someone to do it wouldn't be a problem. But it would be so false. I wouldn't like it at all, unless of course . . . unless it was you.'

A pause. Amanda had seen it coming a nano-second before the words, and was already trying to formulate a refusal which would not offend. She could not but feel the fondness and warmth behind the invitation, and wholeheartedly reciprocated. But the burden of such a commitment was out of the question, and for the second time that day she felt that edge of anger arising unbidden, wanting to be left alone, wishing she had been and that none of this had happened.

'Oh that's so kind of you. Really. But I couldn't do that Gwyneth. I hardly know what to say. I have my work, and really I'm very comfortable financially.' She was conscious of the danger of gabbling excuses and ground to a halt, reaching instead to take Gwyneth's hand. 'It's so sweet of you to ask me, but . . .'

Gwyneth cut in. 'Sweet my arse! It's completely self-seeking. Four nights a week for a trial period of say six months. No fixed duties other than popping in to chat or to read to me sometimes. I'll be taking on a full-time housekeeper to have all our meals prepared and the place cleaned etc, so you'd have plenty time to write. Six thousand pounds a month. Think about it. Now. I think that's Jean. Time for lunch.'

Jean appeared right on cue hollering her hellos.

Amanda rose to her feet, at the same time miming very clearly: '*No*!' Gwyneth merely pressed a forefinger against her lips and imperiously dismissed her with a wave of the back of her fingers. 'Sophie will give you some lunch darling. Come and say goodbye before you go?'

Amanda was glad to get home. Lunch with Sophie had been enjoyable. Sophie had laughed when Amanda told her about Gwyneth's offer. She wasn't surprised. She asked Amanda was she not tempted, but discreetly dropped the subject after Amanda made it clear that she was not. Driving home Amanda had reflected on Sophie's choice of words.

There was much in the offer that could be considered tempting for sure. Sophie hadn't dwelt on the obvious 'money for old rope' aspect, and Amanda could see that it would be an easy place to be *and* to write, waited on by a housekeeper and able to ride out on a thoroughbred hunter whenever she had a mind. But far from enticing, the prospect weighed heavily oppressive, and she felt her anger arising once again. What had any of this to do with *her*? Her life if not fulfilled and joyful had been passably manageable. Why did she have to meet Sebastian? *Why*!?

She thought about him now, his smile, his touch, his generosity of spirit which had captivated her from the outset. What sort of consolation prize would it be to rattle around his house like a museum, offering tlc to his ill widow for handsome remuneration? Clouds of disconsolate gloom, briefly lifted by the activity of the morning were descending once again. She needed a drink.

The morning-room was in shadow at this time of day and cradling a large Remy Amanda observed her gardener mowing the lawns, concentrating on his task and unaware that he was being watched. There were dark patches of sweat on Jesus's T-shirt. Amanda quaffed her drink and returned to her post with another, another cigarette, watching the young man steering the mower in precise lines in order to leave the required stripes.

The two-stroke engine was noisy, and the regular rhythmic pattern of sound and movement had a hypnotic effect, like white noise blocking out unwanted thoughts. How *hard* this muscular young man had fucked Trish! The cognac was slipping down too easily and made her feel warm and woozy. A third large one. Even as she poured it she doubted the wisdom, a recklessness come upon her which chased her troubles temporarily away. The terrace would be in full sun, and suddenly more than anything Amanda wanted to feel the sun on her skin. It was bikini weather . . .

The honey sandstone flags were hot under her bare feet. She put down her drink, generously replenished again en route and already nearly finished. The sound of the mower approaching the corner of the house grew closer. With deliberate intent she loosened the belt of her silk robe, letting it slide off and fall to the ground just as Jesus came into sight close by the terrace.

A thrill ran through her as she languorously moved around the lounger, finely adjusting the position this way and that, pausing to re-check the position of the sun. The sound of the mower had changed to an idle. The hot sun. The thrum of the engine. She was drunk, again, she knew, and knowing it emboldened even more. What the fuck. Why not? He watched her, affecting to check something on the mower, not quite sure, but emboldened too his stolen glances merging into a long appraising look. *Was* it an invitation? Even now his better judgement might have prevailed, but he was a man, and if this *was* an offer he could not refuse. He'd already fucked her friend but this was the greater prize. She sensed his stare, not a dozen steps away, weighing the situation, eyeing her up aroused.

The thought made her quiver and the image of him fucking Trish flashed again into her mind. It was now. She turned, confronted him with her eyes, tossed back her hair, hands defiantly on her hips, a cool defiant stare. A challenge. Did he dare? She would let him if he did.

Even now she feared that he might turn away, continue with his work, but he did not. The invitation, if it was, was irresistible. How he wanted her! He had always wanted her. No pretence now, and for a long moment he returned her gaze, then

155

allowed his eyes to wander, appraising her almost naked body, wiping his hands on a rag fished from his pocket. Yet still he held back. She'd teased him once before.

Her breath quickened as his eyes moved over her. She basked in his gaze, returned it, posed, opened like a cormorant on a rock. He would come, commanded by her look, slave to his desire. This was sin! The stuttering rattle of the idling engine filled the space between them, stretching out the moments. Her bare skin tingled as his lust swept her glistening body. Any small gesture, a word she knew would bring him to her. The mower thrummed, heat pulsing from the baked stone flags, the harsh glare of the sun, and still she stood her ground, daring herself, daring him. Go on! Why not? A woman and a man. Who cared? What was there to lose? Trish had had him . . . *how* he had taken her!

She swayed, steadied. What was there to lose? All was already lost. She touched her belly with the tips of her nails, lips parting, a fingertip touching the fabric of her minuscule bikini bottom. All she had to do was slip it inside, a centimeter, less, half a painted fingernail would bring him. The idling engine phuttered along at the same quick rate, Amanda's heartbeat sped up now in sync, aroused beyond the point where she could retreat.

 But the alcoholic vapours blurred her vision, bending her thoughts like the heat waves distorting the air. This was not Jesus, the gentle Spanish boy who'd dabbed arnica on her eye, but some strange hungry man, predatory, waiting like a pointer, eyes locked on it's prey, straining at an invisible leash, waiting for a sign. She felt her body trapped against the kitchen worktop, the smell of onions, a hand clawing at her breast and neck twisted in a vice-like grip toward the spit flecked hole. A cloud passed across the sun and Amanda shuddered, swayed and took a step. She reached unsteadily for the back of the lounger, her body sagged, no longer the siren mistress reeling in her prey, but foolish and exposed, and suddenly afraid. She turned, defeated, slumped, and made her way unsteady back into the house as the mower throttled up and moved away.

Chapter 13

The days slid by in uniform monotony. They were not punctuated by regular normal activities: breakfast, dinner, shopping, bedtime, but stretched taut like the skin of a drum, aching hours with no relief. Amanda e-mailed Marcia and Trish telling them not to call; she was fine but needed time to herself. Melanie too - taking a break from work, would be in touch. She haunted the house like a ghost, not answering the phone, the mail remaining where it fell.

She wasn't given to rumination, reflection on her loss, grieving in the normal way. It was there like tinnitus, her constant companion, but without translation into words which might in time rearrange themselves into a message of acceptance and healing.

A note on the front door told Jesus not to disturb her, and behind drawn curtains Amanda endured in slow decline. When the alcohol and cigarettes ebbed low she bought online, subsistence groceries an afterthought. She slept wherever it came upon her, overwhelmed by alcoholic oblivion, day and night no longer differentiated other than by darkness and light. Each new awakening was worse than the one before, reaching for another drink to deaden the pain.

There was no drama, no heroic gesture. There was no regret, no penance, not even any conscious self-destruct. There was futility, the nemesis of hope, looking down like a raptor spiraling so high to make no detail visible below, above it only emptiness, skimming the unforgiving icy darkness of the void.

The incident on the terrace had caused something to snap. Her drunken animal desire. The pride before the fall. The shattered delusion disintegrating like a digital image breaking into pixilated parts, released like a genie the wraith which she had so long entertained in her innermost being. A shockwave of bleak nihilism, a dark enlightenment, engulfed by an infinity of emptiness. Lost. Hope abandoned. At last!

A week had passed in a ferment of mindless self-destruct. It could not last. Something had to give, for better or for worse. It was late morning and Amanda had spent the night on the bathroom floor, raising herself every so often to vomit in the toilet, a toxic mixture of alcohol and bile. Eventually she was raising herself only to retch, and at last she fell into a long and fitful sleep. She awoke shivering, the tiles hard against her hip. She lay on. At last she struggled stiffly to her feet. In the mirror a haggard stranger looked back at her, vomit encrusted in her tangled hair, sunken bloodshot eyes dark ringed.

Downstairs she sat numb in the drawing room on

the couch where she'd been bound and tethered not so very long ago. How much had happened in so short a time. She thought about poor dead Sebastian. He had touched her, rekindled her long-since jaded appetite for life. Had she loved him? She thought perhaps she did. She who had silently resolved to renounce the world, to work, to chat and joke with her friends, but never to look for more. She who had resolved never again to submit to the dangerous siren call of love, that flattered to deceive as it lured the unsuspecting sailor onto rocks. Here today, gone tomorrow. The many-squandered thing. Yes, she liked that.

She thought about John. 'Damn you,' she said aloud, and for the first time in many days found herself crying, at first a copious silent flow of hot salt tears, then sobbing great wet snotty sobs, necessitating recourse to her sleeve for the first time since a small child.

At last, the reservoir of tears run dry she was becalmed. She started at the clatter of the letterbox, more paper adding to the ever growing pile. She had to get away, to flee, to fly . . . anywhere. The thought no sooner occurred than it was decided.

How tedious it was to travel. Shepherded like sheep through barriers, liquids obediently separated in plastic bags, the indignity of removing shoes, watches, belts, and all because some deluded madmen thought it was a *good* thing to slaughter

160

random people. And then there was the spoonful of sugar after, the cornucopia of luxury goods to purchase from dazzling displays, all things that would make you happier, indulgent purchases uniformly superfluous to necessity.

Amanda did what was required. She bought some French perfume, her favourite Guerlain. She walked haughtily past the liqueur stores, hesitated, then retraced her steps to purchase a bottle of Remy and a very large carton of cigarettes.

And on to the next stretch of tedium. Sitting by the departure gate Amanda marveled at the travelling public's penchant for queuing. With few exceptions everyone wore holiday gear, smart (and not so smart) casuals. A relatively small number remained seated, their shared superiority not appreciated by their fellow travellers standing in line ready to scramble for their pre-allocated seats.

Armani suit and heels was not, Amanda already regretted, the most practical travelling attire, but she nonetheless maintained her own cool superiority, hiding behind her shades like Jackie Kennedy accidentally wandered into Burger King.

Out on the runways a British Airways plane was taking off, lumbering reluctantly into the air as a red and white Turkish Airlines flight angled to touch down in the opposite direction. Oh for a cigarette.

'Excuse me?'

Amanda turned to the owner of the voice, a young woman who had taken the seat next to her. She was holding a book, and even without looking at it Amanda immediately guessed what was coming.

'Sorry to trouble you, but I appear to be reading *your* book!'

She looked anything but sorry, positively pleased with herself as she beamed the brightest smile which immediately had the effect of quelling the uncharacteristic irritation Amanda felt. She returned the smile, despite herself, glanced down at the book.

'Ah. Yes. Guilty I'm afraid.' She appraised the young woman, waiting for her to ask her to sign the fly leaf, and surprised when she didn't, but instead marked the page and put the book away in the top of her rucksack.

Mid-twenties, old torn jeans and faded T-shirt, tanned and smiling out of a wild lion's mane of blond hair. She had the lightest trace of blond down on her upper lip. She wore no make-up, and was unadorned but for a silver chain around her neck from which was suspended a small silver buddhist wheel. There was a tiny tattoo low on the side of her neck, a bird with a sprig of something in it's beak, which Amanda recognised as the dove returning to the ark to signal the end of the flood.

'Where ye headed?'

Again Amanda was surprised, expecting the usual comment on the book, not the direct inquisition of her travel plans, which in any case she thought should be rather obvious from the flight they were both waiting for. Just in time she realised that the girl referred to the possibility of first stop Dubai, or the terminus, Bangkok. In the same instant she registered what should have been obvious from the first, which was that the girl was Australian, allowing in Amanda's mind for her intrusive questioning to be at least partially forgiven.

'Oh, Bangkok then . . . not sure.'

'Cool. Plenty to go at. It's a great country. Bangkok stinks! You writing another book?'

Amanda capitulated, unsure whether the unpredictability of the conversation was refreshing or annoying. 'Yes I am. Well, it's early days.'

'Me too. It's shit just trying to get over the game line isn't it? Waiting for the flow . . . *is it going to come*!?'

Amanda was relieved from having to answer as the voice from the desk invited business-class passengers to board. 'Oh, that's me, lovely to meet you,' she said rising, wincing at how lame she sounded.

'Sure. See you in Dubai. There's a smoking room there. I'll show you where it is!'

The cigarette carton peeped guiltily from the top of Amanda's duty free bag, and she half-turned and grinned as she made her way. 'Good!'

Having submitted to the statutory force-feeding and free alcohol, Amanda donned her headphones and began to watch a film, though her eyes soon closed and she drifted in and out of sleep. Her physical removal from the place of her travails lightened the load. High up in this big steel cocoon buzzing through the night sky, her recent past seemed like someone else's story. There was a welcome disconnect, suspended in time and space in the care of the attentive stewards, nothing to do but to submit to their ministrations and the protocols of air travel. It was strangely comforting.

Her fleeting dreams, a disparate chain of short cameos involving all the usual suspects, played like a random newsreel. She played herself, and they all acted too, playing their parts, all the world a stage. At last she was riding Hector, galloping, jumping, exhilarated and happy. Achilles was almost alongside and Amanda turned to smile at Sebastian, only to see the Australian girl riding bareback and barefoot, laughing as she kicked her heels into Achilles' foam flecked sides to race him on.

Disgorged into Dubai airport the homogeneous mass of Amanda's fellow travellers fragmented and dispersed, absorbed into the larger mass of humankind busily going about their airport activities. It was like a column of ants arriving back at the nest. Some were hurrying to find connections, some looking to find something to eat or drink; but mostly it was once again time to do some shopping. The concourse was an enormous shopping mall. So they shopped. Seating was at a premium, and Amanda knelt awkwardly in her now creased and slept in suit, trying to find room in her hand luggage for her momentarily regretted duty-free purchases.

'Welcome to the pleasure dome!'

She saw the battered leather sandals and jeans first and knew the face that went with them would be lit up with a smile, as indeed it was. She triumphantly zipped her case shut, and struggled to her feet. 'Four hours of this! I'm Amanda by the way. Oh . . . you already know that.'

'Matilda. Mattie'll do.'

Amanda tried and failed to disguise her amusement and it wasn't lost.

'Yeah; my folks had a sense of humour. Fancy that smoke? You look all in.'

It was an accurate observation. Amanda had managed some sleep but the transitory relief she had felt before had evaporated when she awoke. Herded onto buses and shuffled through passport control she was miserable and beginning to doubt the wisdom of her decision to flee. She followed Mattie for what seemed like a very long way, longing now for a cigarette.

The young woman evidently knew the airport well. Amanda observed her as they went. She was an odd fish. Quirky and quite intrusive in her manner, but engaging despite it. She was slim, a little taller than Amanda. Her olive skin and sun-scorched hair exuded health and well-being. Amanda noticed how gracefully she moved, threading through the mele with cat-like fluidity.

She *smelled* it first as the inconspicuous door

165

opened and a man emerged. Mattie went straight in and Amanda followed. The unventilated room was small with a few plastic chairs and large chrome ashtrays squatting at intervals around the perimeter. There was one long strip light in the centre of the tar-yellow ceiling. A dozen smoking men all standing, and two seated young women glanced at the newcomers.

Mattie and Amanda sat down and lit up, savouring the rush of relief as their lungs filled with smoke. There was little said, concentration high and the forced seedy intimacy inhibiting conversation. Their clothes would carry away with them the stale toxicity of the fetid air, but still they remained, in for a penny, finishing their cigarettes and only then in a hurry to get out. They bumped into a young African man heading the other way and trying to light his cigarette even as he went through the door, prompting Mattie to proclaim with exaggerated irony:

'God, desperate or what!?'

'Pathetic!' Amanda concurred, superior having had their own fix. Mattie led the way and found some sparsely populated seats away from the main concourse, where mute people sat gazing into their phones or the middle distance, and tired travellers stretched out heavily asleep. They sat down.

'You running away?' Mattie didn't seem to subscribe to the usual social rules. Amanda decided it was time perhaps to put this amiable young

166

upstart in her proper place.

'Tell me, are you always so direct?'

Mattie was unfazed. 'You look *so sad* Amanda.'

It was the perfectly weighted dart to deflate Amanda's ballooning indignation, and she felt her body sag tired and heavy, craving sleep, longing for the safe familiar comfort of her own bed.

'Yes. I'm sad. And yes, I'm running away.' She felt her eyes beginning to prickle and looked straight ahead, concentrating on an elderly Chinese couple who were looking about them, belatedly ascertaining that they had strayed from the shopping mall, before turning to slowly retrace their steps. She felt a hand on her arm.

'Sorry to hear that.' It was said quietly and with real concern and Amanda was touched. She turned and looked at Mattie who's hand remained resting on her arm, her face it seemed for the first time not beaming out a smile.

'Aren't you supposed to tell me 'it will be alright' or something to that effect?'

'Yeah well. Maybe it will, maybe it won't. But it *probably* will!' and her smile lit up again, lightening for a second Amanda's burden; the optimism, playfulness; the energy and ebullience of youth.

Different place, different time-zone. The cavernous glasshouse of Suvarnabhumi airport captured the morning sun. Amanda had slept and was lifted by the brightness, and the energy and purpose of the

167

other travelers released at last, all with places to go, people to see.

She donned her shades and trailing her trundling case emerged from air-conditioned transit to hit a wall of tropical heat infused with exhaust fumes. Taxis were drawn up in a long line and she scanned the names held up on cards, relieved not to immediately see her own and therefore able to park her case and join the other smokers, her first one since Dubai.

Mattie had said goodbye after passport control, her only luggage a well stuffed rucksack which she had taken on the plane. No baggage reclaim for her. As she glided away to find the domestic terminal and her flight to Koh Samui, Amanda had paused to watch her go, delighted when some fifty meters away Mattie twirled and waved without breaking her step, her smile conveying that she both expected and appreciated that Amanda looked after her. She returned the wave, her passport held aloft. They had exchanged contact details, Mattie encouraging Amanda to travel south and link up. Perhaps it was the meaningless protocol of travelers in brief transit encounters. Certainly they were unlikely companions, Amanda elegant and expensive, Mattie the archetypal backpacker. Amanda had thought this as she'd turned with a sigh to head off to look for her luggage, resigned to the reality that it was the last she would see of her young friend.

The heat was oppressive. Amanda had finished her

cigarette. She was preparing to retrace her steps to wait in the air conditioning at other side of the glass doors, when a young Thai man immaculate in his white shirt and black trousers walked straight up to her and made a tiny bow, hands clasped together in the traditional wai. 'Mrs Carling?' he enquired.

'Yes,' she replied, surprised, but glancing about immediately realised that it would not have required special powers to ascertain which of those waiting was booked in at the Bangkok Hilton. Her case was commandeered and she was courteously chaperoned to the gleaming taxi. It was mercifully cool and lightly infused with a mix of air freshener and the driver's after-shave.

At the hotel she was handed over, all smiles and wais to an identical young man who took her luggage and shepherded her into the lobby. She could almost have been in any five star hotel in any major city. This one, however, was distinctively eastern with it's diminutive ever smiling staff and a preponderance of cool granite and marble overlain with expensive-looking rugs.

At last settled into her room Amanda sent e-mails to those she hadn't told she was leaving: Trish, Marcia, Melanie, and Gwyneth. Jesus was the only person who already knew. It struck her as she completed this task how very few people she needed to let know she had fled to the other side of the world. How her life had shrunk.

Running away, as Mattie put it, had brought about

a change of perspective. Here in her hotel room in a bustling far eastern city things looked different. It was as if the physical distance and alien surroundings demanded a different view. Amanda was no longer pinioned painfully by the overwhelming weight of grief that had incapacitated her. She listened to the air conditioning vying for supremacy with the open window, through which clamoured the chaos of traffic far below. The familiar canvas of her life was partially obscured, over-painted with a pale semi transparent wash.

She lay on the bed, closed her eyes and with an effort opened them again. She told herself to shower and change, go out to get her bearings, take a tuk-tuk to the grand palace, try some street food, smell the smells, sample the ambience. The best way to deal with jet-lag was to keep moving, fight the exhaustion and set aside redundant Greenwich mean time which bade her rest. Rising onto her elbow she counted to three, building up to swing her protesting legs to the floor. 'Three.' She sighed and dropped back, her head only a second on the pillow before she was asleep.

Bangkok. It was excessive. Beyond the sanitised oasis of the Hilton was a chaos of life, heated to a frenetic boiling point by the relentless sun. It was the 'hot season,' but undeterred the teeming millions swarmed, Thai and 'farangs' alike. Suicidal tuk tuks apparently without brakes dodged people and cars.

Traffic fumes blended with food aromas sizzling from the ubiquitous street hawkers' stalls, and everywhere the faintest underlying smell of whiffy drains.

As Amanda did the rounds of tourist 'musts' she submitted to the city and in the chaos found calm. The Grand Palace, the Reclining Buddha, Chinatown, Thai massage, shopping malls. The days trotted by and 'Lonely Planet' in hand she made countless forays from the cloisters the Hilton, observing the people, over-paying grinning tuk tuk drivers, her inner voices silenced, her emptiness filled up, 'in the moment' if not 'letting go.' When in Rome . . .

But like all good things it had to end. The sight-seeing, the submergence in Bangkok's human soup. It was late afternoon and Amanda had returned tired to the hotel. She showered and sat down in her bathrobe and towel turban to check her e-mails. She was already feeling that it was time to move on; and there it was, from 'waltzing.m@gmail.com'

'Hey Amanda! How's it going? Bkk'd out yet? In Koh Tao (turn left at Koh Samui!) and the diving's great. Really clear and calm sea. Huge whale-shark the other day. Do you dive? In town today but back to beach tomorrow so no internet then till a week or so, so get back soon as? Be nice to see you . . . MattieXX.'

The timing was spot on. Escaping Bangkok for an idyllic tropical isle was an immense attraction.

Amanda and John had learned to dive in the Maldives, and achieved their open water certificates, returning to dive there as well as making a visit to the Great Barrier Reef. The brilliant silence of a coral reef in crystal waters was the perfect antidote to Bangkok. She began to type.

'Hi Mattie. Sounds good! And yes I do (dive). And yes, it would be nice to see you too. Send me info. Off to pack!
Amanda x.'

Chapter 14

The train journey to Chumphon took all of the next day, and then there was the overnight ferry to Koh Tao. The hotel had arranged the train ticket, allegedly first class. This meant that the carriage was a little more roomy and sparsely populated, the seats were *not* bare wood, and there was glass in the windows to contain the invaluable air-con. Amanda was grateful for these small mercies, though wondered as the hours ticked by had she not made a mistake in opting not to fly to Koh Samui and transfer from there.

At each of the many stops local people besieged the train selling all manner of food and drink, knocking insistently at the window, all smiles, well aware where they would get paid the most. They had perfected the beaming friendly smile with a hint of supplication. Amanda duly obliged, sliding open the window driven by hunger to overcome her concerns for the hygiene of the food preparation, or indeed whether it was chicken or rat in her pad thai.

Stretched out on the open deck of the ferry, an alarmingly small boat, she had eventually drifted off to sleep gazing up at the stars, mesmerised by the thrum of the engine and the rush of the churning water in the wake.

She woke and smelled the pungent odour of cannabis. A couple nearby were smoking a joint as were the two Thais, father and son she guessed, who crewed the boat. It slightly perturbed Amanda momentarily that the captain of this small boat may be stoned, but her concern miraculously evaporated after said captain grinned, squatted and passed his spliff to her. He was wiry and weather beaten, probably around the same age as Amanda, though the deep lines on his face made him look older. Nobody else on the boat could have been over thirty. It was a small gesture of camaraderie. Amanda returned his smile and took a couple of long draws as he nodded his approval and whispered 'good stuff!' in what she guessed was probably one of the very few essential English phrases he knew. Instantly stoned she'd returned the joint and lain back surveying the night sky, as her new friend sprang away with quick precise movements, barking orders at the boy in rat-a-tat Thai.

Mattie was on the jetty to meet her in the bright early morning sun, waving as the ferry approached and laughing along with the general amusement as the younger crew member struggled to pass Amanda's enormous suitcase from the bobbing boat to his counterpart on dry land.

'G'day Amanda. Welcome to Koh Tao!'

A Thai youth appeared from behind Mattie and

174

grabbed Amanda's suitcase. He carried it on his head from the jetty before them, seemingly oblivious to the fact that it had wheels. They stopped by a pair of motorbikes where another young man perched smoking a cigarette, laughing at his friend and saying something which he then obligingly translated for Amanda. 'Same same but different!'

'Oh God.! We're not going on these are we? What about my case?'

'No worries. Nut here can take his whole family on the bike, or a couple of pigs, believe me!'

The said Nut frowned, offended: 'No! Whole family *and* two pigs!'

As they sped from the small port out into the countryside the fresh morning air was invigorating. Amanda held tight onto Nut who had somehow balanced her suitcase on the bike between his knees. He drove with abandon, passing his friend and Mattie with a whoop and a wave, the first of several such exchanges during the fifteen minutes journey.

At last the sea came into view again and they were quickly descending toward it via a series of hairpin bends. Just below was a perfectly semi-circular bay with a small sandy beach. A scattering of around a dozen small traditional bungalows on stilts were strung along the beach either side of a larger construction. This consisted mainly of a large covered deck area, a restaurant/bar where a few people sat, glancing up at the approaching bikes. Within the bay the deep blue of the ocean gave way to pale turquoise with a patchwork of darker hues. It was fringed along the seaward perimeter by a line of foaming surf breaking on the edge of the coral reef. A longtail boat with the traditional wrap of brightly coloured fabrics on its prow was moored in the sparkling waters a little way off the empty almost white beach. Two small clusters of palm trees, strangely symmetrical at either end of the crescent half-moon of sand, leaned over the water, lending the scene an absurdly picture-postcard quality as if painted by a child.

The young man who emerged from the restaurant to greet them was very dark for a Thai. He was tall with a swimmers physique, and approached them with easy confidence conveying that this was *his* place. Mattie did the introductions:

'Amanda this is Khala: owner, divemaster, chef, and all round clever-dick good guy!'

Khala shook Amanda's hand laughing and dismissing Mattie's comments with a shake of his head

'Well I'm the owner for sure, but maybe not *that* good! Very pleased to meet you Amanda. Come, you must be hungry.' He picked up her case easily with one hand and led them to a low table, indicating for them to sit.

There were a few such tables and many cushions scattered about on the broad wooden planks worn shiny over the years. Despite the very early hour a small group were breakfasting at another table. They waved and said hi. There was the very faintest of breezes, just enough to gently move the many mobiles made from shells, driftwood, and pieces of broken coral. Amanda sighed and looked at Mattie sitting opposite, Buddha-like in a half lotus and beaming out as usual her iridescent smile. 'Well ? what do you think?'

Amanda gazed about her taking it all in as Khala came back with two glasses of mango juice. 'It's perfect. Thanks for the invitation.' She turned to Khala who was visibly pleased to hear the approval and repeated with a finger raised and serious expression.

'Yes! Perfect! It *is* perfect! You are right!' With which his face melted into a mischievous smile, his eyes glittering like the rippling water. He momentarily seemed to forget the menu and pad in his hand as he looked about him, talking half to himself as he repeated more quietly. 'Yes. It is perfect.'

Amanda caught Mattie's skyward glance, and brought back Khala's broad grin with a well-timed. 'And *you're* right too! I'm fucking starving! What have you got?'

So began what Amanda would always refer to as the 'idyll'. A motley crew of young back-packers willingly marooned in Khala's hideaway, brought there by the winning combination of untouched nature and high quality diving. As the first morning progressed and the others emerged, Amanda felt as if she'd landed on the film set for Jesus Christ Superstar. Latter day hippies every one, tattoos, piercings, hair adorned with fine plaits, dreadlocks or long flowing tresses, each individual having carelessly cultivated his or her own personal style.

The boys nearly all had the unshaved look, and the girls made Amanda think of Joni Mitchell in her 1970's Greek Island sojourn. They were nearly all disconcertingly blond and nut-brown tanned. Except for two Australians all were German or Swiss. Apparently the place had somehow escaped the notice of the Rough Guide and Lonely Planet, but highly praised in an off-beat German guide-book was a poorly kept secret amongst German back-packers and their Swiss neighbours.

But Khala's place, as it was known, was not quite what it seemed. Here the religion was diving, and everyone without exception was a devotee. They were serious. Khala lived in the back of the restaurant where he had a secure store housing diving gear for hire by his residents. The reef deepened beyond the shallow coral gardens of the bay, attracting bigger visitors, reef sharks skulking in from the ocean tempted by abundant fish suppers amongst the coral, dolphin, barracuda and turtles doing the same, trigger fish belligerently defending their patches of paradise from all comers. The sea-going longtail gave access to many ocean dive-sites where big fish, the rare and the elusive were drawn from the deep to underwater rock promontories, where smaller prey abounded.

But for the moment it was time to rest and get her bearings, and Amanda 'hung out' as people appeared in dribs and drabs, gravitating to the restaurant before making preparation to head out to dive. She declined the invitation to join the several hour boat trip planned for that day. Having ensconced herself in the pleasingly primitive leaf-roofed accommodation she sun-bathed on the beach, as the food and drink, diving gear and finally people were loaded into the longtail which noisily clattered off into the bay. It rounded one of the headlands and was gone, leaving only Amanda and a local Thai girl Nang, who had appeared to help with breakfast and to prepare the food for the trip. Nang busied herself in the deserted restaurant, creating order from chaos before disappearing into the kitchen.

Alone at last Amanda's thoughts returned to her real life, the one she had fled from but to which she must one day return. She lay on the beach caressed by the sun, and the said reality felt like a distant dream. It made it easier to contemplate, no longer pressing on her as it had before. Time to think and perhaps achieve perspective from afar, elusive in the thick of things.

She felt a twinge of guilt for so peremptorily deserting Trish who had her own troubles, but even as she did so knew that Trish would bounce back, resourceful more than her girlie persona would suggest. Richard may well have already returned tail between his legs and begging forgiveness. But then there was Gwyneth, *her* troubles not so easily resolved, alone in her mourning and imprisoned in a body whose only function now was to torment her in it's refusal to obey even the least command. Gwyneth who in happier days had been Amanda's double. How strange (or actually perhaps not) that Sebastian had as it were fallen in love with the same woman twice.

In the end she had dismissed the idea of accepting Gwyneth's offer, but now she thought of it again, curious, dispassionate. How might it be? Fleeting though it had been, Amanda had loved Sebastian, of this she was in no doubt. It didn't trouble her in the least that he had all the while loved his wife too. Gwyneth too had quickly realised and accepted her husbands love for Amanda. It was a comfort to her, a bond between them. Both were writers, both passionate about literature. No, it was entirely logical that Sebastian would have fallen in love with Amanda, like falling in love with his wife all over again. But how very very strange this must for him have been.

Her thoughts returning to Sebastian Amanda's hitherto calm, almost disinterested reviewing of her recent past wavered. The hollowness of loss which had been drowned out out by the noisy chaos of Bangkok, lost in the movement of travel, instantly returned. It emptied her, evacuated her body with a physical shock that took her by surprise and made her sit up, heart pounding and casting about her, the empty beach, the featureless ocean, alien and inhospitable now as she tried to breath, the sweat on her brow suddenly cold.

Slowly it passed, a panic attack she knew, and a timely reminder of her broken life. Alone on a deserted beach thousands of miles from home, Amanda knew with resigned certainty that she would never love again. Her beautiful house with it's manicured lawns, her gossipy lunches out, the soirees and dinners with the tennis club set, none of it seemed possible now. Life as it had been before did not seem possible. She had since losing John, become habituated to the cold emptiness of loss, but it was now so much colder, a play in which she no longer had a part. Robbed for a second time. Twice bitten. Once too many.

It was too hot to lie any longer, and Amanda scooped up the mask and snorkel Mattie had lent her. She paddled out to the coral which came right in to the shallows where it was barely deep enough to swim.

The warm clear water was soothing. Large patches of coral, separated by dazzling white sand gave the impression of underwater gardens, where thousands of small fish instead of butterflies and bees tended the coral blooms, an infinite variety of colour and form. A little deeper and a large reef shark louted lazily along the bottom just three or four meters below, meandering away, slowly fading out of vision as if it was dissolved by the sea. Gone. A turtle glided by, it's portliness forgotten in the silent elegance of its flight. A yellow and black banded water snake coiled gracefully on it's way, Lawrence's snake by a Sicilian water trough: 'a sunlit prince.' Amanda's mind settled to the plink of the lightly bubbling water and the sound of her own breathing.

Already it was becoming too hot to lie in the sun, and after a brave attempt Amanda returned to the shade of her tiny bungalow. She was tired and needed sleep. Here she could rest, be with the young people, dive, gather her strength, formulate a plan. Nature would be her friend, her small life a spec in the infinite ocean. She thought again of Gwyneth, her partner in grief who would be her friend. Perhaps there was a way.

The days drifted slowly by. A week, two weeks, three. As Amanda attuned to the gentle rhythms of life at Khala's place, she too slowed, dropping into sync with her surroundings. It *was* an idyll. There was a dream-like quality, and yet conversely life here seemed essential and real, far from the madding crowd.

Something softened inside her. She began to relax. She could breathe. It was not a place that was conducive to nursing grief or fanning the flames of anger. The land of smiles.

And so the seeds of healing could germinate and begin to tentatively take root. Most days they dived, heading off in the longtail to Khala's favourite dive sites. He seemed to have a mental picture of the underwater terrain, a map of the seascape which enabled him to find places of interest deep beneath the waves and miles out to sea. Amanda could not remember on previous diving holidays ever having before seen such dramatic underwater scenery and such an abundance and variety of marine life. She imagined Khala to have magical powers, symbiotic with the ocean itself.

He obviously loved the endless excitement of the divers after a dive. They talked about what they had seen like trainspotters, conversations in German shouted to overcome the loud clatter of the diesel engine as the longtail headed home. Khala grinned, holding the tiller, lazily making small adjustments, interjecting from time to time in his own perfect German. Everyone loved him.

They visited tiny islands, anchoring close to shore, and picnicking on pristine white beaches, snorkeling on the shallow reefs. Amanda learned to meditate, taking instruction from Mattie who often sat in half lotus for long spells on the small veranda of her bungalow. They meditated together, and sometimes snorkeled after, continuing the slow counting of the breath as they slipped across the reef, caressed by the warm sea, the crystal tinkling of bubbles in their ears.

It was a nice group of people. The new age vibe didn't bother Amanda. She took them at face value. They were kind, gentle individuals drawn to ways that expressed this, rather than the other way around. Their life philosophies such as there were leaned toward the eastern spiritual, yoga and Tai Chi, Qigong, meditation, contemplative practices.

It was 'peace and love', and Amanda embraced it, let it in, her worldly cynicism put aside as she perceived that it was neither a fashion nor a protest, just a way. They were thoughtful, kind, defined more by what they aspired to than what they rejected. But there was none of the earnestness Amanda would have associated with the 'type.' They were fun.

'Far away eyes?'

Amanda had come to realise that Mattie had an uncanny way of reading peoples faces and moods, and was not therefore surprised to hear her once again get it right. They were sitting on the beach near the waters edge. It was almost a month since Amanda had arrived.

'Yeah, far away. I was thinking about home, Gwyneth (you know, Sebastian's widow), and my friend Trish.'

'So you're leaving?'

'God Mattie, give me a chance! I was just thinking . . .' but she sighed and smiled, a wistful smile, her protest evaporating and carried off on the breeze. 'Yeah, I think it's probably time.'

Mattie smiled too, her big sunshine smile. 'You *know* when it's time Amanda. No *probably* about it.'

Amanda' narrowed her eyes then grinned. She looked at Mattie watching her, and more seriously now confirmed. 'Yes, you're right. It *is* time Mattie. Time for me to go.'

Mattie reached out and rested her hand lightly on Amanda's knee. 'You'll be fine. Talk to Khala.'

'Of course. He'll need to get one of the boys to take me.'

'No. I mean, just *talk* to him.' The smile still lingered on the edges of Mattie's mouth, but there was an earnestness about her now.

'Yes. Alright I will.'

Amanda had grown close to Mattie. She felt as if Mattie had at some point made a decision to befriend her, probably at their first meeting at the airport flight gate. She for her part accepted the friendship with the same unquestioning willingness, almost as if it were a fait accompli. They were she knew, unlikely friends. The young woman's directness and humour, her 'knowingness', the old head on young shoulders cliché drew Amanda to her. The sparse conversation on the beach was typical. Mattie communicated with an economy of words and sentiment. Amanda had at first perceived this as bluntness, but subsequently revised this view. She realised that Mattie's direct and stripped-down way of talking encapsulated the old conundrum of simplicity being the cradle of the profound.

Mattie for her part had not (as Amanda had initially thought) wanted to speak to her because she had recognised the writer of the book she was reading. It wasn't the usual celebrity thing. But it *was* because of the book. She was someone who saw signs, and divined meaning in coincidences.

The others on the beach clearly respected as well as liked Mattie. She had an aura, disguised in her outward persona, but quickly apparent beyond a cursory acquaintance. Seeing Amanda at the airport had for Mattie been a sign. Signs could be misleading, but it took only their short initial conversation for Mattie to know that this was not the case. Her subsequent actions had proceeded on the simple unquestionable basis that they had been meant to meet, and indeed to Mattie's singular way of thinking, possibly knew one another already. She had asked Khala to keep a bungalow free for Amanda a couple of days before inviting her to come. This was how Mattie understood things, and the reciprocation from Amanda was unstinting as their friendship quickly grew.

It was late in the evening. Amanda was the last remaining after dinner. There was to be a long diving trip the following day. Various casual pairings saw couples drifting off together. Mattie had gone off with a young Swiss guy she liked to sleep with. He wasn't the only one. It was how things were at Khala's, easy, shifting sands. A question, an answer, a kiss to seal the deal and a night of sex.

Amanda had in the first few days graciously turned down such offers, which as a consequence had dwindled away. Mattie had begun to sense her frustration, and encouraged Amanda to take the initiative. 'It's not the usual rules here Amanda. Just fuck who you like. No need to wait to be asked. Jesus any of these guys would go with you like a shot; they're *really* nice!' It was that simple for Mattie, but for Amanda this was a step to far. There would be no holiday romance, or sex at any rate.

She sighed and put down her book. The generator went off at nine, and her eyes were tired from straining to read in the candlelight. She lit a cigarette and looked out to sea, the faintest glimmer of horizontal light still visible where ocean met sky. There was no breath of air. Familiar constellations of stars, shone bright against a jet-black sky, upside down . . 'same same but different' as the Thais loved to say. A shooting star, and then another in quick succession interrupted the vast stillness of space. Billions of stars, billions of miles away, some so far that the light she was seeing had taken many years to get here; some were stars that no longer existed, though their disembodied light still endlessly travelled through the darkness of universe.

Amanda shivered involuntarily at this thought, which might have been a comforting perspective on her small woes, but in the event filled her with dread, futility gaining ascendence, the old familiar friend casting a cold shadow across her soul.

The sound of Khala bumping around in the dive store brought her back. She lit another cigarette as he came through and sat down next to her. He picked up the packet and lit one for himself.

'All ready?' Amanda said.

'Yeah, I think so. Nang will be here early to help with the food.'

They gazed at the small waves breaking on the beach. There were patches of shimmering phosphorescence in the shallows.

'So. You are leaving soon?' Khala said quietly.

'Yes. Mattie told you?'

'No.'

'She said I should talk to you.'

Khala laughed: 'Yeah? She's some woman!'

Right on cue from one of the nearby bungalows came a familiar female voice loudly exclaiming in long and rapturous orgasm. Khala and Amanda grinned, giggled, and Amanda mouthed a whispered 'Hallelujah!' They sat watched the waves, their mirth subsiding, sinking each into their own thoughts.

'How do you know?' Amanda said at last. 'The dive sites, the caves, *everything*. All those places where you just decide to stop the boat. How do you *do* that?'

Khala turned to her, smiling.'I just know. I know things.'

Amanda reflected on this. Of course. He never had a map or any kind of location device, and never really seemed to concentrate too much on where they were. He knew that she was leaving.

'So is this where you will stay. Will you grow old on the beach, the old man and the sea?'

She was half flippant and not prepared for the reply. 'I will not grow old Amanda. I know this. You and I, we are the same. You know things too . . . you just don't know that yet. But you will. And it will be alright.'

Amanda lit another cigarette and passed the packet to Khala. She felt nervous, exposed. 'But only the good die young Khala. Not sure I qualify.'

He lit up and watched intently the smoke curling from the end of his cigarette in the candle light.

'You will know Amanda. And it will be alright. Believe me. It will be alright.'

Their eyes met and he held her with his look. His words resonated within her and Amanda saw recognition in his eyes, knew him too, and understood. A great weight fell from her, a burden that she hadn't known was there, and she felt a lightness in her heart that would never leave.

'Yes. Thank you. I think it will.'

It was almost light when Amanda arose. Nothing stirred, just the endless swish of the waves. She dressed quietly, and took a few seconds to look at Khala, still sleeping. She wanted to commit the image to memory. At last she turned toward the door.

'Hey.'

She turned back. Khala was propped up on his elbow.

'Hey yourself.'

For a long time nothing was said. The clatter of a pan in the kitchen told them that Nang had arrived. A half smile played around Khala's lips, but it was his eyes, deeper than the deepest ocean trench. She felt radiant, warmed by waves of infinite compassion, forgiven without knowing for what, released. This young man.

'Don't worry.' He said at last. 'It's OK.'

'Yes.'

Nang looked up and grinned when she saw Amanda, but then started and hurriedly put down the onions she was about to peel, putting her hands together in a Wai accompanied by a little bow, peering from half-averted eyes. Amanda nodded, accepting the unusual formal show of respect. She walked down to the sea, the sand still cool, and back along the beach through the shallows, the small breaking waves fizzing around her ankles.

Chapter 15

It was strange to be home. Amanda had only been away for a little over six weeks but everything had changed. She'd fled in a state of deep confusion, but returned calm and clear. It was something more than a case of a change of scenery offering safety and perspective, though this had most certainly helped.

As she sipped her coffee in the drawing room her thoughts strayed to Khala's place, to Khala himself, and Mattie. Something had happened. Therapy by association, a meeting of minds, more, a meeting of souls. Amanda had been touched. These two most unlikely people had ducked beneath her defences. It was not so much the case that she no longer felt alone, but that it was alright to be so, empowered within her own orbit and accepting of her fate whatever that may be.

Lighting a cigarette she considered the certainty she now felt with a sense of joyful disbelief, as if she had stolen the right to live and be herself, and it had been the perfect crime! Her path was uncluttered now, and she would follow it without hesitation.

'It's *so* good to see you darling. You look so well. You are different!'

Gwyneth was sitting in her all singing all dancing wheelchair just as she had always been in Amanda's memory, and Amanda had taken her usual place on the sofa. Outwardly it was all as it had been the last time they'd sat and talked. Amanda's hand rested on Gwyneth's, her slender brown arm on the edge of the tray next to Gwyneth's precious I-pad. Her posture although inclined forward was open, her look clear, at one with herself and the world.

'Same same but different!' she laughed. 'It's what they say in Thailand, same same but different!' She repeated it with a comical Thai/Chinese accent.

'Well I'm glad about the 'same same bit' darling. Wouldn't want you to change *too* much. But I'm so glad to see you so well!'

They looked at each other, all smiles. Gwyneth's eyes were sunk with dark rings, but twinkled with pleasure at Amanda's unheralded appearance.

'And you Gwyneth; what about you?'

Gwyneth sighed and her head slumped forward for a long moment as she collected herself. When their eyes met again the smiles had gone.

'I have no reason to live anymore Amanda. But it seems I have to. All part of god's plan for me as you might say. Without Sebastian . . . you know it's not that I was dependent on him. Well I was, but not in a pathetic sort of way; but we would talk, he cared, we loved each other. He gave me reason. He *was* my reason. Do you understand?'

'Yes.

192

'It's a museum here now darling, just a museum, worse, a mausoleum. The life's gone from it. Just the girls keeping me going like one of those bloated queen bees attended by the others that can fly outside, that *have* a life.'

'Oh Gwyneth. You know, I miss Sebastian too. I knew him so little, but I loved him. He brought light back into my life. The thing is, I'd thought that too . . . the museum bit, when you'd asked me to come here . . . '

'Oh Amanda that was foolish of me . . .'

'Wait. I *had* thought that. But things have changed. Sebastian is dead. It's not about Sebastian now. It's about me, and it's about you. Yes I *am* different. Things have changed.'

'So what are you saying? If you're saying what I think you're saying Amanda then the answer is no, I won't hear of it. It was the foolish fantasy of a ridiculous woman. I can't allow you to up sticks and come here to be my nursemaid. No! You have a life. You must live it.'

This was an unexpected turn of events. Amanda could see from the set of Gwyneth's jaw and the fire in her eye that this was not a bid to be persuaded. But she was undeterred.

'And what if I *want* to do that: to come here, to be your friend *not* your nursemaid; to be with you? What if I want to do that?"

'No.'

'Gwyneth please listen to me. When I met

Sebastian and he told me about you . . . well I won't tell you what I thought . . . '

Gwyneth smiled: 'Candy from a baby?

'Only you could say that. Yes, it was something like that I suppose, to my eternal shame. But Sebastian knew something. I don't think even *he* knew what it was, but he *had* to have me come here and meet you. It wasn't just to relieve his conscience. It was something else. There was a reason. Oh I'm not putting this very well. You and I. . . we had to meet. I feel I know you. I want to help you for me, not for Sebastian, not even for you, but because that's my purpose. I think I've known it all along, just a matter of dusting it off so I could see it properly.'

It was a lot to say all in one go. Gwyneth was looking at her curiously now. She was proud, and Amanda could suddenly see her own face, the young Gwyneth in the photo, as if computer imaging had stripped away the ravages of illness. It was there, hiding in the eyes. She steeled herself, resolute, determined that she would not give way, but for a second time was not prepared for what came next.

'Amanda.'

'Yes?'

'Will you take me to Switzerland?'

Silence. Gwyneth's look was calm, entreating, steadfast in her resolve. Amanda held her gaze, a long look. She breathed as she had learned to do, staying in the moment, opening to all that was in this look from this woman to whom her whole life had led her. She rose and walked over to the window where she absently looked out at the summer garden, the proverbial 'riot of colour' basking in bright sunshine. A minute passed before she returned to sit by Gwyneth.

She closed her eyes, but still could see the other's pleading look. Another minute passed in silence. Amanda weighed what she had been presented with. It all made sense. This is what *she* would want if their situations were reversed. She could not argue against it. Furthermore it all now clicked into place. The logic and symmetry of everything that had happened between Sebastian and the two of them was clear. Everything led to this.

'You ask a lot,' she said at last.

'Yes.' Gwyneth slowly nodded her head, 'But I ask only what you can give, and what only you *can* give. I didn't know until just now, until you said what you said. I do know that Sebastian loved you. He didn't know he was going to die. But here we are.'

Amanda started. A shiver had run through her. She saw Khala, sitting with her late that evening, and wondered. He had talked of a subliminal reality that some, he and according to him Amanda too were attuned to, knowingly or otherwise. The conversation had moved Amanda to a different sphere of understanding. So what of Sebastian?

What did *he* know? Where did the influence of the dice of life run out, and 'that which is written' come to the fore, mysterious movements beneath the surface of our lives and loves?

'I will come here. We will be together. If it remains your wish, in the fulness of time, I'll help you.'

Tears poured unchecked down Gwyneth's cheeks, dropping from her chin to form two ever growing dark patches on her white blouse. Amanda sighed and took her hand once more, resigned to the rising awareness within her that the end was already foretold.

'But you can't!' Trish's voice was alarmed and with a whiney whinge like a child watching TV told it's time for bed.

'Of course I can. Don't be silly. *Why* can't I?'

Amanda automatically adopted the parent voice, which far from impelling Trish to a more measured tone had the opposite effect.

'Well you just *can't.* I mean really Amanda it's . . . well it's *weird*!'

Amanda felt sorry for Trish and was trying with limited success not to appear patronizing.

'Oh come on Trish, I really need a change and Gwyneth is lovely, you'd really like her. I'm not committed to anything. I won't be selling the house!' This was not of course entirely true, but a parental white lie.

Marcia looked on, curious but non committal, and

cruelly amused at Trish's apparent high anxiety.

'But you *can't*! I mean really Amanda. You'd be . . .well you know. I really don't see you as a nursemaid, and moving in with Sebastian's . . . well it's just . . . *weird*!'

Amanda caught Marcia's little flicker of an eyebrow and tried to suppress a smile. 'I won't be a nursemaid. There are carers, and Gwyneth's hired a 'woman who does'. I mean I won't even have to cook if I don't want to. It's so nice there, and I can ride whenever I want, imagine!? I'm not going into a nunnery!'

Trish shuffled in her seat and tried to regain her composure, conscious of Marcia's head turned now toward her like a spectator at a tennis match.

'Well no, of course not. But . . . well . . . what *about* the house; and what about Jesus?'

Marcia couldn't resist echoing with the faintest trace of mimic: 'Yes. What about Jesus?'

'Oh shut up Marcia! You know what I mean. Nobody living here, just Jesus by himself, I mean . . .'

Now it was Amanda that couldn't resist as Trish dug the hole beneath her own feet:

'Well in actual fact darling I thought *you* might like to keep an eye on Jesus for me?'

Marcia mid-way taking a sip of wine spluttered into her glass, confirming to Amanda that Trish had not been able to keep quiet about her Spanish conquest.

'Ha ha, very funny. And anyway I might well just do that. *I'm* certainly not renouncing the world to do good works. The faint blush partly undermined the counter-attack, but Marcia relented and stepped in to the rescue. 'Well I'm quite looking forward to meeting Achilles. He sounds just my type!' Marcia was a fine horsewoman, diva of the local hunt.

'Oh he is, right up your street. Quite a handful I think, for a gelding.'

Marcia tossed her head back and flicked out a dismissive wave of the hand. 'Oh that's par for the course. Even without the wherewithal they still mess about. I think they just like the whip!' She paused taking in the amused look from both her friends. 'What? Oh you're both just disgusting.'

Trish picked up the threads. 'Oh. So we can come and visit then?'

'Yes of course you can! Why ever not?'

'*I* don't know. Well. I suppose that's alright then.' She paused. 'Fine. If it's what you want. But I still think it's a bit . . . '

Amanda cut her off: 'If you say 'weird' once more Trish I really am going to have to kill you.'

After her friends had left Amanda cleared away and made tea. She sat outside in the twilight and lit her final cigarette of the day. It was cool with no breath of wind, the stillness heightened by the 'pike pike pike' of a blackbird hidden in the shrubbery settling on a place to roost. She thought about Trish and smiled. She had known her friends would think her decision to be, as Trish had put it 'weird,' but it was the care and concern that underlay the judgement that touched Amanda, and for Trish at least the open anxiety that she may be losing a friend. Her decision to live with Gwyneth had upset the natural order of things, it was 'all change,' and change was a threat.

She stubbed out her cigarette, and went back inside. Without switching on the lights she set the alarm and went upstairs in the gloom, pausing at the casement window on the half-landing to look out over the garden. Silhouetted against the fading light of the after-glow, she was still. The security lights glared on and a fox unhurried trotted across the lawn, leapt the fence into the field and was gone. Darkness resumed, darker than before, a growing camaraderie of stars puncturing the sky.

There was nobody out there. The burglar had served his purpose, like a bit player in a play, there to move the story along, to develop the plot. Had their night together moved his life in some way as it had moved hers? She silently forgave him and climbed the remaining stairs to bed, unafraid.

Chapter 16

At the start of each new day it is always the same. In those first waking moments the mind searches for a foothold in the reality of the day before. So the thread of living is unbroken. Sometimes the heart leaps, sometimes it falls, depending on the way things are. For the wise these movements are less extreme, the way things are being simply that, and not something with which to be overwhelmed, for better or for worse.

Amanda's eyes flickered open and things began to fall into place. Her breathing remained calm, though her heart fluttered with that spark of excitement something new always brings. The light was different in this strange bedroom. She turned over onto her back and pushed herself up on the pillows.

She had expected to be given the same bedroom as before. But this was the master bedroom, Sebastian's and Gwyneth's once upon a time. All his belongings had been removed. Amanda's own clothes now hung in the wardrobes, *her* things were on the dressing table, her robe on a hook on the back of the door.

It was a bedroom from the past, furnished in polished antiquity. The only modern things in the room other than soft furnishings were (thankfully) the mattress, and a huge TV incongruously occupying the centre of the wall opposite the bed.

Amanda was surprised. What did Sebastian watch in bed at night? Did he like sport? Football? Rugby? Did he plough through box sets of Inspector Morse or Downton Abbey? There was so much that she did not know about this man who had been so briefly in her life, changing it forever.

There was an oak desk by the tall windows which overlooked the garden, the perfect place to write. Amanda's laptop sat there, still in it's case. She climbed out of bed and threw open the curtains, took it out and switched it on. She was going to write. Since returning she'd felt the impulse growing inside her. How much time did she have? She didn't dwell on this question, but it was there, in the recesses of her mind: Khala's prophesy of a foreshortened life. Strangely it gave rise to a sense of purpose, all part and parcel of the same pre-ordained nature of things, a perhaps unlikely comfort. She felt more content than she could remember ever having been. She hummed a familiar tune as she showered and dressed. What was it? Mozart. Yes. It was Eine Kleine Nacht Music carrying her high spirits along with it's spritely pace.

The human traffic in the house had increased since her last stay. Gwyneth had given her a written schedule but it was going to take a while to become accustomed to it. The mainstay of the care was still anchored by Becky and Jean, but there was a cook/cleaner who came twice a day, and a rotating night-time carer who slept in the bedroom that Amanda had first occupied, now rigged with a high tech intercom/alarm through to Gwyneth's annex.

Returning to her room after breakfast Amanda sat down to write. She'd hesitated for a half second by Gwyneth's door, but continued on her way as Becky swept by with cheery 'hi' and an armful of linen. She opened the document tagged 'New Novel', but before settling down to scan through what she had already written, opened another tab and googled 'Dignitas.'

It was all there, a clockwork efficient Swiss service to help those for whom life was no longer a desirable option. There were even FAQs, like hiring a car or switching bank accounts she thought. For a second her finger hovered before closing it again. Now was not the time. But she knew in her heart it would come, already resigned to that certainty. But now was *not* the time. She had to write.

She read the first few pages, experiencing the familiar satisfaction she always felt, accompanied by the ever present self-criticism. She was making minor changes as she went, and knew that in time there may be wholesale revisions before the final product. No room for flights of ego here. She was not Mozart. Few were like him, writing the final version the first time around.

Amanda had once read about the forging of a Samurai sword, how the metal was heated, folded and hammered hundreds of times to produce a blade of sufficient strength and flexibility with a razor edge. She liked this as a metaphor for writing.

At the end of the first chapter she paused, rose from her seat, stretched. A cloudless sky again, the garden resplendent in the slanting morning sun. She could see the gate through to the stable-yard where Seamus was pushing along a wheelbarrow. She would ride later. She sat again, for a few seconds looking at the start of chapter two, before abruptly closing the document and creating a new one. For a full minute she stared at the blank page, then without further hesitation she began to rapidly type.

So the days passed by at a sedate and measured pace. Perhaps improbably it worked. Amanda more and more enjoyed spending time with Gwyneth, reading to her, talking, or sharing an easy silence, only their breath, the chirrup of a bird, the bore of a jet. How they laughed, egging each other on to shameful excesses of irreverent humour. A look, a touch, they knew one another and their mutual affection deepened.

Gwyneth's spirits rose. Her bouts of depression were rare and short-lived. She no longer mentioned Switzerland, but Amanda intuited that it was knowing there was an end game that buoyed her up. It was this that enabled her to positively contemplate living whilst she must. The promise of an imminent end. Was this another thing that in a way they shared, a mutual reality? If so it was closer for Gwyneth to be sure, but for Amanda it was an unspoken bond, a sympathy which would support her in the days to come.

She had not told Gwyneth everything about her experiences in Thailand, and what Khala had said to her. She did not know yet what lay in store for her, but embraced and trusted in her fate however it might come to pass.

'Riding later?' Gwyneth clutched her beaker of coffee to her chest with both hands, the straw angled against her cheek as she chatted.

'Yes I think so. I'm addicted. I'll have thighs of steel pretty soon!'

'I'm truly envious, vivid green! Sebastian and I used to ride a lot. We hunted too I'm ashamed to say. That was before we all became a bit more enlightened . . . well some of us anyway. Why don't you try Achilles?'

'Oh, I don't know. I've thought about it but when I get there I always want to take Hector. We have a bond Hector and I!'

'Yes. It's funny. I used to be like that. I'm not sure what it is about horses. I mean they're not the most intelligent beasts but they do seem to have some kind of telepathy going. It's odd. It's a sort of symbiosis isn't it?'

'Yes, your right. That's exactly it. And they can manipulate you, more than ever a man could!'

They laughed, Gwyneth having to hastily spit out the straw so that coffee dribbled down her chin for Amanda to wipe away with an ever ready tissue.

'Sophie mentioned about perhaps coming down for a long weekend, this one or the one after. What do you think?'

'Oh yes, that'd be lovely. I'd like to see her. I bet *she's* an Achilles fan.'

'Absolutely correct. And do you know, he's like a lamb with her. Really. It's what we said.'

'Well maybe they're more intelligent than you give them credit for. Formidable woman Sophie. I wouldn't want to be on the wrong side.'

'Hah! I'm sure you'd hold your own Amanda.'

Amanda pondered. She knew her own capabilities.

'Yes I suppose I would. But I do like her. I can just imagine her presiding over the High Court. Does she . . . *know*?'

It was the first time since Amanda had moved there that either of them had alluded to the plan they'd agreed, but neither believed anything other that it would happen in, as Amanda had put it, the fulness of time. Gwyneth smiled, her twinkling eyes confirming to Amanda that she would not be changing her mind.

'No she doesn't, not yet; but I think we should tell her when she's here. Would you be happy with that?'

'We?'

'Yes, I think so. We both should tell her, unless you'd rather I did?'

205

Amanda thought about it for a few seconds and the question hung in the air. 'No you're right. It makes sense. One thing that did occur to me though.'

'What?'

'Why didn't you ask Sophie?'

'Ah well, for one thing she's a Catholic, so that puts it completely off limits for her.'

'Yes. And for another?'

Gwyneth smiled, and putting down her drink so that Amanda could take her hand. 'Because it was meant to be you.'

There was really nothing to add to this, confirming as it did what Amanda had for some time believed. They had both independently come to the understanding they now shared.

'Yes.' Amanda said at last. 'It was. It is, isn't it?!'

Amanda answered the door to find Sophie with a large overnight bag and an armful of yellow lilies.

'Hello Amanda. Take these from me would you darling then give me a hug. This is Gilles. He's French. He's a philosopher. You'd have met him at the funeral only he chose that particular day to have his appendix removed. Gilles this is Amanda. She's saving Gwyneth from abject desolation. If you're nice to her she may save you!'

All this was said in a flurry of flowers and hugs, Sophie striding regally past her leaving the said Gilles in her wake and indicating with a Gallic shrug that he was used to it. But as Amanda stepped forward out of the shadows to proffer her hand he froze, and she felt a sudden trembling in his.

'Hello Gilles, do come in.'

He didn't move, gazing at her, a strange look somewhere between panic and wonder, absently holding her hand still in his. It was only a second or two, and Amanda waited having become used by now to such reactions, though this one was somewhat more dramatic than most.

Gilles seemed at last to recover himself, inclining forward whilst raising her hand to kiss it with great solemnity.

'Enchante Amanda. What is the phrase the English are so fond of: I've heard a lot about you!'

Amanda smiled and waited for him to go in, but still he hesitated entranced, then bethinking himself grinned and threw up his hands. 'Ah! Pardon, it is just that you . . . and Sophie she did not . . .'

'Yes yes, I know. Don't worry. Come in do!'

They made their way to the kitchen where Sophie was already making a pot of tea. Gilles led the way, apparently familiar with the house. Sophie and Gilles exchanged a look, but that was all and he discreetly desisted from taxing her with her failure to forewarn him. It was all in the look, Gilles narrowed eyes and Sophie's amused raised eyebrow.

He was not tall, but slim and elegant in spite of his crumpled black suit that had seen better days. He had the appearance of being from the south, swarthy, dark complexioned, his face lined. Amanda thought it a face that had lived and probably imbibed significantly of both the grape and the leaf. His jet black hair, a little long and swept back was silvering at the temples, tempering the louche. He carried nothing, hands in his jacket pockets with his thumbs hooked outside.

Sophie placed a pot of tea and some cups on the table. 'I should be doing that.' Amanda said depositing the flowers on the side and trying to think where she'd seen some vases.

'Nonsense. Leave that darling and come and get your tea (they're on the top shelf in the pantry). So how *is* Gwyneth? How are *you?* Are you enjoying the baronial life?' Sophie drew Amanda to the table and sat her down, ignoring Gilles who had also sat down and looked at neither, lost in his own thoughts or bored.

'Gwyneth's fine. Actually she's been in very good spirits this last couple of days, looking forward to you coming!'

'And you?'

'Oh, I'm . . . content!' She smiled happily.

Sophie peered more closely at her. 'Good. Yes. I can see. Good. Tea!' She commenced pouring and Amanda turned to Gilles.

'Do you live in Edinburgh Gilles?'

'Yes, for, let me see, twenty years?'

'Oh more than that darling.' Sophie cut in.

Gilles smiled a comical long suffering smile. 'She knows!'

'But not in the legal profession, I don't think so?' Amanda liked this Frenchman and was pleased at the look of reproach her remark brought and the giggle from Sophie.

'But why not? Do you think I do not look 'legal'?'

'Certainly not.' Sophie interjected. 'No Amanda, he actually *is* a philosopher. You know, looking for the meaning of life etc etc. Professor no less.'

'And how's it going?' Amanda asked with just a hint of mischief hidden in the polite.

Gilles looked at her, impassive, apparently weighing the question. He turned to look for a moment out of the window, as if he might find the answer in the garden, and turned back to his questioner as Sophie distributed the cups of tea.

'Badly.'

Amanda tidied away whilst the others went through to say hello to Gwyneth, then took herself off to change for a ride. Sophie was keen to get out after the journey. Gilles was not in the least interested in horses, except, as he pointed out, being French, to eat.

Seamus was working in the yard when they arrived. 'Well now if it isn't Judge Jeffries of the north! And look at you both now, a sight indeed. Have you no concern at all for an ould man's blood pressure?!'

'I'll give you 'old man' you rascal blarney peddler! How are you Seamus?'

'Och I'm keeping a half length ahead of the years

mi'lady, but their biting at me heels so they are!'

They hugged warmly, Seamus's head only coming up to Sophie's shoulder so that his cheek rested momentarily against her chest like the Madonna and Child, but neither appearing to be in the least uncomfortable.

He led them into the stalls where both horses were already excited at the sound of their voices, Achilles stamping and whinnying loudly.

'Shut up now ye varmint! Sure he's been like this half the mornin'. Knew ye were here so he did.'

Gwyneth was right. When Sophie mounted Achilles quietened. He was still flaring his nostrils and blowing, and pranced very lightly, but he didn't pull as was his wont, and responded obediently to Sophie's easy guidance as she turned him to head off into the country. Once underway they gave the horses rein and cantered cross country to a place where they could gallop and jump.

'Just over there Amanda!' Sophie had pulled Achilles up and he was bouncing and turning, knowing what was to come. 'There are a couple of small fences and a gate in a dry-stone wall, but you can take the wall easily enough. Then there's a high hedge. If you don't fancy it you can dip down to the right - there's a gap there. OK?'

'Yes, let's go!' Amanda replied kicking Hector on but holding for Sophie to pass, by which time Hector was straining to stay in touch with Achilles in full flight. The fences and the gate were easy, but the hedge even some way off looked a challenge and Amanda hurriedly weighed it up. Achilles had flown away and sailed over the hedge some way ahead. Amanda began to pull Hector into a turn, deciding upon discretion being the better part, but he resisted and in a split second she changed her mind, letting him have his head but with a sharp instructive tug on the rein as she calculated his stride toward the hedge. Only when they were airborne did Amanda fully realise two things: the full height of the obstacle, and the incredible ability of her mount, clearing it like Pegasus with room to spare.

Sophie had pulled up and turned to see, full of praise as Hector cantered up.

'Wow Amanda, what a clearance!"

'Yes, well, I have to say it wasn't entirely my decision, but he obviously knows what he can do! He's bloody amazing!'

'Yes he is. I wouldn't have suggested it otherwise. Hector can *really* jump! But you *nailed* it. Fantastic!'

Amanda was warmed by Sophie's approbation. They walked the horses for a while, taking advantage of this first opportunity to talk.

'Seamus is a love. He's an absolute magician on a horse. I've never seen anything like it!'

Sophie laughed. 'Oh God yes. I think he *is* half horse! He's practically a member of the family, and Concepta too. Seamus taught me to ride too many years ago. He's seventy-eight you know.'

'No! Oh there's something definitely strange going on there. Do you think he may really be a Leprechaun?'

'Hmm. Funny you should say that. I've always entertained that very thought myself! And what do you make of Gilles then? Mon petit choux Gilles?'

'Oh he's a card isn't he! Wherever did you *get* him?'

Sophie laughed. '*Got* he is not! Just friends Amanda, but very old friends. He was at Oxford with me and a devilishly interesting Latino renegade I have to say. But we were never lovers. He returned to Paris after, but we always visited, and I was very happy when he came to live in Edinburgh.'

'Yes. So he must be very fond of you.'

'He is. Well, me and malt whisky, and not necessarily in that order!'

They were approaching a gate onto a lane and Sophie dismounted to open it before continuing.

'I'm so glad to see you well Amanda. I have to say I was somewhat concerned for you.'

'Yes, with reason. Things weren't so good. I wasn't going to come here at all, but then when I was away things fell into place rather and I realised it was what I wanted to do. More than that, it just seems . . . *right*. Does that make sense?'

'Yes, it does. I know *exactly* what you mean. Life's rich pageant is possibly not always woven as we go along. Gwyneth *certainly* doesn't think so.'

'Yes, that's right. I mean . . . well I always loved

Hardy, but thought it far too fate fate fate; and here *I* am practically painting by numbers!'

They fell into their own thoughts, the easy rhythmic clop of the horses hooves, a pair of skylarks, bouncing dots high above sending down their song. Amanda broke the silence. 'What about you Sophie? You've lost your brother. *I* only knew him for such a short time.'

Sophie considered this, and at last slowed and stopped, causing Amanda to pull Hector up too.

'Sorry. I didn't mean to . . .'

'No, no it's OK. The thing is Amanda, when Sebastian was up in Edinburgh, when our mother was unwell, he asked me to go through his will with him and review everything. It wasn't a very good time, lots of things to sort out, but he was so keen to get it done I agreed. We stayed up most of the night. He was planning to simplify his investments, winding up certain things and transferring a whole lot to Gwyneth's name, which would make things easier in the event of . . . well. It's been dreadful Amanda. I miss him so much.'

Her voice had faltered and she quickly wipe away a tear as she move Achilles on again. They trotted briskly along, Sophie raising her voice above the clip clop din of the horses hooves. 'Gwyneth said she wants us to have a talk.'

'Yes.'

They were coming to a junction. They stopped to let a tractor rattle past, and remained paused there as the noise of the engine receded leaving only the blowing of their mounts and the birdsong.

'You owe us nothing Amanda. You do know that don't you?'

'Yes. Of course.'

'Good. Come on, I'm famished!' Sophie nudged Achilles into an eager trot, homeward bound.

Amanda had shopped to buy in for a special dinner, glad to have the company and opportunity to do so. She'd proposed that they have it in Gwyneth's annex so that they could all eat together, but Gwyneth had demurred, suggesting instead that they have pre-dinner drinks with her. She was going to tell Sophie and Gilles of their plan. Amanda had not expected the inclusion of Gilles, but could not find any good reason to object, as Gwyneth appeared firmly of the view that he should be present. She was curiously indulgent toward him, and he reciprocated with great tenderness. As the hour approached Amanda was agitated, distracting herself with preparing dinner followed by a leisurely bath.

At last they gathered together. Sophie and Amanda had decided for fun to dress for dinner and were seated on the sofa, elegantly poised, legs crossed, drinks held delicately aloft. Gilles, still in his crumpled suit had pulled up an armchair. Gwyneth presided regally in the centre.

'Good lord!' Sophie exclaimed having taken a sip of her G&T. 'That's a stiff one Amanda. Have you got one Gwyneth?'

Gwyneth laughed and attempted to raise her beaker. 'Yes. Rather weaker than yours I think. Disability strength! Cheers. To us!'

Gilles was on whisky of which he had a very large measure, a good quarter of which disappeared in the first generous glug as they joined Gwyneth in her toast.

'So.' Sophie said, settling back into the cushions. 'I'm intrigued. What are we going to talk about?'

Gwyneth tipped over her emptied beaker as she tried to put it down and Gilles reached across to right it.

'Sophie. My dear Gilles. Since Sebastian's death I have thought deeply about my situation. He kept me going. Not to put too fine a point on it he gave me reason to live. There is none now. I do not wish to continue. I know you think that I asked Amanda to come here to be my companion. That was my initial thought and is in part true. However, whilst Amanda was away I had time to think. I couldn't expect Amanda to give up her life for me. That would be absurd, and in any case to what end, if, as I have said, I do not want to live. I have asked Amanda to take me to Dignitas in Switzerland, in order that they may assist me to die, and she has agreed to help me.'

Nobody spoke. Gilles stared down into his glass, swilling the whisky round and round. Sophie glanced at Amanda, resolute and expressionless but aware of a faint blush heating her face as if she had done something wrong. Amanda waited for the expected protests, but none came. At last it was Sophie who spoke.

'This is quite a shock. I don't know quite what to say.' She paused, thinking. 'Have you contacted Dignitas yet? I mean do they. . . have they . . ?'

It was Amanda who replied. 'No, not yet. We agreed we'd see how things go with me here first.'

'I see. I'm sorry. I really *don't* know what to say!' adding an after-thought. 'Why did you ask Amanda . . .'

'And not you?' Gwyneth interrupted. 'Well for one because you're a Catholic. Sophie I was married to your brother for close to forty years. Of course I wouldn't . . . *couldn't* ask you to go against your beliefs, however irrational they might be!'

Sophie nodded. 'And the other reason? You said 'for one'?'

'Because.' She paused. 'Because, my darling Sophie, this is what Amanda is here to do.'

Sophie nodded again. She turned to Amanda.

'Do you think that too?'

Amanda found herself colouring yet again, but spoke steadily, holding Sophie's gaze.

'Yes, I do.'

Sophie took a large gulp of her drink. Her expression was neither a smile nor a grimace, but a strange contorted combination of the two. She arose and walked across to the window just as Amanda had done when Gwyneth told her. Framed statuesque against the light she looked out, distracted, gathering herself. Gilles, head down continued his apparent fascination with his drink.

'So when's it to be?' Sophie threw it out over her shoulder, almost cheerful as if she might be talking about a party, a wedding, some event that they needed to jot down in their diaries.

Amanda crossed the room and Sophie didn't move when she lightly put her arm around her, still staring out into the garden. 'Sophie? Sophie come, come and sit down.'

Seated all four once more, Gwyneth was business-like. 'Amanda and I need to discuss this Sophie, the timing and all that. It'll take a bit of arranging. I'll have quite a lot to attend to first, and I would like you to help me with some of that. Would you do that?'

The reply was resigned, finding voice in little more than a whisper. 'Yes, of course. '

It was almost as if Sophie was now a small child who had been given a meaningless job to make her feel important and included, and Gwyneth sought to dispel this. 'Good. There's a lot of legal-type stuff Sophie. I can't do it by myself.'

Sophie sighed a defeated but accepting sigh, and managed a weak smile. 'Yes. I'm sure. I'll do whatever I can.'

Gilles had the last word, arousing himself from his reverie and quaffing his drink. 'Bien, it will be difficult and I think perhaps you will need a

Frenchman. I will come too, to assist you Amanda. It's OK. Je suis Communiste!'

'Fuck you Gilles.' Sophie said with incongruous sweetness. She arose and left the room.

Chapter 17

The rain beat against the bedroom window. Amanda had returned to bed with her second cup of coffee, having sat in the porch with the first to enjoy her first cigarette of the day. Sophie and Gilles had returned to Edinburgh the day before. It had been nice having them to stay, but she was glad to have the house back to herself and Gwyneth, returned to normality.

Deep in thought she watched the raindrops coalescing into runnels down the window pane. Things had moved on. The tension between Sophie and Gilles had been short-lived, but the shadow of what Gwyneth had imparted stretched across the rest of their stay. Sophie had spent time with Gwyneth assisting her to begin putting her affairs in order, and suddenly it was all too real, happening, no going back.

Amanda had been thrown by Gilles statement that he would accompany them to Switzerland. Initially she'd thought it was just him being gallant, and that Gwyneth would put paid to the idea; but this was not the case. Gwyneth was very happy for Gilles to be a part of the plan, and Amanda found herself hugely relieved. The transformation of plan into reality weighed on her, and having Gilles involved lightened the load. Amanda had already researched Dignitas online, as indeed had Gwyneth some time before. Gilles was having to catch up, and he and Amanda discussed timescales and a rough schedule of what needed to be done.

Unsurprisingly, whilst it was straightforward it was not a simple process. Gwyneth would need to become a member of Dignitas. There would be searching preliminary discussions. These would heavily focus not only on the reason for her wish to die, but on potential alternative ways in she might be helped. Amanda learned that in the majority of cases, usually involving chronic pain, Dignitas was often instrumental in offering advice from specialist pain relief practitioners resulting in a large number of applicants discontinuing. Likewise many who progressed to being assessed as suitable chose to pause the process, able to reserve the agreement for use at a future date, relieved and reassured, able to go on knowing that there was a solution available.

So Dignitas did not offer a simple free-choice dispatchment service, but a sophisticated multi-layered approach which more often helped people to live rather than to die. But Amanda knew that none of this would apply to Gwyneth. She was not in pain, nor was she desperate and seeking a better way to live. What would the Swiss make of her? Would they agree under such circumstances?

In contrast to the increasing earnestness around her, Gwyneth's mood remained elevated. She joked about not needing to pay travel insurance. Amanda had tried to suggest that there was no rush, pointing out to Gwyneth that they had talked about her taking time with Amanda living there, to take things slowly and at least give herself the opportunity for further reflection. But even as she had said it she'd realised the futility, Gwyneth smiling unmoved.

'For me no Amanda. For me it's a case of: ' better it were done quickly.' Not because I'm frightened, far from it, but because doing otherwise feels like living a lie. And I'm concerned about Sophie. I think *you* understand. But it's harder for Sophie. Teasing it out won't help. But if you really want to take things more slowly then I'm not going to insist. I know what we said, and if you feel . . . if that's really what you want then OK!'

Amanda had been disarmed. Yes she did know that this was the way it had to be, felt it in her bones, a knowledge that was fundamental and didn't arise out of the processes of rational thought. She had returned to the UK changed. Both Gwyneth and Sophie had seen it, and she herself was supported by an inner calm that made all that she had agreed to possible. As Gwyneth had said, it was what she was here to do. Gwyneth was right.

Gilles appeared to take it in his stride, *philosophical* or at any rate accepting. He was serious and diligent, more than that, quietly and unwaveringly determined that Gwyneth's wishes should be respected.

But for Sophie it was not so easy. She was conflicted. Her rational self understood and agreed. But even though far from devout in her Catholicism and not even 'practicing' as such, the teachings she'd been subjected to as a child were deeply embedded, like an irritating grain of grit within an oyster. Now even at the centre of a many layered pearl it still had the power to disturb her, in an indefinable way encroaching on her reality, an unwelcome guest that could sometimes be ignored but never removed.

Then there was the inevitable guilt, that she'd been passed over in this most serious matter relating to her brother's wife, in favour of, as it were, a complete stranger who'd appeared in their lives from nowhere. She was too big a person to feel piqued. It was not a question of petty peevishness that discomfited Sophie, but a sense that all of it signified an inadequacy within her which made her unequal to this particular task.

So she quietly endured an unspoken wretchedness. Gwyneth was aware of it, and that her impending death ironically caused Sophie to suffer far more than it did herself. Procrastination was both pointless and even cruel.

The situation driven forward by Gwyneth herself had it's own dynamic. Amanda had envisaged or at least hoped for a long settling in period to her new life, moving eventually toward fulfilling Gwyneth's wish if she remained determined to press on. But this was not how it was going to be. Things were moving on apace, and there would be no reprieve unless Dignitas said no.

Outwardly things continued much as they had been before. Amanda wrote, rode, spent happy times with Gwyneth who was unswerving in her intention now things were under way.

Amanda and Gilles were in regular contact planning and doing what needed to be done. Amanda had decided that along with Gwyneth herself, she would take primary responsibility for liaising with Dignitas. She felt that this honoured their agreement and her 'calling,' if indeed such it was. Gilles would deal with the practicalities of travel and accommodation, and the inevitable bureaucracy around a death.

It was plain that Gwyneth's current carers could not be asked to assist in a matter such as this. It would be up to Gilles and Amanda to assist Gwyneth to travel. Once there it was possible to acquire assistance from nurses who worked with Dignitas.

It was going to be awkward terminating the employment of the current carers, who were not to know of the reason. Gwyneth decided she'd say she was going to be abroad for an unspecified period, indicating that they might wish to find alternative employment, but would in any case be given a notional retainer of six months pay. Amanda would contact them on her return to let them know that Gwyneth was dead.

All the necessary information about Digintas was available on their website, from initial contact and membership, through to the assessment / decision-making, and beyond to the death itself and potential arrangements after. Gwyneth had no wish to be brought home except in the reduced state of a small box of ashes which would occupy a corner of Amanda's suitcase to be scattered on Sebastian's grave.

That a significant majority of people approaching Dignitas were helped to find alternative ways forward did not encourage Amanda. Neither did the fact that many given the 'green light' were reassured and effectively 'banked' it for potential future use. She knew that Gwyneth would not be one of either of these groups. But she herself found it reassuring that this was an organisation that sought to first help people to live, and explored with them ways to help them do this before moving to agree to help them to die. It dissolved any lurking apprehensions she had about agreeing to facilitate her friends death. She quickly came to understand that this was a highly ethical organisation of great compassion. Alternatives would be considered. There would be a thorough assessment prior to Dignitas agreeing to underwrite their plan. The burden was thus shared.

Gwyneth was also dealing with things herself. Shortly after the visit from Sophie and Gilles, a van had turned up with 'eye-gaze' technology equipment. Over the next few days a technician had been a frequent visitor, returning to tweak and adjust things, having installed and taught Gwyneth how to use it. She was struggling to use her I-pad and the eye-gaze was a boon, enhancing her ability to navigate the internet and send e-mails. She'd quickly ascertained that she could wait an inordinately long time to acquire eye-gaze through the NHS, and paid a large sum to the manufacturer to acquire the necessary equipment complete with technician in just a matter of days.

'Have you joined yet?' Amanda was sitting on the edge of the sofa, a pad on her lap and pen in hand, like Gwyneth's PA.

'Yes, all done and confirmed, I'm a fully paid up suicide applicant!'

'Good!' Amanda smiled. 'We'll need to sort out the medical reports.'

'I've done that too. GP and neurologist both booked in.' She was grinning mischievously. Her mood had become more volatile, and Amanda was taking advantage of one of her 'up' days to have a conversation about arrangements for Dignitas.

'Oh. So when?'

'GP on Thursday at two, then the neurologist next week, time to be arranged.'

'They don't know I presume?'

'Good heavens no! I'll deal with that when I have them in front of me.'

Amanda eased back into the cushions and put down her pen and pad. 'So what if they don't say . . .

I mean, doesn't it all rather depend on what they say? What if they say that you're in good fettle and stable and managing very . . .'

'They won't. They'll say what I want them to say. She who pays the piper . . !'

'Ah. I see.'

Amanda was not badly off, and she had some very wealthy friends. She knew only too well that the phrase 'money talks' had a solid foundation, and that both opened doors and paved the way. She wondered what sort of amounts Gwyneth was paying for her two medical reports. Judging by Gwyneth's confident demeanour it must have been a lot. But she was also backing herself. There would after all have to be a medical basis for what the doctors said, however cooperative they were. She was a formidable woman, confident that she could steer them to the desired conclusions.

'Oh they won't have to tell any lies as such, just to err on the side of the negative, downbeat and going down. I can get them to do that. And they'll send me draft copies before it's finalised. And before I make the payments. ' A raised eyebrow said it all.

'Oh. Gwyneth . . .'

'Well, it's not much use to me after I've gone darling. I'm not leaving anything to chance here Amanda. They'll want to talk to you most likely, and I'll give them Sophie's number. Sophie can be very persuasive, and she knows what to say.'

'Oh.'

'Lot's of 'ahs' and 'ohs'. Are you uncomfortable my dear with me greasing palms and leaning on people? I don't want you to tell any lies, just to . . .'

'Just to exaggerate a little: downbeat and going down?'

'Yes. Something like that.' Suddenly Gwyneth's expression was apprehensive, pleading, the face of a small child begging indulgence from a doubtful parent. Amanda sighed.

'I'll do my best. It's difficult.'

'I know. I know. But it's my one chance Amanda, my *only* chance.'

'Yes. I know. I will . . . I'll do my best.'

'Thank you. Really.'

What was never going to be easy now seemed too close to a reality for comfort, and the need to massage the story in order to achieve the desired end was not something that Amanda had anticipated. The down payments to medics also jarred, and her discomfort was considerable.

'What about the Dignitas doctors?' Amanda said at last. Gwyneth was brisk and business-like.

'Well my reading of the situation is that so long as they have the right medical information and prognosis, I can just tell them the truth. I really do want this, need this, and I think that's what they want to know. That it's not going to get better. There's no pill for it, and it's only going to get worse. I'm of sound mind and it's my consistent wish. That's what they want to know. We've both read their stuff. I think we can trust that they'll understand. Anyway, I'm willing to take that chance. As for the rest, my own esteemed medics, I *have* to make sure that they tow the line, because it's *their* information that will release Dignitas to be free to decide. At the end of the day Amanda it's officialdom, always the same. Everyone needs to be able to cover their backs.'

'Right!' Amanda picked up the pad and her pen and stood up. But catching Gwyneth's eye, dropped them back onto the sofa and bent to envelop her in a hug, Gwyneth's hands touching so lightly on her sides, unable to muster the pressure to return her embrace. 'Oh my darling I'm so sorry!' She murmured into Gwyneth's hair, holding onto her, fighting back the tears, regretting her pique. Who was she to judge?

It was alreadyAugust. Amanda had arisen and walked out early in the morning. She'd had a restless night and awake at first light was unable to get back to sleep. The coming test she faced weighed on her mind. That she had no doubts didn't help. The stark fact remained that she was embarked upon a complicated difficult process in order to do one thing: to help her dear friend to die. She'd stopped by the stables, all quiet with the doors still locked, then out along the tiny lanes that criss-crossed the countryside all about.

It had been a dry sunny few days, the vivid green

of June had long since given way to faded hues, and now the year was beginning the long slow downward tread to winter. Amanda mused in melancholic mood. How quickly the summer became tired once the sap had risen and buds burst into leaf and flower. New life, luxuriously rampant for a such a short time so soon in check. Youthful exuberance reined in, the vibrant blades of spring so quickly dulled. Forecast in the hiatus of high summer, even in its brash promise of endlessness, there is decline.

It was already well advanced, the linen white bramble blossoms transforming into darkening fruit. It was there in the meadows where ewes moved impatiently away as large portly lambs butted at their mothers' shrunk udders, no longer cute and tottering on pipe-cleaner legs, but ever hopeful for a meal.

The cycle of the seasons. A perpetual motion of change: warm and cold, light and dark, predictable and inevitable. Always the same. Summer days expand and expand then shrink away, imperceptibly at first but gathering apace as autumn suddenly is here, urging all living things to hurry and prepare for darker times. But spring would come and it would all start over again.

Amanda thought such things as she walked. All was quiet. The dawn chorus had long since fled the fields and hedgerows. Some of the erstwhile singers were tardily feeding second fledgeling broods, every waking hour devoted to this task and no more time for tunes.

The sunny spell had seen the haymaking come and go. The clamour of machinery, tractors and trailers clattering back and forth along the lanes between field and barn. Everywhere stubble fields stripped of their harvest, silent now save the occasional bleat of a sheep, and the distant drone of an invisible plane far away in the endless blue sky.

'Gilles?' Amanda had to ask the question as Gilles did not speak when he answered the phone.

'Yes, it's me. And it's you Amanda. Bonjour.'

'Hi. It's not too early?'

'For what?'

Amanda smiled and sank back into the armchair. She knew that he would wait for her to answer and let him wait a little longer.

'I went for a walk this morning. I was thinking.'

'Ah oui? It's a good time of day to think.'

'Yes.'

Amanda could hear the rasp of a lighter and pictured Gilles lighting a Gitanne as he patiently awaited her thoughts. She reached for hers and did the same.

'Is that your first?' Gilles too had heard.

'No. Gilles, I *have* to do this.'

'Yes. I know.'

'But *you* don't.'

'Yes, I know that too.'

'I just wanted to say, I wouldn't mind if . . . you know. You made a very generous offer, and have already been an enormous help. But I don't mind taking Gwyneth alone if you . . . '

'. . . would like to change my mind?'

'Yes.'

There was a long pause during which Amanda suddenly imagined that Gilles might be thinking that she was telling him that she didn't want him to come, which was anything but the truth. She was suddenly anxious he might withdraw, needed to explain that this was not actually her wish. But it would be very awkward now to do that without appearing to put pressure on him in the opposite direction. So she held her peace and waited.

'Amanda.' He was going to withdraw. She sighed.

'Look, it's alright Gilles. . .'

'Amanda. I don't *have* to do this, as you say. It is not part of my *purpose.'* He emphasised 'purpose' with a hint of irony. Amanda suspected that Gilles had no truck with fate, meaning, purpose, a grand scheme, despite seeming to accept hers.

'But you see, I have a debt to repay. It is an opportunity to restore my honour.'

He stopped. A long pause this time.

'Gwyneth was my lover for many years Amanda. She was so beautiful. I was mad for her. As she became ill it became more difficult, but even then we continued. But as her body changed, so I found excuses not to meet. You see how shallow we

231

French men are! She knew, or at least, it did not take her long to realise. You know, women are much better at 'faking it' than men!'

The self-reproaching bitterness in his voice gave the lie to his joke, and Amanda opened her mouth to reply but no words came and she again waited.

'So Gwyneth called it off. She 'fell on her own sword'. Oh you know . . . it was for Sebastian . . . she wanted to focus on the two of them . . . you know the sort of thing. I accepted it of course. Nothing was ever said of the truth. Yes. The truth!'

Amanda still waited. Now it all made sense. But she felt that more was to come.

'So. You may understand. I do it for myself as much as for Gwyneth. I am still as always a self-centered egoist. I haven't changed.'

'Oh Gilles, don't say that. Thank you . . . for telling me. It's fine. I understand. We will be together. I'm so happy to have you help me!'

'Merci Amanda. Please . . . Sophie does not know. I have to go now.'

The call abruptly ended, Amanda's goodbye spoken to a dead line. Gilles having made his confession peremptorily fled to nurse his newly opened wound. What new twist was this? A strange mix of emotions and so many thoughts sought to crowd into Amanda's mind. She was having to re-jig her image of Sebastian and Gwyneth's marriage, no longer the perfect relationship blighted by illness. Did Sebastian know? *He* had never been unfaithful, she knew that. He had loved his wife, idolised her, Amanda suspected. And Gilles, what of Gilles? So different to Sebastian. 'Mad for her.' And now atonement for abandoning the beauty that had become marred by illness, perfection no more.

And at the centre of it all, Gwyneth. She had wanted Sebastian to have a lover. Was she atoning too? Amanda remembered how Gwyneth had been when she had expressed doubts about informing Gilles of the plan. Had she perceived the burden he carried with him, the weight of their unspoken 'truth?' And what about her?

She made her way into the living room and picked up the photo of Gwyneth in her riding gear. She was just a few years younger than Amanda, but the same, exactly, her double. She looked at it for a long time.

Chapter 18

Following the conversation with Gilles Amanda lay on her bed, going over it all in her mind. Gwyneth, the orchestrator moving powerfully at the centre, writing the parts for the principal players, destinies fulfilled, atonement achieved. Resolution, forgiveness, redemption flowed from the unfolding tragedy of her life and death.

And yet she barely moved at all, literally or in any other way actively moving things along. She just *was*, there at the centre, a very ill woman walking her own path, a guiding light, a compassionate heart.

How must it have been for Gwyneth? Devoted to Sebastian, her clandestine affair with Gilles must have caused her pain as well as joy. Was she likewise 'mad' for Gilles? Deserted by him then, and her cuckold husband stepping up to care for her as her illness ate into her humanity. Finally Amanda herself then drawn in, the doppelgänger. Had Gwyneth played a part in this? Confined to a chair or her bed, she had all the time in the world to ruminate on her loss, her own deception, the goodness of her husband, as her body slid into relentless decline. And at last she had found a way to make things right, to repay her debts, and in doing so had glimpsed her own redemption beyond the final twist of fate. The tangled web had acquired a crystalline symmetry, Amanda the final piece of the jigsaw, created in one another's likeness, their paths destined to intersect.

But answers prompted questions. Amanda's total focus had been on the task in hand, helping her friend to end her life. But what then? For the first time she pondered life beyond Gwyneth.

She thought of Mattie who'd not long since e-mailed. She was back in 'Oz' fruit-picking, Koh Tao having moved into the monsoon season. She thought of Khala remaining there alone, leaden skies, driving rain, heavy surf pounding onto the beach. And suddenly she was back there once again, deja vu, Khala propped on his elbow in the early morning light; Nang hands solemnly clasped averting her eyes; the tiny wavelets swishing warm around her ankles. All would be well.

But for now there was much to be done. Gwyneth drove things forward. Gilles assisted. Gwyneth had had her initial phone conversation with Dignitas following their receipt of the medical reports. Amanda and Sophie also had conversations with them. There was a further follow-up conversation with Gwyneth, and the very next day confirmation that they could move forward to arrange the two face to face interviews with the Dignitas doctors who would be responsible for the procedure. They would take place over the course of a week in Switzerland, and if the procedure was agreed it could take place within a couple of days of the second interview. Dates were set and the hotel was booked for a fortnight. Gwyneth had no intention of returning home to reflect further. Her affairs were in order. The die was cast.

In Geneva airport Gwyneth looked unwell. Her eyes were closed and she was pale, enduring as best she could the exhaustion and indignity of being moved around like freight. She was squeezed into a wheelchair not designed for someone so large, and her head lolled forward.

Their suitcases were stacked on a trolley, and a fresh faced young Swiss man designated to assist politely waited. Amanda held Gwyneth's hand. Gilles had gone too find her own wheelchair, separate from their baggage and travelling freight.

At last, after what seemed an age, he arrived with the chair just as they were simultaneously approached by a young man and woman:

Mrs Carling?'

'Yes.'

'I'm Frida, and this is my colleague Ralph.'

Gwyneth opened her eyes.

'Oh, Mrs Hartley,' Frida smiled. 'Hello! This chair is not very good. Shall we help you into your own and then we can go to our vehicle?'

What seconds before had felt overwhelming, now

seemed manageable, and Gwyneth managed a smile.

 'Yes my dear, thank you.'

Gwyneth's hotel room resembled at a glance any other but for the incongruous bed which would have been more at home in a state of the art modern hospital. It was spacious and uncluttered with wide doors allowing easy access to maneuver the large wheelchair. There was a large specially equipped wet-room including an elaborate hoist, another by the high-tech bed.

Frida and Ralph assisted Gwyneth to the bathroom and then to change and get into bed. They worked together efficiently, cheerfully talking all the time to Gwyneth and each other. Frida had smiled and demurred when Amanda offered to assist, expertly going about their business. Amanda and Gilles took their cue and retreated to the balcony for a smoke.

'Merde!' Gilles' lighter sparked without lighting as he repeatedly and ever more frustrated tried to light Amanda's cigarette.

'Fucking useless. He threw the offending lighter to land with a clatter on a small coffee table. 'Have you a light?'

Amanda smiled: 'Yes. In my bag. Gilles?'

'What?'

'Give me a hug?'

 He smiled, shook his head and laughed, comically throwing his unlit cigarette over his shoulder as he gathered her up.

'We made it!' She said as they clung to one another.

'Yes. Bien sur.' A few seconds passed, and Gilles was the first to speak:

'Amanda.'

'What?'

'Have you a light?'

They leant on the rail and gazed out over the lake, lost in their own thoughts. A ferry cruised along far out in the surprisingly large expanse of water, and small random sailing boats with colourful sails skimmed along like butterflies.

The hotel was an old building, one of a type dotted along the lake shore, enormous stone houses with steep alpine gables. They were set in lawned gardens shaded by large trees, and nearly all now become guest houses and small hotels. Another one was the Dignitas base, where Gwyneth would have her interviews and spend her final hours. It was not what Amanda had expected, envisaging a clinical modern building in the heart of the town.

She glanced over her shoulder. Ralph was folding down the bed, Frida and Gwyneth out of sight in the wet-room. She wondered how many occupants of this room had finally chosen to die, here for the same purpose as Gwyneth, each with their own story, their own reasons, but united in this one thing. There was obviously a sufficiently regular demand for the hotel to have gone to some trouble to provide the specialist facilities and equipment needed.

Amanda was smoking one of Gilles' Gitannes, and

accepted a second. He had not spoken since their embrace, quiet too when she took her second cigarette and joked about him leading her astray. She was glad he was there. It would not have been easy to be doing this alone. She knew that it was harder for him to be there than for herself, and admired him for it.

At last the glass door slid open and Frida stepped out, closing it behind her. 'That's everything done. I think Mrs Hartley is going to sleep now. She's very tired after the journey. Here's my number if you need anything. I'll be back at five pm?'

Amanda took the proffered card and stubbed out her cigarette in a large black ashtray atop a heavy slate stand.

'Yes, thank you so much.'

'See you later!' Frida said cheerily, turned briskly and left, Ralph in her wake raising a hand in a little wave through the glass as they departed.

'Moi aussi.' Gilles now wearily scrunched his stub into the ashtray. 'I think I'll have a lie down.'

'Are you OK?'

Gilles mouth turned down in the reverse of a smile, hands turned upward as he waggled his head from side to side:

'Oh, comme ci comme ca.'

He forced a wistful smile, touched Amanda lightly on the cheek and was gone.

Amanda and Gwyneth were in connecting rooms. Gilles' was a little way along a square gallery resplendent in old oak and looking down two floors to the hotel reception foyer which was furnished like an Edwardian drawing room.

After Gilles left, Amanda unpacked and lay on her bed, suddenly overcome with fatigue. The connecting doors were open so she could see Gwyneth now sleeping peacefully after the rigours of the journey. A long sigh slowly escaped her. They had made it. Now she could step back for Dignitas to do its work. She slept.

When she awoke all was quiet. Gwyneth slept on. She found her book and took it to sit with her, suddenly conscious of the limited time that they would have together, and wanting to be there when she awoke. It was very quiet, not a sound from within or without, just Gwyneth's softly rasping breathing.

Half an hour passed quietly thus. Finishing another chapter Amanda glance up to find Gwyneth's eyes fixed on her, her tender look lighting up in a smile as their eyes met.

'Oh, you're awake. Sneaky! How long have you been awake?'

'Oh just a couple of minutes.'

Amanda marked her page and put the book on her lap.

'Are you OK? Good sleep?'

'Yes to both! So happy to be here at last. Thanks for bringing me. And Gilles, my dear Gilles. You've saved my life . . . so to speak!'

Amanda laughed shaking her head. 'You really are incorrigible!'

'How *is* Gilles? Having a sleep?'   'Yes I think so. He went as soon as Frida and Ralph did, wanted a bit of time. I think he's struggling to be honest.'

'Yes, I'm sure. It's very difficult for him.'

Amanda waited, wondering if Gwyneth was going to say some more. When she didn't Amanda made a snap decision:

'He told me Gwyneth. He told me about . . . well you know.'

Gwyneth studied her, nodding her head slowly.

'I see. I thought he might. That's good. I don't think he's ever told anyone. So that's good.'

'It must have been very hard.'

'Yes. Yes. It *was* hard. I . . . my heart was broken Amanda. But I survived. I 'got over it'. I had Sebastian, his love, *our* love. It never faltered, ever. I was unfaithful, yes. But I always loved my husband. Poor Gilles. He never found someone. Oh I'm sure he hasn't been a monk. . . he's French! But he's been so alone with his books and his whisky and cigarettes. He's remained faithful to his loss!'

Amanda took her hand.

'Yes.'

A minute or two slipped by, Gwyneth's eyes far away, her mental footfalls tripping back across the years.

'I so want him to be free Amanda, to put down his burden. Coming here, I don't know, but I'm hoping that it will give him release. He did what any man would have done. I was hurt of course, but I don't blame him. I think he's never forgiven himself.'

'No.'

They sat in silence. What more was there to say? Amanda thought about Gilles' joke about being a communist, and considered the irony of his very Catholic guilt. What grand passion must he and Gwyneth have shared to take her from Sebastian's side? Whilst love could cloth itself in such a varied and resplendent array of colours, loss is only ever naked and alone.

Chapter 19

Frida and Ralph had their own key and came and
went throughout the next day. Gilles had reappeared in the midst of the lunchtime visit. He was
clearly uncomfortable and stationed himself on the
balcony, making his excuses after only one
cigarette. At Amanda's suggestion he had agreed to
explore the town and scout out a decent restaurant
for the two of them to have dinner, evidently glad to
have something to do.

   It was a day to relax and recover from the journey
which had taken it's toll on Gwyneth, and again she
slept in the afternoon. Frida had Gwyneth choose
dinner from the hotel menu, and it appeared like
Swiss clockwork half an hour after she and Ralph
did early in the evening.   Amanda hovered
anxiously. She was dressed to go out and It was
almost time to meet Gilles in the lobby. Gwyneth's
nightly Lorazepam was on a small white saucer on
the bedside cabinet.

   'Shall I give you this before I go? Are you sure
you're going to be alright? We can easily get
something sent up?'

   'Don't be silly, of course I will! Yes, give it me
now. I'll be out like a light before you reach the
restaurant.'

Frida had reassured Amanda that she would call by mid-evening. It was an unnecessary precaution as Gwyneth always slept heavily under her nightly sedation, but appreciated by Amanda who's anxiety levels were raised. Still she lingered.

'Yes I know. It's just that *here . . . now.* I don't like the thought of you being by yourself.'

'Look after Gilles Amanda. He needs it more than I do. And enjoy your dinner.'

Gilles was nowhere to be seen in the lobby but appeared from outside just as Amanda was about to sit down.

'Ah, there you are!' They kissed times two in the traditional French greeting, and Gilles, evidently cheered by the imminence of dinner took a small step back, his hands still resting on Amanda's shoulders:

'You look so beautiful. I think I must walk behind you!'

Amanda raised an eyebrow. 'Flattery will get you everywhere.'

She ignored Gille's grin and sailed past.

'Come on, reprobate!'

They were both happy to be temporarily relieved of their duties. They'd become closer during the three months since Amanda had first seen Gilles lurking behind Sophie in Gwyneth's front porch. There had been many calls and written communication between them. Embarked together on an enterprise to secure the death of someone they both loved, they leaned on each other for support, unable to look to anyone else. Like hostages they had kept each others spirits up. It was one thing believing that what they were doing was the right thing to do, and entirely another to carry it through. The burden was heavy and they shared the load.

Their conversations mostly skirted their feelings, lightly brushing past each other in the darkness they both experienced. But it was enough. They each understood the other's reticence, and in their coded messages each reassured the other that they were not alone. It was not to avoid, but to survive.

They strolled along the lake shore in the evening sunshine. Gilles had booked a table in a small restaurant with a balcony overlooking the water. At last in the very eye of the storm, they chose to talk about anything but that which was most pressing. Aperitifs then a long leisurely dinner.

Their was an easy intimacy between them. Gilles talked about his life in Paris. Amanda's suspicion that Gilles for the most part lived the cloistered life of the academic don was confirmed. Relationships it seemed were few and short-lived; one night stands, younger women, easy for a teacher with so many adoring students searching for the meaning of life.

Amanda wasn't shocked. She knew the sexual freedom of academia. She teased him that he had 'groupies,' and Gilles laughed, replying that he had 'needs.'

'Now you know many things about my life, but

you are still a mystery. I know a little, but not the essence. You have just *appeared*. And yet . . .' He looked at her, a long admiring look.

They had paid the bill and were smoking a final cigarette. It was twilight on the lake and a pair of mallards skimmed the inky water silhouetted against the afterglow.

As she lay in bed Amanda thought about Gilles, entrapped in his loss. There was a similarity to what she had experienced after the death of her husband. But Gilles' anger had been directed inwardly at himself, whilst hers was toward John. Her eye for symmetry reminded her that Sebastian had been the source of her own liberation from despair; perhaps Gwyneth would at last be the same for Gilles.

They had allowed for the following day, Sunday, to be a recovery day following the journey. The first appointment at Dignitas was on the Monday morning. It was early and Frida and Ralph were attending to Gwyneth.

Amanda had again retreated to the balcony for a smoke. The door slid open and she was joined by Gilles. She was wondering whether scheduling an intervening day might not have been a good idea. Gilles was morose, and she too felt stressed.

'Lets take her out,' she said, 'We can't just sit around here all day. The elephant's just too fucking big!'

Gilles agreed, and Amanda stubbed out her

cigarette and went in to organise it. Gwyneth was all for it, and Ralph suggested a ferry trip around the lake. The wheelchair wouldn't be a problem and it was a beautiful day, perfect to sit in the stern of the ferry and enjoy the sunshine. It was decided. There was a departure in a little over an hour which they would be able to make.

It was the perfect diversion. A lazy day steaming around Lake Geneva like holiday makers on a day out. Basking in the summer sun, sipping drinks, taking in the splendid views.

Gilles had perked up and amused his companions with his droll observations. Unlike in the hotel where he appeared fazed by Gwyneth's care needs and steered nervously clear, here he was attentive. He brought her drinks and snacks, fussed over her not being cold in the breeze which was cool despite the sunshine. He reminisced about a similar trip they had taken around Lake Ullswater in the Lake District with Sebastian and Sophie, and the laughter when Sebastian's straw fedora had blown off, last seen bobbing in the churning wake of the boat. As is so often the case this sparked other reminiscences.

Amanda took herself off, ostensibly to take some photos from the bow and to sit inside for a little while claiming to be cold. She had brought her book and said she was going to read. She wanted Gilles to have this time with Gwyneth. Returning some time later she could see them both from inside the cabin, Gilles holding Gwyneth's hand, talking, both smiling and so relaxed. She smiled, a wistful smile tinged with sadness, her eyes starting to mist, and retraced her steps to leave them to their memories.

Frida and Ralph met them on the pier, waving to them all smiles as the ferry swung around to dock stern first. Gilles insisted on pushing Gwyneth along back to the hotel. It was a good twenty minutes and Gwyneth was not a lightweight to push, but he waved Ralph away joking that it was his workout for the day and would save him having to go to the gym.

Back at the hotel when Frida and Ralph had departed, Gilles and Amanda sat in the bar whilst Gwyneth was having an afternoon nap.

'Thank you Amanda. You were very thoughtful on the boat. I appreciate it.'

'I'm just happy that you were able to have some nice time together, to talk.'

'Yes, c'etait bon. It's a long time since we talked like that. Really, thanks.'

'And so. Tomorrow.'

'Yes, tomorrow.'

'They will want to speak to us.'

'Yes. I know.'

'What if they don't agree?'

Gilles pondered this, looking into his whisky and swirling it around the glass.

'Then we will take her home.'

Amanda began to speak but stopped. How quickly had the normality of their afternoon jaunt evaporated now, faced with the reality of their mission. Gilles ordered more drinks and they sipped in silence.

'She seemed so happy today.' Amanda said. 'Oh I know it's *because* she can see an end. I know it would be horrific for her to fail, and she'll go downhill quickly. I know, I know all of that. But it makes it so hard too. I don't know quite how to say it. Do you know what I mean?'

Gilles quaffed his drink.

'Yes. I know.'

There was nothing more to say. They were locked into a situation that had it's own dynamic. Having started the process they were now helpless observers. It would run it's course and there would be an outcome.

Gilles knew this. His quiet resignation. Que sera sera. And in that moment Amanda had no doubt as to what the outcome would be. Gwyneth, the master tactician had planned and executed a campaign that was not going to fail at the final hurdle. It was a foregone conclusion. She recalled Shakespeare's famous lines: 'All the world' a stage, and all the men and women merely players.' Yet again the recognition of a greater scheme calmed her.

'What?'

Gilles was looking at her inquisitively.

'Sorry?'

'Why do you smile?'

'Oh. I was just thinking. It's as if it's already

happened. It's as if it's always happened, and we're just seeing the official record being written, the ledger updated. Not just this, *all of it*. Gilles, they aren't going to say no.'

Gilles smiled too, a tired sad smile eyes downcast, slowly nodding his head in agreement. He sighed and their eyes met. 'Yes. I think so too.'

It was Gwyneth's wish to attend the appointment alone, and Frida took her. There was no expectation that there would be any immediate outcome, and Gwyneth may just as easily have been going off to a routine appointment with her GP or dentist. It was a grey day and the view across the lake was obscured by mist which coalesced into a fine soft drizzle. When they returned they were unexpectedly damp, but chatting away in good spirits.

'How did you get on?' Amanda wasn't quite sure what was the best way to phrase the enquiry and kept it general and innocuous, not expecting in any case that there would be a decision made so quickly.

'Oh fine darling. Where's Gilles?'

'He's in his room, shall I . . ?

'Would you darling, thanks.'

Amanda's heart rate had instantly sped up. They were not dealing with local council officialdom in rural Sussex. Things were different here. If it required Gilles to be there and it was 'fine' that could only mean one thing. She and Sophie had already spoken on the phone to someone from the

Dignitas team, but she had understood that they would want to meet her, and Gilles too, so she had't expected anything to happen till then. On her return with Gilles, Frida asked Gwyneth if she'd like her to go, and Amanda was certain then what she was going to impart. A great heaviness came upon her.

'No do stay Frida. It might be helpful. My dear Gilles, darling Amanda . . . do sit down you're making me nervous!'

They complied obediently. Frida remained standing close by.

'They've told me that they will help me. I have to have a second appointment on Thursday for me to confirm that I remain of the same mind, but that will be a formality really. So, I'll go on Saturday!'

She said the last sentence with such glee that Amanda actually laughed, incongruous tears streaming down her cheeks as she arose and hugged her.

'Oh that's wonderful. I'm so happy for you!'

At last extricating herself Amanda sat down again and Gwyneth turned to Gilles. The colour had drained from his face and he stared blankly ahead not meeting her eye.

'Gilles?' Gwyneth said, gently edging her hand toward him. He took it and suddenly knelt beside her, his forehead resting against the arm of her chair. He wept. With an extraordinary effort Gwyneth lifted her hand to flop onto Gilles head, her swollen shiny fingers hardly moving as she tried to stroke his hair. 'Gilles, darling, it's alright. Shhhh now. It's alright.'

Amanda caught Frida's eye and as one they exited to the balcony. Frida slid the door closed. She joined Amanda leaning on the rail and looped an arm around her waist like an old friend.

'She's happy.' Frida said. 'I think it is the right decision.'

'Do you? I thought you had to be sad to want to die.'

'No, you can be happy too. I think she would be sad to live. *Then* she would be sad.'

'Yes.'

Frida turned her face toward Amanda. 'I think you are at one with this.' It seemed a peculiarly correct use of English, one of those instances where ironically the non-native speaker is more precise than a British person would be.

Amanda smiled. 'Yes I am. It's the way it has to be. I've known that for a while.'

It was brightening a little. The mist still obscured the lake, though the near shoreline was now visible. The very tops of the dripping trees in the garden appeared to be touching the clouds, and all was silent but for everywhere the muted percussive symphony: drip, drip, drip.

'Gilles is very distressed.' Frida said at last.

'Yes. He thought he had abandoned her a long time ago. Evidently he didn't.'

They gazed out into the distance. The mist over

the lake was thinning and the sun was burning hazily through it with a diffused pale yellow glow, into which the ferry steamed like a phantom, the Marie Celeste, there for a moment . . . two . . . three . . . gone.

Chapter 20

Sitting at her desk, looking out of the tall windows at the rain-soaked garden, Amanda recalled the view from the balcony in Geneva, Frida's arm slung around her waist, the ferry coming into view and vanishing like an apparition. Alone in the empty house in rural Surrey it all seemed like a dream. She wondered what Frida was doing now; no doubt kindly caring for another tired hopeful hopeless person, looking to find relief in ending their life.

It had been a turning point. Gilles was gone when they re-entered, Gwyneth wearing a serene smile which hardly ever left her for the rest of her few remaining days. Those days saw Gilles mostly withdrawing to his room except for his visits to Gwyneth. He was solemn, more often than not sitting quietly holding her hand, in contrast to Gwyneth's easy relaxed calm. She reminisced, laughed, reminded him of things from their past, sometimes eliciting a smile, a 'd'accord,' or occasionally a small contribution of his own.
Sometimes they sat in silence.
As the days passed Gilles too seemed to relax, staying longer, a few words, a smile, even managing to laugh when Gwyneth gently teased him as was

her wont. She observed him, sensed his struggle, sometimes quietly saying his name, telling him 'It's alright.' She was an irresistible force, and slowly, like the stirred up sediment in a liquid settling once again, his expression became clear and at peace.

Amanda was her normal self, reading to Gwyneth and chatting to her. Gwyneth didn't want to go out again, and spent a good deal of her time in a quiet meditative mood, sometimes appearing to be asleep as she listened to her own breath. Frida invited Amanda to meet her for coffee in the town, and they had dinner together. Gilles declined their invitations, only venturing out to sit by the lake with a book, smoking his beloved Gitanes.

It was a warm sunny spell, and Gwyneth sometimes asked to be wheeled out onto the balcony from where she would watch the activity on the lake and the birds flitting in and out of the trees and banks of rhododendron in the garden. Amanda watched her, her calm focus on both the details and wholeness of her surroundings, a focus heightened by having always one eye turned inward, assessing her own consciousness of the existence of the world beyond her, soon to be without her.

The Thursday appointment had not thrown up any difficulties. Gilles and Amanda had as expected been given an opportunity to talk to one of the Dignitas doctors, but this was less for the doctors to acquire their view, than to offer *them* the opportunity to talk about their feelings, as well as to discuss practical arrangements. Both Amanda and Sophie had had lengthy telephone conversations with Dignitas staff before the trip to Switzerland, and the emphasis now was on doing what was to be done and caring for all concerned.

On Friday, the day before she would die, Amanda had sat down next to Gwyneth on the balcony. 'So, what's the meaning of life?' She had launched the question intending to be flippant, but in the space of these few words realised not only that she meant it, but that she hoped for an answer.

Gwyneth did not disappoint. 'It's listening to your heart, being able to live and love when you can, and able to let go when you can't.' The reply had come straight back at her.

On the morning of the Saturday, they had organised for Gwyneth to have a private face to face conversation with Sophie on Skype. Directly after that they had gone to the clinic. Gwyneth had decided that she wanted to die sitting in her chair rather than in bed as was the norm. This had been agreed. Frida had kissed her and left the room, and Amanda and Gilles sat together to one side.

The doctor had a conversation with Gwyneth to offer her the opportunity to halt or delay proceedings. He was kindly but stubborn, coming back to the question several times before he was satisfied that there was no question of doubt in Gwyneth's mind. She'd resolutely smiled and

politely refused. At last he gave her an an anti-
emetic to prevent vomiting once the lethal drug had
been taken. Having done so he and the nurse in
attendance withdrew in order for the three friends to
be alone.

Gilles had embraced her, a long long hug.
'Forgive me.' Was all that he had said quietly in her
ear, his voice steady now that the end had arrived.

'We lived and loved Gilles, and have nothing to
regret. There's nothing to forgive. Nothing. Do you
understand?'

He nodded still holding her.

'Do you understand?' She was insistent demanding
a reply. Gilles stood back, raised her hand and
kissed it:

'Oui. Merci cheri. Je comprends.'

'Listen, and remember. You must live!'

He bowed his head and quietly stood back, his
whispered assent barely audible. It was Amanda's
turn to say goodbye. Gwyneth spoke first.
'Goodbye my friend. Thank you. I owe you so
much. And don't forget!'

Amanda was holding Gwyneth's hand, and she
nodded, feeling even then the echo of those words in
the cool dawn on a beach thousands of miles away.
She knew that Gwyneth referred to what she had
said on the balcony the previous day.

'No. I won't forget. Goodbye Gwyneth. Thank
you.'

They embraced. At last Amanda opened the door

to let the doctor and nurse know that they were ready. The doctor again asked Gwyneth if she would like to stop, to delay, to postpone what was about to happen until a time of her choosing. When she once more declined he discharged the contents of a syringe into a clear glass beaker containing a sugary drink, and assisted Gwyneth to grip it and take the protruding straw into her mouth. She sucked with purpose and the liquid having disappeared he removed the beaker and gave it to the nurse.

Amanda and Gilles stood on either side, holding Gwyneth's hands. She smiled at Amanda and finally turned her smile to Gilles. As her head began to droop forward she tried to speak, one word slipping through the closing door of her consciousness as the light was extinguished:

'Live.'

The silent tableau held as Gwyneth's breath shortened, weakened, and after a minute or more, ceased. The doctor reached across and felt her neck, nodded, and left the room. Amanda placed Gwyneth's hand gently on the tray stroked it lightly, then leant in to kiss her on the forehead. Gilles did the same, exactly, following Amanda's lead in every detail. She took a step away intending to exit, but Gilles remained. She went to him and took his hand, led him quietly from the room and closed the door.

They left hand in hand, anchoring each other, and continued without pause along the lake, wordless, united it would seem in a wish to put distance between the corpse and themselves. The reality was not how either one had imagined it would be. They had killed. They had not poured the poison, held it to her lips, made her drink, but the lifeless corpse cooling and beginning to stiffen even now, the corpse that late had been their friend, had by any measure died at their hand. They fled from the shock of this knowledge, quickened their step and kept going until they reached their own hotel where they still did not stop. They climbed the stairs, and entered Gilles' room.

On the balcony they smoked. Sometimes theory cannot prepare for reality. There were no words. They'd both known what they were about. They felt no guilt. But all the compassion and mercy in the world could not cushion the shock. Amanda paced, stubbed out her cigarette and lit another. She was like a caged lioness, Gilles seated like a pile of crumpled rags, staring into space.

'I think I'll take a walk down to the town.'

'Yes. Bien. But we must phone Sophie.'

Gilles' presence of mind to remember this was a relief. Amanda had feared he might not deal with things, but in fact it was he who now took responsibility. She sighed, and felt her own burden lighten, only by a straw, but enough. 'Oh yes. Of course. Shall we go inside?'

Gilles phoned, put it on 'speaker' and placed it on the coffee table between them.

'Hello? Gilles?'

'Yes, it's me. It's done.'

'Oh.' The ensuing pause was interminably long. Amanda broke the silence. 'She was very happy Sophie. Smiling. She was . . .' she sighed and continued. 'She never faltered, not for a moment.'

'Yes. Yes. Good. Well . . .' Sophie's voice broke and trailed away. Amanda visualised her trying to gather herself, determined to be strong. She wanted to help. She could see that Gilles was not going to. In the end they both spoke together.

'Sophie she . . .'

'I'd sort of . . .'

They pulled up short, and Sophie continued. 'I'd sort of thought, with you having said how happy she's been, that they wouldn't . . .'

She re-grouped excessively brisk now, as she too fled from the reality with which she was at last confronted. 'So you'd said the cremation was going to be tomorrow? Will you come back then or wait till Monday?'

Amanda began to answer, that it would probably be Monday, but Gilles cut across her. 'We thought we may stay a few days Sophie. It's booked and paid for, and it has been . . . you know.'

'Yes, of course. Good idea. It must have been very hard for you both. You . . . you've . . . I'm so sorry to have . . . thank you; thank you. Take care of yourselves. Talk soon.'

Her voice broke and the line went dead before either could speak. Gilles pocketed the phone and their eyes met. Amanda's expression was querulous, and she waited for Gilles to speak. He sighed.

'There is no right or wrong. Amanda I don't know anything anymore. But I would like you to be with me, for us to be . . . together, for the little time we have here. If you would like?'

His look was calm, steady, and Amanda immediately perceived quite different to how he had looked at her before. Or had she just not seen? Right and wrong. Her skin tingled as from nowhere appeared the image of Gwyneth in her riding gear, smiling, her hand still holding her crop as she smoothed her hair back from her face. How was it that he had put it: 'I was mad for her.' She smoothed her own hair back, distractedly mimicking the photo.

Was it this that he saw, the doppelgänger, his lost lover returned beyond her death that had set him free? Amanda didn't care. On the contrary the idea made her aroused. Her pulse raced and colour returned to her cheek. There was a tremor in her hand, her breath short. The outcome seemed, like many things before, as inevitable as it was unexpected.

'I'm not Gwyneth Gilles.'

'No. I know that.'

'Just for the time we are here then?'

'Yes, just now, just here, making love.'

'Yes. I would like that very much.'

They were children again, young lovers, shy,

unsure now how to manage that first touch, suddenly in thrall to the urgency of their budded lust about to flower, but yet tight furled.

A few long seconds passed. It was now. It had always been now. As if by some subliminal signal they simultaneously rose, stepping hurriedly forward so they collided awkwardly, grabbing one another so tight, holding, holding on.

'Oh Gilles! *Oh Gilles*!'

'Amanda! Ma cheri!'

The close press of their bodies fused as one. She burned, woman, desire sprung from nowhere, all consuming, obscuring everything. No right or wrong. No thought but for one thing, this man locked in her arms, with whom she'd shared so much, his erection pushing unmistakably against her belly, she pushing back on it with short hard thrusts, her flood gates breached.

'*Oh Gilles . . . yes . . . yes. Oh Gilles*!'

She loosened her arms around his neck, nuzzling her mouth against his, parting her lips and so his, tasting his taste, a quick tentative touching of tongues. It was the briefest prelude to the sudden hunger of an endless savage kiss. More an assault than a kiss she tore off his jacket as they devoured one another momentarily pausing to gasp for breath only to collide ferociously again, restraint abandoned, muted cries, kissing, biting, the clash of teeth, their pain unleashed sublimating into such wild passion in which to find relief. She gasped as his hands slid up the back of her skirt grabbing her bum as she grabbed his belt, backing up against the wall and pulling him onto her.

'*Here! Fuck me here!*' she panted, tugging on his zip as he hoiked her skirt up around her waist. It stuck halfway. 'You try . . . please . . . fuck me. . .OH!' She cried out as he roughly grabbed her crotch, gripping her hard till it hurt. He was incoherent, grunting, biting her neck as he wrenched aside the drenched fabric of her pants to frig her as she struggled frantic now with his zip. '*I can't. . . it won't. . . you do it*! *Fuck me! For god sake Gilles*! *Get it out*!'

But suddenly he broke away, breathless, agitated, a step back, two, turning away to adjust the disarray of his clothing and cover himself. He was trying to say something but no words came, and he walked across to the window. His palms pressed against the pane his forehead too, and he was still.

Amanda started, as if from a short sleep, still against the wall, her skirt up around her waist, knickers torn all askew.

She hurriedly adjusted her dress, fleeing the scene to perch stiffly on the edge of the sofa, perplexed, embarrassed confused, legs crossed, a trembling hand smoothing back her hair as she tried to regain her composure.

'Amanda? Amanda.' He was beside her, his hand reaching for hers, but she demurred. 'I'm sorry. I'm so very sorry. It's me, my fault. I want you so much .

. . so much!'

She was taut like a bow-string. Even now she breathed heavily, her eyes smouldering on fire still, yet fearing that his next word would be 'but.'

He reached out and caressed her cheek. She didn't move, staring straight ahead, poker stiff. But when her own hand distracted touch her cheek where his had, he reached out and gently took it.

They sat, quietly, hand in hand, and slowly, little by little Amanda's tension leeched away. She turned to look at him at last, such pain, such longing in his eyes. 'Amanda. Forgive me. My darling. I know . . . I know I have no right. Just a little time? Only a little. Can you wait? Amanda, cheri?'

She breathed a long sigh, her body quivered, slackened and her head bowed. His hand was smoothing her hair. At last she retrieved it, kissed his palm and pressed it against her cheek, her eyes swimming with tears in which his face disolved.

'Of course. I will wait for you Gilles. We have time.'

Returned to her room to shower and change, Amanda sat on Gwyneth's bed, waiting for her accelerated body to slow. The minutes passed. She tried to piece together what had happened, but it was a blur. She breathed as she had learned to do. She could not remember having ever been so turned on and so denied. But gratification was only deferred and she longed for it even now.

She lay down and placed the palm of her hand on the pillow, her face nestled into the hollow where Gwyneth's had been. A grey hair. She picked it up and held it between her finger and thumb. It was over. Gwyneth was at last at peace. It was over, and relief flooded over her, lifting her up light as a feather in it's gentle swell. A great weight had fallen from her. She touched the hair with her lips, a final goodbye, an elegy, a prayer, and placed it back on the pillow. Now she could live again, and they were tears of joy that darkened the linen as she whispered aloud: 'Thank you Gwyneth.'

There were things to attend to. They had to return to Dignitas. They would have a further appointment later in the afternoon to deal with the inevitable officialdom. But first were to meet with a counsellor to whom they had been already introduced .

The counsellor was a quietly spoken woman in her early sixties. She expertly opened up the conversation without directly guiding it. It was for the bereaved to take it wherever they wished, or wherever it took them, the counsellor only there to hold open the door.

'Thank you for coming. I met your remarkable friend Gwyneth, and know she was happy to die. But she was your friend. So you have lost a friend, and helped her to go from you. You may not need my words, but if I can help you now in any way, it is my privilege to do so.'

After the counsellor's short pre-amble, like at a Quaker meeting a comfortable inviting silence prevailed. As is so often the case, not feeling that you have to do something makes you want to. It was a conversation of happiness and smiles when at last Gilles began, talking warmly about the boat trip on the lake.

The sun streamed through the windows and they laughed, drank coffee and celebrated their friend's death. The counsellor beamed, her twinkling smile not unlike Gwyneth's. She was so happy for them, a joy for her too to know not only that their work at Dignitas could have offered such a singular gift to Gwyneth, but that they were also able to assist and support people as courageous and selfless as helpers such as they. They could be proud of what they had done. The ultimate sacrifice, she reflected, was not laying down one's own life, but being prepared to lose a loved one, and helping them to go from you.

They did not need to be forgiven. They had after all done no wrong. But there was in the kind understanding of this wise smiling woman, permission to forgive themselves, to expunge any clinging mote of guilt.

They left buoyed up, hand in hand again, but how different now! On the lake shore Gilles stopped, drew Amanda to him and kissed her, a fleeting soft touch of their lips. The smiles that had hardly left them since their interview now shone, and before Gilles could turn away Amanda's arm looped up

266

around his neck and she kissed him back harder, a long tender kiss, a marker put down for what was promised.

'Happy?' She asked him as they resumed their walk.

'Yes. I am!'

'That's good. So am I!'

The ferry ploughed into sight far out on the lake, heading for the jetty half a mile along the shore. Amanda quickened her pace and broke into a run pulling Gilles along with her. 'Come on, we can catch it if we run!'

Chapter 21

They checked out of their hotel and booked into a place on the lake. Amanda was married for a long time, and had always been faithful. But she had had more than her share of lovers as an undergraduate and during her early years in academia. Her late teens and early twenties happened close on the heels of Woodstock and 'free love,' and university life even as a teacher lived up to it's liberal reputation. But she was used to the innate reserve of the English. She had never had a so-called 'Latin lover,' and was not prepared for Gilles.

Many French people are indistinguishable in their appearance from others in North Western Europe, but then there are those who in both appearance and temperament favour their southern neighbours. Gilles was such a one. His origins were in Marseilles, and beneath the sophisticated Parisian savoir-faire his temperament ran warm. As a lover he wore his emotions on his sleeve and there could be no mistaking his intentions.

Amanda was surprised at the sudden change. The attentiveness with which she was treated, the touching, looks, words, a latent sexual charge quietly imbued into *everything* without any hint of vulgarity or intrusiveness. It made her feel like a woman who was (as indeed she was) adored and wanted, those first moments of awkwardness a distant memory.

The day was heavy with expectation and deliciously so, as they did the normal holiday things knowing what awaited in the night.

There was an unspoken understanding that it *would* be in the night when they slept together, when they made love for the first time. But there was no coyness between them as they showered and changed in their room that evening. Amanda had a long shower and washed her hair, to find Gilles already changed and sitting on the edge of the bed, as she appeared in her robe, hair up in a towel.

'I think I'll go down to the bar. You can have some peace to make yourself even more beautiful.' He said it without any hint of irony, and Amanda sat on his knee and kissed him.

'Alright my darling. I won't be long.' She kissed him again then off to the wardrobe to peruse her clothes. Gilles hadn't moved. Amanda selected two tops and two skirts. She had them in her hand as Gilles kissed her and headed for the door with a little backward wave.

'A tout a l'heure.'

He was closing the door behind him when Amanda called after him. 'Oh, Gilles.'

He reappeared in the doorway. 'Yes?'

She let her robe slip to the floor and naked pulled the towel from her hair, shaking it out behind her as she replied: 'Oh. Silly me. Forgot what I was going to say! See you in the bar.'

She found Gilles seated on a bar stool, turning toward her as she approached and kissed him.

'Cheri, you look so sexy. You have been hiding!'

It was all tastefully done to arouse and entice, and Amanda appreciated the compliment. She *felt* sexy, and sensed admiring glances from others, causing her to tingle with excitement at her own effect.

'It's for you. As was the preview.' It was all she said but with a look that said much more.

After dinner they had liqueurs on the terrace with the statutory cigarettes. Their urgency was hidden in the casual way they took their time. It had been a leisurely dinner, but knowing what was to come the sexual frisson between them was palpable.

They were alone on the terrace seated side by side looking out onto the lake. They'd finished their cigarettes and liqueurs. Gilles had looped his arm around Amanda's shoulders. 'So. You are a stripper?'

'Yes.' she said, matter of fact, 'My husband used to like it.' Gilles turned to look at her, her half smile, a trace of sadness flickering around her eyes. She had never told anyone this before.

Gilles divined it. He tenderly squeezed her shoulders, and kissed her hair. 'Moi aussi cheri.'

Amanda leaned into him, tilting her face up to his. 'Kiss me.'

It was a long loving kiss gathering intensity as

they fell into it, Gilles' hand sliding up her top and under her bra. He squeezed her breast, and tweaked the stiffened nipple so she squealed, breathless when at last their lips parted.

'I love your tits.' he whispered.

'Yes. . . yes . . . for you.' she replied, '. . . and this.' As their lips met again she pulled his hand from her breasts to guide it unceremoniously up her skirt opening her legs. She pushed forward to the edge of the seat, and moaned softly as he slid two fingers easily into her already wet cunt, frigging her, slowly easing them in and out.

It was the start. They were unleashed, reckless on the rebound from their brush with death, inhibitions evaporated, carnal intentions already declared.

'Can you see . . ?' She breathed, quivering, still deliciously impaled, as Gilles glanced over her shoulder toward the door.

'Oui. C'est bien.' They were daring, oblivious to the chance of discovery. Amanda gripped Gilles' wrist with both hands and pushed against the knuckle till she stiffened, a series of tiny trembling gasps, hips vibrating, ecstatically penetrated as he found the spot deep inside and she stifled a cry.

Voices from within and they hastily broke apart, but with one mind were already scrambling to their feet, almost colliding with an indignant elderly couple; into the lift and they were already devouring one other as the doors closed.

Their room door slammed . . . tearing at each

others clothes . . . naked at last. '*O fuck! Oh fuck! It's so . . . ohhhh! Fuck*!' Amanda gasped in disbelief as she grabbed Gilles' cock, dragging him to the bed, her expletives in wonderment and apprehension that her fingers were barely able to encircle the shaft.

'Fuck me . . . fuck me!' she threw herself on on her back pulling back her legs. Gilles gripped her behind the knees to pin her doubled back. *'Quick . . . get it in . . !'* She'd reached between her legs to grab his cock waving huge like a threat, pulling him to her.

'*I have it . . . ohhhhh yes*! *Get it . . .*' She gasped as she slotted the shiny bulbous end deliciously into her opening, stretched even now so tight and barely inside. '*Oh my god*!' she quailed, yet in the same breath urged him on. '*Yes! Yes! GO ON*!'

He'd stooped so the crooks of his arms pinioned back her legs, gripping her wrists tight against the pillow, her body now a willing receptacle, pants somehow snagged around her ankle waving like small white flag triumphant in surrender.

They froze thus face to face, panting, hesitating, fevered eyes met, Amanda's wide, pleading, waiting; a momentary hiatus; the eye of the storm. It was now. A last: 'Go on then,' she whispered so quietly it was barely audible: 'Fuck me Gilles.'

He lurched forward into her. One swift thrust, it stretched her so she screamed as if in childbirth, her forehead beaded with sweat, head rolling from side to side, eyes closed, a long primal howl rending the air. He stopped, startled, throbbing deep inside her, but her eyes flashed blazing wild. '*Don't fucking stop*! *Fuck me . . . FUCK ME*!'

Goodbye Gwyneth. They had held her hands and watched her die. But there was no regret ridden ruminating. There was sex; not a guilty pleasure displacing their grief, but if anything *un homage* to she who they both had both loved. Gwyneth's twinkling eyes which had so encouraged them to live and be happy when she breathed, continued to do so now that she was gone. When they talked about her it was with joy and laughter. The sun still shone, the birds still sang, just as before, but the warmth was warmer, the birdsong more melodious. They were happy.

'I wish I'd known her before she was ill.' It was still quite early and they had wandered down into the town for breakfast. The pavement terrace basked in the sun but it hadn't yet properly warmed up, and a light breeze off the lake had persuaded Amanda to have a pink cashmere cardigan draped around her bare shoulders. 'What was she like?'

Gilles raised his eyebrows, and looked into the distance, moved his head from side to side as was his wont. 'Don't you know?'

'No, how could I?'

'She was like you.' He said it matter of fact as if it

was a given, obvious, what a silly question to ask.

'No that's not what I meant. I know she *looked* like me, and she was a writer, and we have a similar sense of humour etc etc. But what was she *like?'*

'She was like you Amanda. *Just* like you. She laughed like you, held herself like you. She flicked her hair back the way you do. She made love . . . like you.'

Amanda narrowed her eyes and studied him. There was no tease. She pondered it, sipped at her coffee. Why was it that nothing surprised her anymore? She looked again at Gilles who had put on his shades and was eating a croissant with great delicacy, causing her to grin, amused and very happy. 'Well in that case I hope you aren't going to fall in love with me Gilles.'

'Why not?' He replied and took another bite.

'Because you've already done that once, and it didn't turn out too well!'

Gilles pondered this for a moment before leaning across to plant a very loud kiss on Amanda's waiting, pouting lips.

'What can I say? It's too late.'

Those days following Gwyneth's death were a pause, a hiatus. They had scaled a perilous peak and were returned to base camp. They relaxed, made love, enjoyed being unexpected tourists. But for each of them there was something very different happening, their paths diverging even as they

274

became close to one another for this short time.

For Gilles it was a separation. He had arrived at a watershed where he had put down the burden under which he had for so long laboured. He was like a young fully fledged gannet on a cliff top, exercising his wings in the sun in preparation for the journey which would see him depart forever to a new life with his very first flight.

Separating from Gwyneth was something that in her life he had not been able to do. Even with her death it may have been difficult. The yoke of guilt fed by an idealised version of what she had been before could be hard to dislodge. People labour under such self-inflicted torment all their lives, and Gilles had been deeply entrenched in his own particular hell.

But the cure was to hand. Amanda to Gilles was like a homeopathic remedy. Her living replication of the person he had so deeply loved, provided the opportunity for Gilles to reverse time, to return to the loving he had lost and somehow in doing so to invisibly repair the damage he had done. The spark had continued beneath the ashes of his shame, and here with Amanda, it was re-kindled, something fine and beautiful unsullied by life. The circle thus joined up he could with dignity and grace say goodbye to the love he felt he had betrayed but had never quite relinquished.

Amanda had already travelled some way along her own path. Whereas Gilles looked outward,

Amanda's reflections took her into herself. Everything for her was tested against an inner understanding of what her journey now was. She looked for resonance, for a thread of connection, and found it in her tryst with Gilles. Her senses had become alert and she trusted her judgement, prepared to allow things to play themselves out if they felt right. What was happening between herself and Gilles was a natural part of the whole thing, whatever the whole thing was. And as Gilles began at last to move on from his doomed relationship with Gwyneth, Amanda found herself moving ever closer to her.

Gilles' remarks about her similarity to Gwyneth might easily have alarmed her. But she did not find it so, and did not fear for *him* as she might well have done. On the contrary, she sensed within herself an ever closer affinity to her friend. Alone she often thought about her. They *had* become close. From the very first moment it had been there, an indefinable connection. Now she was happy that Gilles may as it seemed be making love to Gwyneth as well as to her. She recognised a completeness within herself, and mused that Gwyneth too may have experienced something similar, two notched pieces of wood which fit perfectly together, tokens of identity which traders of old had used to identify themselves in order to pay and claim their dues.

'Are you looking forward to going home?' They

were sat up in bed, post-coital. They held hands and as she spoke Amanda brought Gille's to her lips and kissed it tenderly. The curtains were open and he morning sun streamed in in as they looked out over the sparkling water of the lake ruffled by a stiff breeze and flecked with white.

'Yes, I think so; in a way. It's time.'

'Yes.'

Gilles had an unlit cigarette in his mouth, his protest because Amanda wouldn't let him smoke it in the room as he wished to, and he didn't want to leave her to go out on the balcony where it would yet be cool. He turned to look at her:

'Yes?'

She smiled: 'Yes! What's wrong with yes?!'

He blew out a phhh and shrugged.

'Je ne sais pas. It doesn't say very much. "Yes." What is: "Yes"?'

'Yes!' She said again, teasing him now, and leaning in so that he looped his arm around her and she rested her head on his chest. 'What are you looking forward to? What will you do when you get home?'

Gilles considered this. 'Well first I want to drink a glass of Lagavulin, maybe two! Then I have to think about my future. I want to be with Sophie for a little while. I would like to help her. It's very difficult for Sophie. She loved Gwyneth. She has struggled with all this. I have to help her find peace. Et apres . . .'

'You must think about *your* future?'

'Yes. I think perhaps I may return to Paris.'

Amanda turned her face up to his. 'Paris?'

'Yes. It's in France. I am French. I think I may go home!'

Amanda grinned. 'Gilles? Are you telling me you stayed *all this time* in Edinburgh because of Gwyneth?'

The cigarette had been bobbing up and down when he talked and he scowled now as Amanda removed it.

'Gilles?'

'Yes. No. I don't know. Maybe . . . *yes*!' He grinned. 'Yes. I am a sad case. A person from a pop song. Lost in love, lost out of love, just lost. I could not leave. Phh! But now, now it's finished. Now I can go!' He snatched at the cigarette, breaking it as he did so. 'Merde!'

Amanda snuggled back into his chest. 'Will you miss me?'

'Mais oui, bien sur. You have a great body . . . and you are a wonderful fuck.'

She smiled and he felt it against his chest. They were quiet for a while.

'Amanda, I will miss you very much. You are my friend; my comrade in arms; et je t'aime.'

She planted a kiss on his chest. 'And I love you too.'

'Good! It's agreed. Come on. I need a cigarette.'

They donned the hotel bathrobes and made their way out onto the balcony. They sat quietly, smoking. A wind surfer zipped over the agitated surface of the lake, the yellow sale vibrant in the early morning sun. At last comforted by nicotine Gilles resumed.

'But we are free, Amanda. You. Me. We have come too far, known *such things*. We may love . . . we do I know, but it cannot be everything, any more than it can be nothing. It is a fact, not a way of life. It is not a solution. I think you knew this before I did. But I have caught up with you, so there! *Hey*. .!'

He protested protecting his cigarette at arms length as Amanda leapt from her chair onto his knee. They kissed long and passionately, Gilles' cigarette falling from his hand which slid up between Amanda's legs, obligingly parting with a little moan as his fingers found the cloying ripeness of her cunt. She writhed and pushed herself down onto them with a groan, rotating her hips, gasping, panting in his ear. 'Come on then. Come on. Fuck me again . . . *ohhhhhh yes* . . . *yes*! I'll take It . . . while I can!'

Chapter 22

Rain beating against the bedroom window aroused Amanda from her reverie. The house was so different without the 'help.' She'd foregone breakfast opting for coffee and cigarettes, wandering aimlessly from room to room. She had intended to return home, but decided to stay having received word from Sophie that she wanted to come down to see her.

She opened her laptop and logged into her e-mails. Time to catch up. She'd been incommunicado since a couple of weeks prior to going to Switzerland, and it was time to re-connect. She was organised, a notepad and pen to hand on the desk.

It was nice to hear everyone's news. There was nothing extraordinary to grab her attention, and ordinary life was like a warm blanket wrapped around her, comfortable to hear all the chatter from her dear friends. Trish had been keeping an eye on the house perhaps rather more than she really needed to, calling there regularly. Marcia had commented on this in a very Marcia way. It amused Amanda who thought of Trish playing Connie to Jesus's Mellors.

It was not till Amanda had methodically worked through her e-mails to the most recent that she saw one from Mattie that made her sit up. She was in London, planning to spend a few weeks in Europe, and asking if they could meet up. Amanda dialed the number and was thrilled to hear Mattie answer straight away.

'Hey Amanda! You back in Blighty?'

'Yes. Just. I've been . . . oh well it's a long story. Tell you when I see you; soon I hope?'

'Sure thing. Thought I'd head up soon as, if it's OK with you. Just a couple of things to do here, ye know . . . Royal Garden Party and stuff like that. What about Saturday? You gotta bed for me?'

Amanda was laughing.

'Hey, what's so funny? You been smoking something you shouldn't? Always thought you were a dark horse!'

'Oh Mattie I've *missed* you.'

It was all arranged. Mattie would come up in a couple of days once Sophie had returned home and Amanda decanted back to hers. It was good news and Amanda looked forward to seeing her. She knew that Mattie was the only person she might really talk to, and even that remained a 'might.' She would see how she felt when the time came. She didn't feel the need to share or have someone else express a view. But Mattie was different.

Having likewise gone through her phone messages and spoken to Melanie she made more coffee, at a temporary loss as to how she was going to fill the rest of the day. Sophie was in court in the morning and planned to catch an afternoon train. She didn't feel in the mood to write, and the rain still lashing down precluded any possibility of a hack.

She wandered through to the annexe with her second cup and sat down in her usual place. There was a gaping space where Gwyneth's chair had been. They'd left it in Switzerland, Frida very grateful for the donation of such a useful and valuable piece of kit. She didn't feel sad. Quite the opposite she felt mildly elated and found herself speaking out loud. 'So now you've gone. Where are you? Spinning through the ether somewhere? Nowhere? Here?!'

She giggled at the thought of Gwyneth the ghost returned. Gwyneth would have no doubt made some witty remark at the idea, her laughter testimony that she was never one to desist from appreciating her own jokes.

She should do something: check that there were clean sheets on Sophie's bed, and there was dinner to think about. It was a plan. And yet she sat on, listening to the rain, louder in here as it hammered on the glass connecting tunnel, the door left ajar. Her skin tingled and she focussed on her breath, quietly on the out-breath reciting alternately the two lines of a mantra she'd learned in Thailand: 'May I be filled with loving kindness. May I be well.'

It was unseasonably cool for August. The rain had continued throughout the day and Amanda had lit a fire in the living room to provide cheer as much a warmth. She and Sophie retired there with a cognac after dinner.

Over dinner they'd discussed Switzerland. Sophie listened attentively, interjecting with questions, gently extracting from Amanda a forensically detailed account. She probed when Amanda described Gwyneth's resolutely cheerful and positive demeanour, asked what the doctors had exactly said, seeking reassurance that all possible measures were taken to offer a reprieve.

Amanda knew that in part what lay behind the questioning were Sophie's ambivalent feelings regarding her own inability to assist, having been as it were passed over. She had a strong sense of duty and personal obligation, and to have been unable to help Gwyneth in her final hours was her own private Gethsemane. Now her lawyer's craft was employed to quietly go about the task of laying to rest any shadow of a doubt that it may have been a mistake.

After dinner and on their second bottle of wine they'd delinquently smoked in the dining room. Amanda had given a clear and accurate account, carefully painting a picture from which Sophie could derive as far as was possible a real understanding of how it had been. Sophie had shed a tear or two. But feelings of sadness and loss were mitigated by Gwyneth's triumph in shaping her own destiny. She had given Amanda a hug when they rose to go to sit by the fire, a quite 'thanks' whispered in her ear.

Replete, soporific, they were hypnotised by the fire and relaxed in an easy silence. Sophie spoke first.

'I'm sorry to have landed on you so soon Amanda. You must think me rather intrusive, needy even!' Sophie was back to being Sophie, brisk, business-like, self-possessed.

'Hah! Needy! *That's* a good one. I'm very happy to see you Sophie. And I'm glad that you came whilst I'm still here. It feels right.'

'Yes. Indeed. And in fact that relates very neatly to the reason I jumped on a train so smartly.'

'Well I'm glad you did.'

Sophie smiled, nodded, paused, and Amanda intuited that there was something afoot.

'What? What is it?'

'What I have to tell you Amanda is in my capacity as sole executor of Gwyneth's will. Gwyneth has left you this house, and a large amount of money."

Amanda was acutely aware of Sophie's level gaze.

'But why? What about you? What about . . .' she was going to say Gilles but quickly bethought herself. 'I don't want it. I don't . . . no, sorry Sophie, I can't possibly agree to that.'

Sophie laughed. 'My dear Amanda, over and above it being de rigueur not to speak ill of the dead, it's absolutely *impossible* to argue with them. That's what the will says, and that's what you have got! And don't worry about me darling, I'm not

284

impecunious, and in any case she has left me a very large amount also, and Gilles too, though I shouldn't strictly be telling you that as I haven't told *him* yet, so please keep it to yourself.'

It was a lot to take in. Amanda needed to re-group 'Good lord. I think I need a top up. Sophie quaffed hers and proffered her own glass. Amanda waved it away. 'I'll just fetch the bottle!'

They resumed, drinks replenished.

'Why? Is there nobody else? What about the horses? What about Seamus and Concepta? It's just . . . really I can't possibly agree to this Sophie.' Amanda was uncharacteristically thrown, and less than gratified at Sophie's apparent amused appreciation of this.

'Oh I'm sure Seamus will be very pleased to have you as his new employer, and there is a clause in the will for him and Concepta to be provided for very generously when the house is eventually sold. Anyway, Seamus thinks you virtually *are* Gwyneth. As to the *why*. Don't you know? She loved you. She saw herself in you . . . we all do. It's uncanny. Perhaps it's her bid for immortality!'

Amanda perceived that Sophie disguised in her flippancy an inescapable undertone alluding to things that a hard-nosed lawyer could never fully subscribe to, and yet could not ignore.

'And in any case Amanda,' her tone changed, 'It was an enormous service that you did. Very few people would have done what you did. Gilles would not had it not been for you. I *did* not. It was an act of complete selflessness and love. You may pardon the phrase, but it is worthy of Gwyneth's eternal gratitude. And if you will also pardon my presumptuousness, I would add to that my own too. It is entirely reasonable and fitting that Gwyneth should honour you as a beneficiary of her estate. I'm very glad that she did so, and will hear no more about it.'

This was Sophie at her imperious best, 'Judge Jeffries' as Seamus had put it, summing up in the High Court and her word law. The new reality settled like a layer of snow stolen quietly upon the landscape which was thus transformed. They sipped their drinks. The fire glowed red in the unlit room, darkening now as night appeared early with the gloom and rain.

'Alright. I need to think about it.' was all that Amanda could say. But even as she said it she knew how things would be.

It was a flying visit and Sophie returned to Edinburgh the following day. After dropping her at the station Amanda walked in the gardens. It was a fine day and she called by the stables to say hello to 'the boys,' She was glad that Seamus was not in evidence and she had the place to herself, but decided none the less not to linger, continuing her lazy perambulation through the garden, lost in thought.

Her first priority on returning from Switzerland had been to call to see Seamus and Concepta. They'd sat in the cottage kitchen where over the compulsory cup of tea Amanda explained to them what had happened. She gave them a letter penned to them by Gwyneth. They had received the information in stunned silence. Concepta read the letter first then passed it to Seamus who then had to search for his reading glasses. Having at last read it he made his excuses and went off to continue with his work. The colour had drained from his weather-beaten face, and suddenly he looked old and drawn. Amanda had half-risen and called after him, but desisted when Concepta rose too and placed a hand on her arm: 'Leave him now my dear, he needs time.'

Perhaps Gwyneth had anticipated this very scenario, for whatever she had written seemed to have the effect of closing things down, relieving Amanda from any need to become mired in a difficult conversation about the rights and wrongs of what had happened. She had come prepared for just this, especially knowing that Seamus and Concepta were both staunch Catholics. She was relieved though puzzled when neither Seamus nor Concepta protested or sought to involve her in discussion. It seemed that even beyond her death Gwyneth could move things to happen in a certain way. Amanda had left shortly after Seamus did, having unsuccessfully tried to bridge the silence which ensued as Concepta grim faced busied herself about the kitchen.

Now as she wandered through the gardens, she contemplated having to make a second visit as, the new owner, their new employer. This was not something she looked forward to. It was this prospect that had abbreviated her visit to the stables, and that preoccupied her now as she absently dead headed roses and took off her sandals to feel the grass warm on her feet.

It was one thing, difficult enough, delivering sad news of the death of a dear friend, but quite another to have to announce that having only known said friend for a time countable in months rather than years, you are the principal beneficiary of the will.

And yet as Sophie had pointed out to her, this would almost certainly be seen by the old retainer and his wife as by far the best outcome for them. In any case, she did not feel able in all conscience to put off informing them of the will. Over and above their sadness and grief, they could not be but anxious about their own future, closely tied as it was to the disposal or otherwise of the property. It would have to be today. Sophie had offered to do it but Amanda had insisted and Sophie acquiesced. It was something that Amanda knew she must not side-step. She had very quickly intuited that if she was to be accepted and beyond reproach, like Bathsheba Everdene she must step resolutely up to the plate and face her potential critics.

Waking that morning Amanda had not felt in doubt, but neither had she decided on her course. The idea of her ensconcing herself here for her remaining days hung in the air, a tantalising daydream. She could not help but feel excited, but waited for that very feeling to settle. In the meantime her plan to return to her own house was shelved. Mattie could come here instead.

Re-entering the house she again wandered through the quiet deserted rooms, but this time with a different eye. She inspected each room as if viewing a house she might wish to buy, downstairs first then up. It was a large house. Sophie had distracted her, but now she was stunned, taking in all she saw but not processing, engaged at an elemental level, alert but in a dream-like state.

At last Amanda found herself in the bedroom she had first slept in, where Sebastian had brought her coffee and perched shyly on the edge of the bed, held her hand. The memory filled her with warmth and sadness. She lay down there like Goldilocks, and within a minute had fallen asleep.

She was neither surprised then nor disturbed when a small noise awakened her. Entering quietly as if reluctant to disturb her was Sebastian, a tray of coffee, a Paisley patterned china mug in green and blue edged with gold. He caught her flickering eyes and abandoned his stealth, his face creasing into the warm smile she knew so well. 'Sebastian thank you so much. I can't tell you how glad I am to be here.'

He squeezed her hand and held it in both of his. 'Me too. I . . . well I think it's right for you to be here. Amanda I . . . oh listen to me your coffee will be cold!'

He stood to leave but Amanda held onto his hand, trying to speak but no words came as the fingers dissolved in her grasp, the image fading like an unfixed photograph exposed to the light.

There was resolve in her step as Amanda made her way through the stable-yard and along to the cottage where she was expected. The late afternoon had turned grey and a breeze had sprung up, disturbing the treetops and tossing her hair. The horses were in the paddock and the place seemed eerily deserted. One of the loose box half doors wasn't fastened and banged in the wind. Wisps of straw lifted and twirled, dropped and lifted again. She veered off to bolt the door.

She carried a briefcase containing copies of Gwyneth's will. Just as there had been really no point when her course had been seriously in doubt, there had neither been a point when she had made a decision. But she knew what she was going to stay. As Sebastian had said, it was right for her to be here, and she hoped that Seamus and Concepta would, in the fullness of time at least, come to the same view.

Seamus was uncharacteristically stiff and formal.

As before they sat at the kitchen table with mugs of tea. Amanda was calm and business-like, sitting straight backed and meeting their eyes.

'I thought perhaps it would be best for you first to have a look at the will, and then we can talk. I've highlighted the parts that relate to yourselves. You will see that Gwyneth has left the whole of the property to myself.'

She gave a copy of the will to each of them, and settled back to wait. She had dropped a bomb which had exploded in complete silence, a half smile and a nod from Concepta and a sharp look from Seamus the only reaction to her announcement before they settled down to read. It was a lengthy document and would take a little time for them to take in. This time Seamus had his glasses at the ready. Only a minute or two passed when Seamus sat back and took off his glasses, head bowed, waiting for Concepta who also finished shortly after.

Amanda realised that perhaps out of innate respect for the privacy of others, not least Gwyneth herself, they could only in so short a time have read the parts that she had highlighted. She must therefore enlarge on matters relating to herself. This she did, at pains more than anything to reassure that nothing was going to change, and that it would be her intention to ensure that their own position would be secure.

Concepta was her warm maternal self. 'Well that's very nice my dear, and we're very grateful. Of course it's all come as a big shock. A big shock.'

'Yes.' Seamus echoed. 'Thanks. A big shock. Yes. Well. That'd be that then. I've just got to get on now . . .'

He made to rise but sat again as Amanda interrupted, her voice louder than usual and speaking with a calm authority. 'Wait. Wait a moment please Seamus. Look, I didn't *want* this to happen. I didn't expect it. I certainly didn't know I was going to be left anything at all, let alone the house. You must believe me. Gwyneth wanted to put an end to her life, and nothing could have changed that. She was very happy, believe me. Even at the very end. Nothing anybody could have said would have changed her mind. We had to help her. It would have been a cruelty not to. We would have condemned her to a slow unhappy death, and the rest of her life spent in deep depression.'

It was the one and only time that Amanda made any attempt to justify what had happened. Seamus sighed, a very big sigh, and his body sagged. Now he looked at her directly, pleading, overcome with grief and confusion, his eyes glistening with tears. 'But that! *That*! How could she do that? Och I know you're right . . . she had a mind of her own that one, oh yes, wrong-headed she could be and no mistake! But it's a big shock for us Amanda. A *big* shock.'

The moment had passed. Amanda reached out her hand and grasped the back of Seamus's which lay on the table like piece of burnished oakwood. It turned, opened, and his strong gnarled fingers grasped hers tight, holding on as if he feared he might be be swept away. Suddenly he looked old, and it pained her more than anything to see his distress. She searched for words but none came, and Concepta came to the rescue.

'Come on, the pair of you. What's done's done. We may as well just say it's for the best and that's it. She knew her mind, and that's that. Who's for another cup of tea?'

Seamus recovered himself and briskly arose, shrugging off his vulnerability and taking his tears with him to wipe away out of sight of the ladies.

'Not for me. Places to go. Horses to see. We can't all be sitting around like you ladies o' leisure!'

'Huh! Chance 'd be a fine thing! Leisure indeed and you wandering around all day with that wheelbarrow as if you're doing anything at all!'

Chapter 23

Mattie took things in her stride. Her clear look took everything in, her positive sunny nature not given to excesses of enthusiasm or judgement.

'Nice place!' They'd drunk tea and were strolling through the gardens, taking a circuitous route to the stables to meet the 'boys'. Amanda had met her at the station, happily re-united with hugs and kisses and not a little amusement as Amanda took in the new look. Mattie's head was completely shaved having spent some time in a Thai monastery. She'd become an anagarika, an unordained novice, and decided after the six month stint that she quite liked what she called the 'Sinead O'Connor look'. Amanda had regaled Mattie with the bones of the story as they'd driven home and over tea.

'Yes isn't it? It's all come as a bit of a shock really.'

'Yeah, I can imagine. Quite a nice shock to have though. I wouldn't mind a shock like that. You gonna keep it?' Mattie linked in, Amanda comfortable with the close contact, their hips touching as they walked. How lovely it was to be with the direct no-nonsense Mattie, the very traits which had on first encounter had so non-plussed her.

'Yes.' She said this without thinking. 'Oh. Did I just say that?'

'Yes you did.'

'Hmm. I don't actually know when I decided.'

'Maybe you didn't!' It was pure Mattie.

'Yes. Come on. Come and meet the boys. Seamus might be there. You'll like Seamus.'

Hector and Achilles were both poking their heads over the stable doors and greeted them as they approached.

'Wow! They're beauties!' Mattie said, caressing Achilles velvet nose. Seamus arrived right on cue pushing a wheelbarrow to which it amused Amanda to think his hands were welded by some mysterious spell, only able to release them when there was somebody else about. She surmised that it was for this reason he always appeared, grateful for the opportunity to have a chat so that he could flex his fingers freed for a little while.

'Well now would you look at this, a lovely head of hair and a lovely head be Jaysus!'

'Seamus, this is my friend Mattie. She's Australian.'

Seamus pulled a rag from his pocket and wiped his hands before shaking hands with a smiling Mattie. He had, to Amanda's great relief, recovered some of his old self.

'Ah they have some fine horses over there to be sure. I had a ride once in the Sydney Cup. Never a chance but I wasn't last! Do you ride Mattie? Sure I could have these fellahs sorted out in no time. Ye'd have to know what your're about mind, they take a bit of seeing to. Amanda here's got the measure of them but that black divil there has a mind of his own so he has.'

'Oh yeah.' Mattie replied. 'Was brought up on a ranch. Nothing quite so fine as these guys but I know my way around OK.'

Seamus was paying close attention and the reply seemed to satisfy him. It was decided. They went off to change while Seamus prepared their mounts.

Mattie sashayed into the kitchen parading her 'English lady' riding outfit.

'Whaddya think?'

She got Amanda to take a photo

'Come and look at this.' Amanda said. She led her into the living room and handed her the photo.

'Oh yeah. Nice pic. Must've been a while ago though. Thought you only met them this year?'

'It's not me Mattie. It's Gwyneth.'

Mattie didn't react. She looked at the photo again, longer this time, and then again at Amanda.

'*Shit*!'

Mattie was perceptive. She knew Amanda had changed. Like a snake she'd sloughed her old skin, left behind in the leaf litter of her life. The transformation was both subtle and profound. It was good for her that Mattie appeared when she did. They talked and meditated, rode together and went for long walks. Mattie 'got it', and that made everything so much easier. She still hadn't decided what she was going to say to Trish and Marcia. How could she tell them them that she had assisted her dead lover's widow to commit suicide and then inherited her house and a small fortune?

So a few days with Mattie provided much needed calm, time to let things fix like a photograph in a developing tray, the image emerging darkly from the blank page, detail strengthening until at last it looked real.

There were no more 'visitations' as Mattie had labelled the waking dream about Sebastian. Amanda was in the habit of sitting in Gwyneth's annexe, and she and Mattie meditated together there. Mattie commented on the 'vibe' which Amanda had herself since returning perceived, happy that Mattie felt it too.

She spoke to Mattie about the strange affinity she felt with Gwyneth, and how everything in her life seemed to have been leading to this. Mattie had sung the words of a song by Joni Mitchell:

'And you can complete me, and I complete you.'

Amanda knew it and laughed, agreeing that this was exactly how it felt.

Mattie was heading to India. She would be taking a circuitous route across Europe to start with, and then planning to fly off from Greece or Turkey in the autumn. Amanda gave her some money, insisting that she had more than she knew what to do with, and Mattie had beamed appreciatively, not for her coy refusals. It would make a big difference to her on what she described as her 'quest'.

On the morning Mattie was leaving Amanda drove her to the station. They hugged on the platform as the train drew in.

'One day, I'll be where you are Amanda. I hope. But anyway I'm going to enjoy the trip, whether I get there or not.'

The train pulled out. The handful of disembarked passengers had dispersed and the platform was deserted. Amanda watched the rear of the train shrink into the distance till it was gone. She fingered the little token Mattie had given her, a piece of polished jade on a silver chain. Would they ever meet again?

Amanda had procrastinated before taking the plunge and returning home for a few days. There was a lot to do to prepare for putting it on the market. She'd spent a few days there and had Trish and Marcia round for dinner. The reaction from Trish had if predictable, been less extreme than expected.

Richard had skulked home suitably remorseful for his unfaithfulness, and fulsome in his declarations of love and devotion, such that Trish was experiencing something of a revival. She had taken the opportunity to tell Richard that their very large garden needed a gardener. They'd shared the responsibility before, and it had been suitably neglected, making it easy for Trish without suspicion to import her young lover for a couple of days a week. She looked stunning, and the amorous attentions of two men apparently agreed with her.

So for Trish, the strange behaviour of her increasingly strange friend did not have the impact it might otherwise have had. The opportunities in terms of increasing Jesus's days of employment once Amanda's house sold were clearly not lost.

Marcia was altogether more thoughtful. Amanda's situation and journey interested her. She was quieter than before, a curious far away look, a hesitance, the usual cutting wit less evident.

It was agreed that they would visit Amanda in her new home for a weekend soon at a time to be arranged. The estate agents sign went up outside the house on the day before Amanda left. She went out to look at it when the van had gone. Fore Sale. A two word epitaph for the ending of a large part of her life.

The downhill tread of late summer into autumn was well underway. Change was heralded in the sharpness of the morning air, the golden slanting light from a lazy sun no longer riding high. A late warm spell coaxed the crispening leaves into a wonderful array of colours, a last hurrah before surrendering to an early frost and several days of wind and rain that stripped the trees of most that yet clung on.

Amanda was writing every day. The calendar showed 15th October, and she sat at her laptop gazing out the bedroom window at the lawns pasted with yellow horse chestnut leaves, and the bright red almost luminous leaves from two magnificent acers. The wind had not abated and battered rain against the window panes, great rat-a-tat sloshes as tens of thousands droplets were hurled against the glass. Skeletal treetops twisted and swayed, and more than once the electricity momentarily failed flickering the house lights, on now even in the day such was the gloom.

It had been a quiet reflective time. What had gone before had taken it's toll more than Amanda had realised. Sophie took on a great deal of work tying up loose ends, more than Amanda was ever aware of, and this left her free to write and adjust to her new situation, to recuperate. This wasn't difficult. She felt at home and that it was where she *should* be. And after all, she had been living there for some time before. But it was very different. No Gwyneth, no carers, and she the owner. She was used to being alone, and now more than at any time in her life, found solitude comfortable. She was at one with herself and her surroundings, and each day brought her joy.

She had taken on a housekeeper and a cleaner. Being freed up from having to think about shopping and cooking was a boon. The housekeeper was Mrs Fellows, a spritely local lady in her early sixties who'd been recommended by Concepta. Amanda grew to like her, and enjoyed chatting to her each day when they met to decide what was to be done.

Very soon Mrs Fellows was managing the house herself, and other than some discussion of menus the daily chats were mostly about the price of coal and the state of the nation.

Sophie had written to everyone who needed to know of Gwyneth's death and informed them that there would be no funeral. Amanda hadn't asked what she said, and forwarded to her unopened the handful of sympathy cards that had found their way to the house. Amanda wrote to the carers to let them know that Gwyneth had died peacefully whilst abroad.

Marcia and Trish visited separately in the end. Trish's visit had seen something of a return to the old girlie camaraderie, and Amanda was happy to indulge. They'd eaten well, drank lots, and reminisced excessively. Trish candidly confided about her life and loves, the despair which she had endured after Richard's departure, and her Phoenix-like resurrection from the ashes.

Marcia had wanted to visit separately and resisted being swept along by Trish's hopes for them to come together, contriving various excuses and encouraging Trish to go ahead herself. Amanda sensed that Marcia's visit might not be so easy.

Her surmise turned out to be correct. The horses rescued them from their difficulties for a large chunk of Marcia's visit. She seemed on edge, distracted, and Amanda struggled at a loss as to how to respond. They rode out together several times. Marcia's horsemanship was supreme. She spurred on a never reluctant Achilles to feats which Amanda would not contemplate on her mount, more than once genuinely concerned for her friend's safety, whilst Marcia herself seemed dangerously oblivious.

Marcia evidently wanted to know things, but she was sensitive to Amanda's reticence. Did she want to say things too? If so she failed to find a way and gave little away about her own situation. It was a difficult dance they stepped together, and Amanda sensed Marcia's deep unhappiness, as if she'd lost her bearings and was struggling to find a way.

When it was time for Marcia to go Amanda was relieved. How long had they known but not known each other? Their friendship had been tested by time but was now painful to them both. There was an awkward embrace by Marcia's Porsche. It was a warm day and she'd lowered the hood. Amanda waved a last wave as it disappeared into the trees along the drive. A hand shot up to reciprocate, and she was gone.

Amanda knew that she would not see Marcia again, and was not surprised when she heard from Trish a few weeks later that Marcia had left her husband and home, whereabouts unknown.

It would soon be Christmas. The comings and goings were over, and the household routine settled.

Mrs Fellows was firmly ensconced as if she had always been there. Amanda sat at her desk, surveying the now so familiar scene. Life went on. There was already an offer on her house that she had accepted. Gilles was planning his imminent return to Paris where he'd been offered a professorship `at the Sorbonne. Sophie was working hard in the Scottish capital dispensing justice. No word about Marcia. Trish continued to enjoy her men and her changed fortunes. She planned to make another visit but in the event was never quite able to find the time. Mattie was in Greece and soon to be jetting off to Bombay. Amanda aroused herself and opened a new document, before her a blank page.

Chapter 24

The weeks flew by and arranged themselves into months. Amanda quietly slipped away, from her old life. She visited Sophie in Edinburgh and their friendship strengthened with the passage of time.

The house was her retreat and she was content with her life of seclusion. She often spoke with Gilles, though had not yet made it over to Paris to visit him. He did not press her. Their closeness remained and Amanda was his confidante. She knew that he was enjoying his new found freedom and did not lack for female company. He was engrossed in his writing, a new philosophical work, which was a well-guarded secret even from Amanda.

There were occasional updates from Mattie on her travels, fallen in love with India and telling Amanda that 'it' was definitely there, just a matter of finding out what 'it' was.

Like Gilles Amanda too was secretive about her new work, even with Melanie who had become resigned to the fact that this one was not going to be turned out within an agreed timescale or with the ongoing oversight Amanda usually afforded her.

Her days were quiet and she was content to write, to walk, to ride, to meditate, her life itself a meditation. She'd sit for long periods in the annexe or in the stables, on a bench in the garden, slowed to a softly pulsing rhythm that was neither sound nor detectable by any sense, just *there* within her as she let go.

It was a year to the day since Gwyneth's death. Sophie had travelled down the day before to be with Amanda. They'd strolled down to the church and placed some flowers on Sebastian's grave where Amanda had sprinkled Gwyneth's ashes. They were walking homeward. It was a grey day but warm, on either side stubble fields from which the hay and barley had been cropped and spirited away.

'Penny for them?'

Sophie had linked in and Amanda glanced at her and away again with a little laugh.

'Oh I was just thinking how right it all was, how right it all *is*!'

Sophie sighed a wistful sigh. 'Hmm. Yes. It took me a while. But you're right of course. After Sebastian died what was left for her? You know Amanda she was *such* a vibrant woman before she became ill. Really. What was left? It would be hell for anybody, but for *her* . . .'

Sophie had stopped, turning to Amanda who drew her in for a hug and for a second held her close.

'You've done so well Sophie, travelled far. I know how hard it's been for you; more than for me, or for Gilles.'

As they fell into step again Sophie thought about

this. She'd struggled, and was quietly appreciative of Amanda's understanding and praise. Nobody else would ever be allowed to speak to her in the way Amanda did. She'd penetrated Sophie's defences, their mutual respect softened over time to a sisterly love.

'Huh!' she said at last. '*I* just sat at home. It was you . . . Gilles. *You.*'

'It was easy for me,' was all Amanda offered, and they walked on in silence, a solitary lark invisible up in the cloud, but joyfully sending down to them his song.

They returned to Edinburgh together. Sophie had some free days and Amanda was easily persuaded. She'd fallen in love with the city, the old town, the Royal Mile, the castle perilously perched on it's rock presiding over all. Arthur's Seat, a small mountain in the middle of the capital muscling up against Holyrood and the parliament buildings, the old and the new. Like Bruges or Amsterdam Edinburgh had an easy charm and intimacy, nowhere in the city too far to walk.

They lunched outside at the Grassmarket and strolled down the Royal Mile, sat on a bench in Princes Street Gardens eating ice cream in the sunshine. Cocktails at the Voodoo Rooms and on to Harvey Nicholls. It had been a long time since Amanda had shopped for clothes.

Returning home on the train Amanda was looking

forward to her solitude once more. The city break had been fun. She'd enjoyed the thrum of town, the Botanic Gardens and the art galleries. A classical concert provided a rare feast of Vivaldi and Amanda's cherished Bach. But she looked forward to home. Her eye caught the Harvey Nicholls bags on the luggage rack and she couldn't suppress a smile. They'd each bought posh sexy dresses and outrageously high heels, egging each other on, fueled by lunchtime wine and cocktails. The following day she'd nearly taken hers back, but let it be. She'd try them on again when she got home. . .

The autumn months had slipped by uneventfully, Christmas already come and gone. It was Boxing Day and Amanda rose early intending to ride out on Hector.

She'd resisted Sophie's invitations to spend Christmas with her. Sophie was also organising a Hogmanay soiree for which Amanda had likewise proffered her apologies, laughing at her suggestion that they both could wear their risque Harvey Nicholls purchases! She didn't feel like socialising, happy with her own company. There was something peaceful about the deep stillness of the 'bleak midwinter,' and Amanda wasn't the least bit tempted to fall in with festive tradition and make merry.

There was no evidence in the house that it was Christmas, other than a handful of cards on the table in the hall. Amanda's routine, such as it was, was for the most part unaltered. Mrs Fellows was notable by her absence. Amanda's one concession to the festive season had been to join Seamus and Concepta for Christmas dinner, bending to Concepta's steel will, and savouring her wonderful cooking and a glass or two of the fine vintage Burgundy bought in her honour.

There had been a sharp fall in the temperature overnight, and Jack Frost had painted the world white. The breath of horse and rider puffed out in great white clouds. The ground was frozen hard so Amanda was forced to rein in her impatient mount to proceed at a sedate pace. Not a soul was abroad. A large vixen broke close to the horse causing him to start and rear, the fox unfazed trotting unhurriedly across the field to disappear through a gap in the hedge.

She walked Hector along the bank of a stream which had several small waterfalls where the ice had thickened reeds, hanging now under the weight liked bunches of fat glass sausages. Icicle daggers long and short clustered like tubular bells upon which nymphs surely played tinkling tunes eerily in the dead of night. The large stones in the stream were glassed over, and opaque white ice had crept from the bank to cover all but a narrow dark channel snaking in between.

Walking Hector along the frosted field, she felt his restrained power; he skittered and pranced as she held him back. *He* gave no thought to the crystalline beauty of this frozen scene, wanting only to run in exuberant celebration of his own existence, to feel the blood coursing through his veins and the earth fly beneath his hooves.

"Beauty is truth; truth is beauty." Amanda did not quite agree with Keats in this, and yet, so often found herself moved by sights or sounds, or elevated as now by an ambience . . . the stream, the frost, the movement of the horse, the stillness, the cleansing coldness of the air. She was open to it, her senses alive like never before.

She was not lonely. She enjoyed her solitude. Alone. It appeared to Amanda to be an outcome in her life, a culmination of circumstances, a necessary state in which her inner being had found release.

Peace. It was a precious gift. She was at ease as she guided the horse, calmer now, along the frozen bank.

Her thoughts strayed to Sebastian's 'visitation,' the joy with which Gwyneth had taken her leave from the world. She thought of Khala. The unhappiness of her life before, had created a tension which itself held things in place giving it the semblance of order and calm, but never peace. Like the surface tension of water, invisibly creating the illusion of solidity. Only when a pebble is thrown do the resulting ripples reveal the water's true nature.

She carefully walked Hector over the frozen ground. The gradient by the stream was becoming steeper and littered with stones where it had cut a small valley into the rock. With a tug on the rein horse and rider swung out along the contour of the gently sloping hillside. The way ahead was open pasture glistening with a trillion tiny diamonds as the sun broke through. Hector snorted and skittered seeing before him the wide featureless space and remembering his purpose.

Amanda relaxed her grip on the rein and the horse immediately quickened his pace to a trot. She let him have his head but didn't speak or kick him on, and after a short experimental trot he snorted and reared, pirouetting on his own axis before moving off at a slow canter.

He moved easily despite the steepening gradient as he angled up the slope. A drystone wall came into view, still some way off, and Amanda measured the distance. They were not moving fast enough to jump it and the angle was all wrong, and she tensed prepared to rein Hector in if he upped his pace. But instead he tacked off to the left following the line of the wall directly up the hill. He kept up the same work rate but it was harder going against the gradient.

At last they approached a transverse wall which blocked their way and Hector slowed to a trot and finally a walk into the corner. He looked over it, tossing his head, steaming now from his exertions and blowing out white clouds of breath, apparently waiting for Amanda to tell him what to do. She leant forward and patted his neck, watching his ears twitch as she praised him. She pulled on the left-hand rein and brought him around, but let it remain loose, smiling as he elected for a sedate walk back down the hill. The sun had gone and clouds were thickening. Snow was in the air.

The iron grey clouds had solidified, and as dusk began to leech away the weakened light, snow began to fall. A few tentative flakes at first, reconnaissance, a small expeditionary force floating earthward like ash from a bonfire. But as the darkness quickened the invasion began, a countless host silently parachuting to earth under cover of night to transform the land.

Amanda sat in the growing gloom of the unlit living room, curtains undrawn, the flickering firelight casting moving shadows around the walls. She'd showered and lounged in her robe in one of the cavernous armchairs, feet warmed by the fire. She breathed, noticing her breath, her body, conscious all the while of the silent cascade of unsure feathered flakes barely visible now beyond the window panes. They floated softly ever downward, blending in a silent prayer into the gathering night.

The phone rang and she answered, simultaneously reaching to switch on a lamp. It was Mattie.

'Hi Amanda. How's it going?'

Amanda hadn't spoken to Mattie in over a year. They e-mailed regularly, but hearing the familiar voice now threw her. She knew from a recent e-mail that Mattie was still in India and temporarily settled in an Ashram in the province of Kerala. It would be late in the evening there.

'Oh . . . well. As ever! How are *you*? *Where* are you? What's the matter?'

The rapid succession of questions betrayed Amanda's sudden presentiment that this was not a social call.

'Some news Amanda. Thought I should let you know straight off. Khala's dead. Took the longtail out and made his final dive. He'd stopped taking people to stay this year. Just him. No worries Amanda. He knew what he was about.' There was a long pause. 'You still there?'

'Yes. Yes. Thanks for letting me know Mattie. It's a shock. But you're right. No worries. Listen, should I call you back?'

By the time she 'd phone back Amanda had collected herself. She found herself speaking louder; the connection was poor and it was as if Mattie was speaking to her through a tunnel.

'Did he leave a note or anything? How did you find out?'

'Well it could have been weeks ago it happened, nobody's quite sure. A guy I know was in Koh Tao and took a bike ride over to see what the score was for some diving. Nang was there sorting stuff. Yeah he'd left her a note. She hadn't been across there for a while since there were no guests and all. Just said it was time; said he was returning to the deep. Hey . . . you knew didn't you? So. No worries. I'll miss him.'

'Yes. Me too. I won't say I expected it. But you're right, I knew well enough. Thanks for letting me know. I really appreciate that Mattie. He was special.'

'Yeah. A one-off. I took a bit of a hit when I heard.'

'Yes. It's a shock. He was special. I owe him.'

'Me too.'

They paused a short reflection, sharing a moment of remembrance.

'How are things with you?' Amanda continued at last.

'Oh good! I think I'm getting somewhere! Hey listen Amanda it's late here and I got a boy with a boat waiting to take me back a'ways. There's no signal anywhere near where I am. Just wanted to tell you right away. You especially . . . you know. . .'

'Yes, I do. Thanks. Keep in touch. Be well.'

Quick goodbyes and once more the familiar quiet of the house. She turned off the light again and let the darkness wrap her in it's folds. The grandfather clock in the hall ticked. In the space of minutes night had fallen, the falling snow no longer visible through the open drapes.

She sat for a long while, listening, alert. Had he been unwell, anticipating his approaching end, or had he just decided it was time for reasons she would never know; or no reason at all impelled by

313

his own sense of destiny? The fire had died down and her eyes grown accustomed to the dark.

At last she made her way to the front door and entered the porch. Beyond the stone arch heavy flakes of snow were plummeting downward, no breath of wind to disturb them from their vertical descent. Amanda sensed the movement more than saw. She listened. It was a silence that could be heard, millions of mute collisions as each flake fell to earth.

She loosened the belt of her robe and let it slip to the ground, stepped out of her slippers and walked naked onto the drive. Already there was a thick carpet of snow and it filled the air tentatively touching her naked body in countless random expirations, melted in a moment by her heat. Slowly she made her way as in a dream onto the lawn in silent measured tread, there to be still, a statue one with the night.

Attuned to the soft clamour of snowflakes upon snow that raged in the deafening silence all about, she extended her arms and tilted her face skyward, turned in a full circle, once, twice, thrice. Her tracks unseen were already becoming blurred and indistinct. Now she was still, head thrown back, eyes closed, arms extended, a ghostly crucifixion, pale transfiguration shrouded in darkness. Thousands of feathery flakes icily caressed her cooling nakedness, melting less quickly now than before. Her hair was soon white like a bridal veil, her skin tingling, snow accumulating on her out-stretched arms, her face, her cold taut breasts, her pubic hair. From out of the booming silence another sound . . . the swish of waves on a distant beach. She saw him, felt his touch, heard his words. 'Don't forget.' Her body shuddered and she cried out.

Chapter 25

The daffodils were already in decline, and warmer days were tempting buds to loosen and unfurl. A few new fledged beech leaves delicate and fresh shone translucent in the morning sun. Regeneration, the rising sap of growth, the urgency of new life. Songbirds proclaimed their territory in strident song, their fluttering fights tumbling back and forth across the borders of adjacent territories until unseen lines could be agreed. Hawthorn was sprouting lime green tufts, and cows at last turned out of musty byres to tender new grass charged about fields bucking and bellowing uninhibited in their joy.

Hector and Achilles spent the days out to grass. Amanda dutifully rode them both, though continued to favour Hector. Seamus picked up the slack with Achilles, sometimes accompanying Amanda on her rides. She wrote every day, and the end was in sight.

Mattie had e-mailed to say that she had ordained as a Buddhist nun and travelled to Thailand to join a monastery there in order to complete her training. The occasional phone calls and e-mails with Trish had dwindled, news and 'catch-up,' fondness still but acceptance that their paths had diverged. Marcia was living in the south of France and this was all that Trish knew. The news had been conveyed by

Marcia's husband, himself largely in the dark and having conceded to agree to be divorced when it had become clear that Marcia was not going to return.

The news about Khala's death had affected Amanda. She knew that like Gwyneth he would not have met his end with anything other than calm and even joy. "Returning to the deep." She had pondered this simple message. There was no need to interpret it, to figure out what exactly he meant. She knew. The strange affinity she felt with this young Thai man had stayed with her, a piece of the jig saw puzzle of her new life fallen into place amongst the others as if placed there by an unseen hand. His death did not cause Amanda to feel sadness, but she did feel more alone, another important thread cut. What was it? It had caused a shift. She wavered, unsure, curious. There was something and she didn't know what it was. She remained alert. Waited. Que sera sera.

Mattie's words had stayed with her: 'One day, I'll be where you are Amanda. I hope.' They had implied that Amanda's journey was completed, that she had 'arrived.' But it was not so. She knew this, sensing her story had yet some way to run. Patiently she waited. She often thought of Gwyneth, always with the warm glow of love. Their stars had aligned, their destinies intertwined, and in the joining there was redemption. She felt her presence in the house, and had kept the annexe exactly as it had been before. She regularly put scented lilies in there, the perfume wafting over her whenever she went there to meditate or just sit.

The days counted themselves off, adding themselves up into groups of seven as the weeks slid by. Soon it would be two years since Switzerland.

Gilles was planning to return to visit Sophie and friends in Edinburgh, and they were both going to spend a few days with Amanda, to visit Sebastian's grave and to mark the anniversary of Gwyneth's passing.

She looked forward to seeing Gilles. Whenever she thought about their time together in Switzerland her spirits lifted, so happy to have shared it with him, her temporary lover, her comrade in arms! If he had persisted in his invitations to visit him in Paris she would have liked to go. Amanda loved Paris and knew that she would have enjoyed having Gilles show her his home city. But after his initial invitation he'd been reticent on the matter which went largely unmentioned in their regular conversations. So she let things be.

They would always be close, a special bond between them that Amanda felt with no other, fused inseparably in Gwyneth's leaving-taking, a hand in each of theirs. Amanda was aware of Gilles' women. She'd wondered if having her there might be awkward for him, but dismissed this as foolish, and concluded that he like her was adjusting to what had become for both of them, life after Gwyneth. She knew that in their different ways both she and Gilles had crossed a Rubicon when Gwyneth died.

So the prospect of Gilles and Sophie's visit was a happy one. Amanda planned with Mrs Fellows sumptuous menus including the best wine and champagne, and of course for Gilles, the ample provision of a choice of his favourite malt whiskies.

She looked forward to the aroma of his Gitanes, and even decided that for the brief period of his visit she would allow herself to join him, confident in her ability to stop again, having already done so with remarkable ease. What could be better than an after dinner cigarette and Cognac with her two dear friends? Whatever exalted state of being attributed to her by Mattie, Amanda was *not* a nun, renunciant of worldly pleasures, and she looked forward with excitement to the coming visit.

Gilles' visit to Scotland was also timed to coincide with Sophie's sixtieth birthday, and Amanda had agreed to return north with her friends to be at the planned party, and the thought of a short stay in the city also lifted her spirits.

It was yet a couple of days until Gilles and Sophie would arrive, but preparations were well under way. Amanda worked with Mrs Fellows in the kitchen and waltzed around the house with Vivaldi playing loudly, arranging a large delivery of flowers for all the downstairs rooms and the bedrooms of her two guests. It was a minor extravagance which pleased her, frugal as she had been with her considerable wealth, and Mrs Fellows laughed at her evident excitement. 'Glory be Amanda . . .' (she had always on Amanda's insistence used her Christian name, a little uncomfortably at first, though Amanda always referred to her as 'Mrs Fellows'), ' . . .it's so nice to see you so happy!'

'I'm always happy.' Amanda replied, truthfully.

'Well yes, I know dear, but it's nice for you to have your friends here. It'll bring a bit of life to the old place!'

Amanda agreed. It *was* going to be fun, and although she was indeed happy, she would have been the first to admit that she didn't have much *fun* and looked forward to it. Seamus and Concepta were away for their annual seaside holiday, planned of course to coincide with two race meetings nearby, but would be returning in time to see Sophie and Gilles, and to have dinner all together.

Amanda was restless, and strolled up and down the station platform. It was early afternoon and quiet, only three people waiting. An elderly couple sat quietly, a young man paced, glancing at his mobile, peering up the line in the direction from which the train would come. Amanda decided that the couple were waiting to meet someone, perhaps a son or daughter returning to visit. The boy would be boarding the train to go to London, people to see, places to go.

At last the train appeared in the distance and slowly materialised from a dot into a large silver and red cylinder as it slid into the station. People within peered out. Doors opened and a young woman fell into the arms of the boy, whilst the elderly couple boarded. There was no sign of Sophie and Gilles, and Amanda looked to the left and right as if watching a tennis match, momentarily perplexed. A rotund uniformed woman had appeared from the station masters office, whistle in hand half raised, surveying the length of the train. At the last second another door opened and Sophie stepped out, as if she had all the time in the world, waving to Amanda as Gilles appeared behind her. The loud prolonged blast on the whistle as the door clunked shut communicated the official's irritation, marching off as the train eased away.

Sophie was pulling along a small case and Gilles overtook her as they neared Amanda, dropping his own small bag and beaming a huge smile as she threw her arms around him.

'Did you miss me!?'

'Ah!' He replied, as they embraced and kissed, 'I have thought of you every day. My life has been empty. J'ai ete desolee!' He was still beaming brightly and holding her hands, and despite herself a pale pink flush brushed Amanda's cheeks.

'What . . . *every* day?' She teased.

Gilles eyes twinkled with mischief. 'Bien sur . . . sometimes *twice*!'

'If love's young dream has finished perhaps I could have a turn? Hello Amanda!' Sophie stepped forward and they hugged as Gilles picked up his bag.

Walking to the car Gilles continued. 'You know Amanda, we were nearly going to London! Sophie was asleep (and snoring) and I am only French!'

'Nonsense! Gilles you do exaggerate. I must have dozed off for a minute and *Gilles* was engrossed in his book rather than looking at the station sign! Anyway, we're here now. And I'm famished!'

The house was silent. Mrs Fellows was to return to cook dinner, and Gilles and Sophie had both gone up for a nap after their late lunch, tired from the journey. All the preparations were already made, and with the disappearance of her guests Amanda was suddenly at a loose end. She wandered out into the garden and down to stables. The horses were turned out in the paddock and enjoying the sunshine. As usual they maintained a distance from one another, and as Amanda approached the gate Hector trotted over to her whilst Achilles trotted away. She stroked his velvet nose and he blew appreciatively.

The stable yard was deserted. No horses and no Seamus bustling busily about. Entering Hector's stall she sat down on a straw bale and found herself remembering the first time she had been there with Sebastian, wet after their ride, the flirtation . . . the kiss. There was a timelessness about the stables which had been up-kept faithful to the original design. Any wood that had been replaced was in keeping, the one round window and the hayloft just the same as they would have been in the times of 'Tess' or the 'Woodlanders.'

She drifted off, soon deep in thought. So much had happened in the few years since love had unexpectedly flowered once again in Amanda's barren life. She thought about this. The voyage of discovery beginning here with Sebastian and Gwyneth had spread Amanda's soul beneath the sun, banishing her darkness, opening her to such riches.

Had she ever really loved before that? Perhaps not. She could not be sure and it didn't matter anyway. We love how we can, and her love for John had been what she could do then. But now she'd changed. She could not be angry with Sebastian as she had been with John, or indeed with Gwyneth who had ended her own life.

And then there was Sophie and dear Gilles. Gilles who had been released from the oppression of his love by the death of his one time lover; who had flown into Amanda's arms and shaken her awake with the passion of his loving and his magnificent cock. She shivered deep inside at the thought. It had been a long time since she'd experienced such a feeling. Beneath her solitary ways she was still a woman.

'Penny for them?'

Sophie's tall figure was silhouetted in the doorway, arms folded, leaning against the door jamb.

'Sneak! How long have you been there?'

'Oh not long.' Amanda made room as Sophie came

across and sat down next to her.

'I knew I wasn't going to sleep. Thought I might find you here.'

'I was thinking about Sebastian.' Amanda offered sort of truthfully, at least truthfully enough for it not to be an outright lie lie. 'We had our first kiss here all wet and steamy after being caught out riding in the rain!'

'Ha!'

'It was odd really. I didn't feel guilty at all; you know, with Gwyneth and everything.'

'Of course not. It was probably Gwyneth's idea!'

They looked at each other. Amanda had never talked about this with anyone before.

'Yes. It was. But I didn't *know* then.'

'Oh I think you probably did.'

They had turned to each other, close. Sophie's pale grey eyes held Amanda's, tender with love. The brief interchange that had just taken place had crystalised for both what they each had known in their hearts. That they were survivors of a strange story, had played their parts, and now were invisibly bound to each other. Love flowed from the tragedy of death, life went on, the story not yet told and still running its course. As one they looped their arms around one another and kissed on the lips, the softest of pressure, as if it was the most natural thing in the world. Looking once more into each others eyes, Amanda could see that Sophie's swam with tears.

'Come on,' she whispered, 'I'm going to be blubbering in a minute! Let's take the boys out.'

They arose, Sophie producing a tissue to wipe away her tears, then managing a child-like lost smile, which prompted Amanda to step in and hug her tight. 'It's alright my darling. It's alright.'

The fickle English weather had moved on by the time they changed and saddled up for the ride. Clouds had blown in from the west and a breeze ruffled the treetops. Agitated rooks took to the air, hanging and flapping like bits of torn bin-liner. By the time they'd left the stable-yard the first drops of rain were beginning to plop heavily to earth, and by the time they returned they were soaked.

Like schoolchildren on a rainy blustery day Amanda and Sophie were high as they returned to the house and clattered through the back door into the kitchen, straight into the outspread arms of Gilles who'd heard their giddy approach. They giggled and submitted happily to the embrace despite Sophie's uncharacteristically innuendo-laden cajoling:

'So you like wet sweaty horse-women mon petit choux?'

Gilles was equal to it. 'Mais oui bien sur! But I am spoiled for choice. You will just have to fight for me! . . *ouch*! Quoi!?'

Sophie's riding crop had cracked down on the back of the Gilles' thigh and he danced comically away rubbing it. 'What did I say?!'

'Do you want me to rub it for you Gilles?' Amanda sweetly offered bearing down on him, only to be nudged aside by Sophie. 'No let me!' By which time Gilles was fleeing into the hall.

'Au secours! You are *mad women*. It was just a joke. And now I too smell of horse!' He dodged away and skipped off up the stairs to their derisory laughter. Sophie announced that she was going for a shower.

'Me too.' Amanda sat down to pull off her boots. 'Shall we go mad and dress for dinner?'

'Of course,' came the reply, Sophie leaning down to whisper conspiratorially, her lips close to Amanda's ear.

'I've brought *the dress*.'

'*Oh my god*! Then I suppose I'd better fish mine out!'

Amanda was showered and dressed, sitting at her desk checking her e-mails when there was a knock at her bedroom door. 'Come in.'

Sophie entered and perched on the edge of her desk. 'How's the writing going?'

'Oh, well I think. What's the matter?'

'Oh, there's a problem. I've had a call about work. They need a senior sheriff for a case coming up tomorrow. It's all set to go and my colleague has rather inconveniently had a heart attack. He's in Edinburgh Royal. I won't bore you with the details but suffice it to say there's only me. I'm going to have to fly home.'

Amanda sat back in her chair: 'Oh. That's . . .'

'I'm so sorry darling. I'm totally pissed off but there's nothing to be done. The only other two possible sheriffs are out of the country on their hols. And all your preparations . . .'

'Don't be silly. Can't be helped. I was just thinking. We could pop down to the grave this afternoon and I'll take you straight on to the train? Anyway we'll be up for your birthday so we can have more time then.' She was disappointed having prepared and looked forward to the visit, and Sophie sensed it.

'No, you two do it tomorrow. There's a lot I'll have to read tonight. It's complicated and even my fabled ability to wing it won't save me if I don't acquaint myself with the basics! And it'll be nice for you and Gilles to have a bit of time. But go on, give it an outing. *That* should cheer him up!' She'd spotted Amanda's Harvey Nicks dress already retrieved from the wardrobe and draped over the bed.

Amanda looked to see whether there was a 'look' but there was none. 'Hmm. I'll think about it! Let's have a look at flights'

Her pc screen already glowed with the bright orange and white livery of Easyjet. Pierced by a pin prick of sadness her heart skipped back to another time when she'd booked someone else on an Edinburgh flight.

327

Chapter 26

Sophie's unexpected departure changed the party mood. Amanda and Gilles had not been alone together since Geneva. What had been planned as a convivial dinner for friends reunited was now dinner for two. There had been a subtle shift in the ambience. The earlier high spirited jokiness had been supplanted by a quieter mood. At first there had even been a hint of awkwardness, despite their closeness, or perhaps because of it. It didn't last for long.

Amanda had been making tea after her return from the station, Gilles leaning in the doorway, watching as she found herself self-consciously wittering in a most uncharacteristic way.

'There! Good. Now. I'll just leave it a minute to brew. And er...oh! Would you like a biscuit? I think we have some Hob Nobs . . . '

Gilles crooked his finger: 'Vien.'

'What?'

She obeyed and he waited till she was up close, and even then continued to peruse her with his annoyingly querulous look.

'Well? *What*?'

'Are you nervous Amanda? There is no need cheri. You know, I am really quite harmless.'

Amanda laughed.

'Oh god I'm sorry darling! (*And I'm not!*) It's just thrown me a bit . . . Sophie having to dash off and all. Yes. We're going to have a *lovely* time!'

Even when she'd been outwardly equivocal at Sophie's dress suggestion, Amanda knew for sure she would wear it. Why not? Any lingering apprehension had evaporated with Gilles' mildly (but unmistakably) provocative remark. She wanted to look good . . . and more. It was unexpected and she was enjoying feeling excited. Showered before dinner she shed her robe and naked perused her body in the full length mirror, turning this way then that, already tingling as she began selecting lingerie to adorn it.

Geneva hovered on the peripheries of her consciousness. It had only taken Gilles' intonation of 'cheri' for her to tingle with the recollection of what they had shared. It had caused her to blush on the station platform, but alone together now it excited her. She had not overcome sexual longings, nor did she want to. Although much had changed for her since Geneva, this had not. A woman committed to going where life led her she did not shy away from her own nature. Desire stirred within her, and she embraced it.

She knew that she would sleep with Gilles if he wanted to. Certainly her attire would do nothing to dissuade him if he had any such aspirations. She would ensure her own would be well understood.

She trusted her own unquestionable charms, and well remembered the heat of their passion together, her and Gilles, not so very long ago.

But even so there was also a flutter of unease. They had both said things that at the time had appeared to preclude further intimacy, perhaps (or so they had thought) for good reason. But no sooner had this thought occurred than she swept it aside. What would be would be, and she relaxed, surrendered to the flow.

She brushed her hair in long strong strokes, bunched it in a fist and held it above her head, critically assessing the effect in the mirror. Yes, she would wear it up, easy to release it at the right moment . . . always effective! Two discreet dabs of Guerlain on her neck, and two more in her décolletage, et voila!

She was apprehensive as she came downstairs. She felt a tad foolish wearing heels in the house and dressed to kill, but her overwhelming excitement more than trumped such considerations. There was music coming from the living room. Gilles must be there. She would try out on Mrs Fellows first, but hesitated in front of the mirror in the hall.

The daring dress was a strapless tube of navy satin, which only just contained her breasts, pushing them upward with startling effect. If it teetered on the side of indecency, it was sent plummeting over the edge by the steeply plunging V in an already daringly low neckline, which precluded the wearing

no regrets. She assumed that it had been the same for Gilles. Yet now they were alone together and everything had changed.

For a long time Amanda had trusted her instincts, surrendered to her intuition. She did so now, now that slumbering desire had blinked awake within her. She'd dressed with only one thing in mind. She was showing herself to Gilles in such a way that he could not mistake the signs. From the moment Sophie had announced her departure everything had changed for Amanda, surprised herself at her own willfulness. Gilles would soon return to Paris, Amanda to her solitary rural life. Their agreement would not be jeopardised. But now she wanted to feel his weight pressing her into the bed, his mouth on hers, his cock filling her cunt.

Mrs Fellows had departed when dinner was served. The many candles on an ostentatious candelabra were burning low, and a second bottle of wine already uncorked. They had spoken little as they ate, but the silences were comfortable. The fleeting touch of Amanda's fingers brushing against Gilles' cheek was held between them. He body was open to him. She felt his eyes on her now. They sipped their wine; the food was finished. She waited.

They occupied one end of the enormous dining table, and even placed as they were on either side were some way apart. The seconds ticked by counted by the slow tick of the grandfather clock.

Once again Gilles was peering into his glass, swirling the wine around so that it caught the flickering flames in its deep claret gleam.

What now? Still she waited, calm, assured. At last he seemed to rouse himself. He smiled warmly, swept Amanda with his eyes as European men do, his gaze loitering with intent. And yet, there was something else. A single ruby pendant nestled deep in her endless inviting cleavage, the ample swell of her breasts almost translucent in the candlelight, rising and falling like a gentle ocean swell with each breath. She returned his gaze.

'You are beautiful.' He said it again, but this time almost apologetically, as if it was despite himself, and for a moment Amanda's certainty wavered.

'Gilles. Oh Gilles. I hope you don't mind . . .'

'What? That you are beautiful? Why should I mind?' He smiled, a little ruefully perhaps but the familiar mischievousness not too far away.

'No. Not that. I meant I hope you don't mind how I've been . . . that I've dressed like this. I just thought . . . well anyway, you *know* what I thought; and if we. . . . if you want to, well there are no strings attached. I know what we said.'

He didn't respond, once more peering into his glass. Had she gabbled? Why was he so quiet? Suddenly she feared it was all going horribly wrong. She'd misread the situation, and for the first time in a long while feared her judgement may have let her down.

'Look, Gilles, it's alright . . .'

'Shall we go outside for a cigarette?' he cut in. He'd fished out his Gitanes and placed the packet on the table, the distinctive blue and white design visible through his fingers.

Amanda sighed, deflated and struggling to disguise it with her attempt to smile. 'We can smoke here if you like. See, there's an ashtray.'

'As long as I can look at you cheri, in the evening light, or here in the candlelight. Comme tu veut. It is *all* I want. It has been a long time. Too long.'

Relief flooded and with it a new boldness, as Amanda's desire rebounded from defeat, instantly aroused, possessed of a certainty that brooked no hesitation.

'Do you want me Gilles?'

'Yes.'

'Now?'

They arose as one and she took his hand, suddenly knowing what to do, leading him unhurried through the glass tube into the annexe. There was a large vase of lilies that filled the room with their fragrance. Twilight was approaching but the light held. Here was where they had sat with Gwyneth and begun to plan her death. No wheelchair now, no bed, but otherwise the same.

They stood by the window to where Sophie had fled on hearing what was to happen. Gilles took her in his arms and they kissed. They held each other, quiet now, his arm around her, looking out.

Amanda's head leant against his shoulder. Her hair nestled into his neck, and he breathed her familiar Guerlain mingling with the scent of lilies. A black and white cat that lived in the stables was slinking fluid across the lawn; the 'pike' of a blackbird somewhere challenging the night whilst settling down to roost.

'Can you feel it?' Amanda said.

'Yes. She is here.'

'Yes.'

The light was fading and a single star punctured the cloudless sky, the crescent moon ascendent in the east perched low on the horizon.

'Will you take me here?'

'Yes.'

Amanda craned up to find his lips, and he gently turned her to him as they tenderly kissed, their fire yet held in check but the flames licking higher with their quickening breath. So slowly Gilles was sliding down her back the endless zip that contained her nakedness, until the dress sloughed from her, her skin milk white in the pale afterglow, the final pallid light of day slowly surrendering to the gathering dusk. She brushed his lips with hers.

'I want her to be with us; to see; to know.'

'Yes.'

'Will you think of her?'

'Yes.'

'As you think of me?'

Once more they kissed, an endless kiss that

336

threaded through time to a mountain lakeside far away. Her naked breasts pushed against the fabric of his jacket, his hardness pressing on her belly, the wetness of longing already seeping from her to welcome in his love.

'Gilles?'

He held her close now. Soon they would be enjoined. Their bodies vibrated in the quickening night. Only their breathing. But then, within the deepening shadows of the silent room, the soft muted sound, hardly a sound at all, of a petal prematurely dropping from a lily. Amanda had only bought them yesterday. Her heart leapt; and instantly she knew already what he would say.

'It is the same.'

Gilles was still asleep. It was light so early now, and even the little light that squeezed through the narrow gap above the heavy drapes was sufficient to awaken Amanda. She still had on her stockings and her fingertips absently slid across a lace top and onto the silky skin above. It was she knew what men liked and she smiled to herself: such simple suggestible creatures! She lay for a long time looking at her sleeping lover, needing a pee but not wanting to disturb him. Most days she rose early with the dawn, but today envied Gilles' peaceful slumber, having tried already and failed to doze off again herself.

She quietly arose and donned her robe.

Downstairs, kettle on, she made her way to the annexe and scooped up their clothes. She placed them in a small pile on the stairs and made coffee. The cigarettes were on the dining room table and she lit one, returning to the annexe with her drink.

Seated on the couch where she'd so often sat talking to Gwyneth, she watched the smoke from her cigarette curling lazily upward. Outside the dawn chorus was in full swing and the low rays of sunshine were slanting in illuminating the lillies on the coffee table to her right. She reached forward to flick her ash in the ashtray perched on the corner, and there was the fallen petal a little way beyond. She stretched to pick it up and touched it to her lips.

It was right here that he'd taken her from behind on the floor, her elbows braced on the cushion where she now sat. A tumultuous fuck. It hurt. He cried out when he came, an anguished exiting from himself, emptying into her over and over. She shivered at the recollection and even now began to be once more aroused, suddenly aware of the ripe cloying stickiness between her legs, remembering the explosiveness of her own kaleidoscopic orgasm as he pounded her.

'It is the same,' he'd said. She remembered how in Geneva at breakfast on a sunny pavement terrace he'd told her that she made love 'just like her.'

'Same same but different,' Thai people would say. They understood. How perfectly they put it! Dear Gwyneth. She kissed the petal and carefully placed it back where it had fallen, breathed a tremulous 'thank you,' and made her way quickly to the stairs.

Upstairs all was quiet. She padded silently across the landing and peered through the partly open bedroom door. Gilles slept on. He'd roiled the duvet so that only a corner covered him. He lay on his back and she crept to the bed and carefully lifted it back. His cock stood proudly erect, just the sight of it causing Amanda to catch her breath.

She carefully eased herself onto the bed, and gently gripped his shaft. Surely he would awaken now; but on he slept and with bated breath she tightened her grip. *Still* he slept. She trembled with longing, could *feel* her juices running, moistening her cunt to take him into her, to have him pushing up her deep into her darkness. She could no longer wait. Even as he blinked awake she was astride him, slotting his cock into her opening, dropping onto it like a stone down to the root. He so stretched her she gasped, rigid, trembling, teetering on the brink of pain and sublime delight. Eyes closed, hands braced on his chest she slowly rotated, grinding onto him, her sweet spot found, pressed, pushed against waves of pure joy surging through her.. Already she was coming, her body jolting into movement as if an electric current passed through, her hair tossed flailing wildly about possessed, as he looked on, passive, transfixed.

She lay in her lover's arms. Still no word had yet

passed between them. Amanda had lifted herself off him and brought him off with her hand. Gilles' turn now, his eyes fixed on her but somewhere else, immersed in the pleasure of Amanda's rythmically pumping hand. She had observed his face, distracted, panting, moaning aloud, and had turned at the last to watch in fascination as white spurts leapt from him into the air to splash hot then cold on her fist. Now she snuggled in, replete. The calm *after* the storm. Gilles could see the whorl of hair at her crown, the diminishing rise and fall of her head on his chest as gradually his own breathing slowed. Her hair was spread on him like contours on a map. His gaze turned upward to the featureless ceiling, seeking out any defect: a wisp of spider gossamer, a flake of paint; a tiny hairline crack ran all the way form the ceiling rose to the cornice interrupting the monotone magnolia.

'Amanda?'

She didn't stir.

'Amanda. We need to talk.'

But there was no response. She slept.

Chapter 27

They walked along to the church having decided to do their remembrance at noon. For some reason it seemed appropriate to set a time. They were in good time but it was some distance and the steady pace set on a hot sunny day soon saw Gilles' jacket slung over his shoulder, and the tie he'd insisted on wearing pulled loose. They were lost in their private thoughts, easy together but acutely aware of one another too. Their unexpected coming together had swept away their settled calm like a tsunami carrying away coastal sands exposing the rock beneath. It was a shock. 'With every action there is an equal and opposite reaction.' Einstein had it: they had recoiled. What was the other thinking?

Gilles had left Amanda to sleep. He'd breakfasted on coffee and Gitanes, and disappeared with his book, whilst Amanda had retired to the annexe to sit and meditate. They had collided with an energy and impact that had sent them back into themselves. What now?

Amanda could feel Gilles' reticence. She felt quiet also, but agitated too. For the first time in a long while the surface water of her calm and settled life was ruffled. Was it a mistake? What *was* he thinking?

At the graveside their reflections were private. The sun beat down; no sound. A lone chaffinch had appeared for a second on a neighbouring gravestone. It eyed them: mad dogs and Englishmen, before fluttering away. Amanda had eventually left Gilles there and wandered into the church. It was cool and a relief to be out of the glare of the sun, the comforting church smell of candles and incense somehow reassuring. Gwyneth had no time for religion or an after-life, and Amanda neither, but the thread of continuity through the generations offered by the old country church was, if not 'meaning', a connection which transcended time.

At last she shivered, roused from her reverie and arose to leave. Surely Gilles must have finished by now. Her eyes took time to adjust to the brightness and she made her way carefully to the graveyard. He was nowhere to be seen. She called his name, but no response, just the cheeping of a blue tit darting in and out of the hedgerow. Making her way to the gate Amanda shaded her eyes and peered along the road, where she made him out sauntering along, already some distance away. She muttered to herself annoyed.

He did'n't respond to her shout, but turned when she called out again, louder this time, and began to walk back as she set off to meet him.

'I thought you had gone home.'

'*Of course* not. I was in the church.'

'Oh. I didn't think . . . I thought it would be locked.'

They walked along. The silence weighed more than before. In Geneva they had linked arms, held hands, promenaded like lovers do, but now they were separate. Amanda turned to speak but glimpsing him apparently deep in thought she thought better of it.

Back at the house Amanda went to put the kettle on. She still felt irked, more so for not quite knowing why. 'Would you like some tea? I think I may go for a hack. You haven't kissed me today.'

It had just come out; an accusation; petulant and spoilt she immediately knew, but did not know how she could take it back despite the sharp sting of regret even as the words were out.

Gilles lent in the doorway as was his habit, taken aback, unsure at first how to respond. Amanda still had the kettle in her hand, the other resting on the tap.

'Well. I don't know Amanda. I thought . . .'

'You thought that you will soon be returning to Paris so what's the point?' It was more clipped than she'd intended, but despite herself could not stop and pressed on as she continued to fill the kettle and get the tea things out, throwing her words over her shoulder. She knew she was in a hole and yet as so often happens was digging still for all she was worth. 'You thought it might *complicate* things, after what we said? It won't Gilles. I'm happy for you to fuck me whilst you're here . . . I wanted you to. I still want you to. And when you go . . . everything is alright. We are not children. You have your life and I have mine. We are not *in love*!'

She turned and lent with her back against the side. More regret; an endless flood of it, rueing her outspoken little speech. He did not move; speak. She sighed, a sad smile, arms folded around her tummy, head tilted to one side, inquisitive, placatory, wanting so much now to make amends. 'Oh Gilles. Gilles it's alright!'

The kettle was boiling and clicked off. Gilles was still, his eyes downcast. He still had his jacket hooked over his shoulder. She wanted to go to him, for him to come to her and take her in his arms. Why had she spoken so?!

At last he seemed to awaken and met Amanda's eyes; a forced smile.

'D'accord. C'est bien. I'll er . . . I need to . . . excuse me.'

He was gone, and Amanda's head slumped forward, her arms hugging herself, but little enough comfort to be had.

Achilles headstrong as ever was pulling every which way, challenging Amanda to subdue him if she could. With Seamus away she had decided to give him a run out 'to be fair,' she told herself, but actually that was not quite how it was, and she rode her wayward mount hard. She'd galloped him along the flat, but now he pulled straight toward the high hedge she had jumped Hector over when out with

Sophie that first time, and she eased off the rein and gave him his head. She hadn't tackled it since that day. Achilles was not quite the jumper Hector was, and Amanda was less familiar with him, but she felt his power beneath her, snorting as he accelerated toward the obstacle.

She was pulling hard on the rein to stop him from veering to the right, shouting encouragement to him. He straightened up but was going too fast and she tried to rein him back, losing the battle as the gelding lengthened his stride, eyes rolling mechante. There was less than three hundred meters now and Amanda's mind raced. It was a mistake. Even on Hector she would not normally have tackled this jump out riding alone. But she couldn't hold him and knowing she could not take the jump pulling back so hard she surrendered, dropping her hands to his neck where she pushed in time with his stride: '*Come on boy. Come on. Come on*!'

The approach was straight, and avoided the highest part of the hedge. Amanda gauged the distance as to whether the stride was right. It wasn't. The last one would be too near, he would refuse and turn sideways into the hedge; she would be thrown; it was too late.

Sebastian's final seconds might well have been like this, riding impatiently as she was, at odds with himself and plagued by elusive doubts. She closed her eyes; too late, braced for the impact. But suddenly the thunder of hooves on turf had gone;

345

peace; silence; and she opened her eyes to find she was in flight. At the last moment Achilles like a dancer had checked infinitesimally, a half-step and he was set, sailing into the sun, his fetlocks brushing the topmost fronds of white flowering May. Amanda was crying out 'YES!YES!YES!' as time slowed and an endless age passed before the jolt of Achilles' hooves re-connecting with the earth. She reined him in and now he slowed, blowing hard, submissive having had his way. Oh she of little faith.

Back in the stable-yard Amanda turned Achilles out to rejoin Hector in the paddock, watched as they cantered toward each other, snorted, skittered, and headed off in opposite directions like magnets reversing their poles. She stowed the saddle and hung up the bridle

In the stable doorway she paused and leaned. The yard was quiet without Seamus tootling about. What now? She wandered back into the stable and sat on the bale of hay where she'd sat with Sophie. A sparrow flew in, perched momentarily on the half-door to Hector's stall, eyed Amanda quizzically and fluttered off out again.

What now? She was calm. With Achille's impulsive charge and incredible leap, all of Amanda's preconceptions had been disturbed, like a snowstorm in a shaken glass bauble, settling again as as her mistrusted steed had re-connected with the earth, but the landscape now subtly different to before. Her puny efforts to change the course of the galloping horse had been to no avail. She recalled the moment of surrender, the falling away of her fear as her resistance had turned to encouragement, joining with the horse in his charge. He knew what to do, a small adjustment, a valiant leap, banishing doubt and sailing into the infinite.

She arose and with a purposeful stride headed for the house. Entering through the kitchen door all was quiet. She'd given Mrs Fellows the day off, and Gilles was nowhere to be seen. She crossed to the living room. The Miles Davies cd case was still out. The dining room, table still uncleared, 'returning to the scene.' On to the annexe where she stood distracted. The silence was oppressive. She felt a rising sense of dread and ran to the stairs.

Her bedroom door was open and instantly she knew before entering what she would find. The bed was neatly made and the note she found propped up on the dressing table shook in her hand as she read:

Amanda, ma cheri,

I must go. It's for the best. I am not what you think, and you, you are beyond me. I know that now.

So, it's better that we part. I'm sorry.

Gilles

A cry pierced the stillness of the house, startling

347

her. Her voice, but no longer hers, no longer the woman in control and at one with the world. Her limbs moved involuntarily, racing her down the stairs to tear around the kitchen . . . bag . . . car keys . . .

The tiny station was deserted. It was that time of day. The glare of the sun separated light and shade in unforgiving contrast, confusing the eye which attempted to adjust to both and managed neither. Amanda's heart sank. Her mind ran on. Was this the right platform? She knew it was, but ran to look along the other anyway. Empty. She stopped, and her agitation gave way to a slow icy desolation that crept from her tummy spreading upwards and down, a gentle tide of despair within which whispered a small chiding voice: 'Too late. Too late.'

She reached out to steady herself against a steel support. A goods train roared through shattering the dreadful stillness which settled then more dreadful than before. Amanda sat, casting about her. She closed her eyes, trying to retreat into the dark; numb. At last she arose to retrace her steps.

Her eyes had adjusted, and it was only then on returning to the northbound platform, that she perceived a small hunched figure sat in the shade at the far end next to a coffee machine, insinuated into the rectangular silhouette. As she approached Gilles looked up.

'Gilles.' Her voice was unsteady and she said no

more as she covered the last few meters and sat by him. He contrived a strange apologetic smile, his eyes red and dark complexion pale. But now he looked once more at the ground at his feet, forearms resting on his knees as before, fixing a spot of paint with his empty gaze.

'Gilles. Gilles please don't go? I need you. I . . . I love you, am *in love* with you. I always have been, since Geneva. All this time. I've been such a fool!'

Amanda's voice broke and trailed off. Her hands moved uncertainly toward him, stopped, gripped together now, knuckles white as if she might wring out her pain.

Dark spots were appearing on the concrete between Gilles' feet, and when he looked up tears were streaming unchecked down his cheeks.

'You appear to have stepped out of a photo.' He said, weakly.

'Oh.' she replied remembering her attire and to what he referred, 'You think I'm . . .'

'Non.' He interrupted, his hand so quickly rising to her mouth to shush her.

'Non. I do not think you are her. I never thought you were . . . her. It was my fear. It is I who am the fool. It was my protection.'

Amanda wept. She took his hands and lowering her head washed them with her tears, sobbing silently, until he gently raised up her chin.

'You see Amanda, when I was in Paris it was like this, always like this: I thought of you every day.

My life was empty. J'ai ete desole!'

She was confused; processing the words, trying to locate them for she knew them already. Where? When? And then she knew. It was here, two days before, when Gilles had alighted from the train. He had told her he loved her then, and she had not heard. But it was not too late.

Chapter 28

It had been a miserable summer, too much rain, too many dull grey days, and all the while very little relief from a cool blustery breeze which had ruined the lupins and delphiniums, and in the course of one afternoon completely flattened the hollyhocks. So the early autumn sunshine when it came was a treasure to be exploited to the full.

They'd breakfasted in the garden. Gilles and Amanda remained outdoors, reading, whilst Sophie rode out with Seamus. She was down for yet another short visit. Her visits had become more frequent since her retirement, and Amanda and Gilles looked forward to and encouraged them.

'Tea anyone?' Mrs Fellows had cleared away, washed up and prepared lunch, and was evidently looking for something else to do, unable as Amanda had found over the years, to do nothing.

'That would be lovely, just so long as you join us and have a break!' It was their usual script, Amanda encouraging Mrs Fellows to relax, and Mrs Fellows supplying the usual reply.

'Nonsense Amanda I've got far too much to do. And in any case sitting in the sun doesn't really agree with me. You two enjoy it. I think I'll pop out to do some shopping.'

Tea supplied and Mrs Fellows duly departed, Amanda at last put down her book and looked across at Gilles recumbent on a sun lounger, still engrossed in his.

'Be a darling Gilles and move the parasol? I'm catching the sun full now and have no cream on.'

Gilles smiled and did as he was asked, leaning down then to kiss her. 'Is that OK?'

'Oui mon petit choux. Parfait!'

He opened his book and found his place, but for the moment held it flat against his chest. 'Did you speak to Melanie?'

'Yes. She thinks it's going to win. Well you know that. Anyway she says it doesn't matter as it'll romp into the Booker short-list, which in her humble yet always mercenary opinion is worth far more euros! She doesn't really approve of the Orange; thinks it's patronising to women.'

'Pff! Everyone now is looking for something to be offended about. But I agree about the Booker.'

Amanda's novel had been published in the spring. It was the second part of a trilogy, following on from the huge success of the first part, Death Dance, published two years before. This one, Phoenix, had received massive critical acclaim already. Amanda had resisted Melanie's best efforts to encourage her to participate in marketing PR, and already was making good progress with the final part of the trilogy, yet to receive a title. It was of this that she now spoke.

352

'I really should be getting on with it instead of sitting out here. But it's so nice to have a bit of sun. What a miserable summer it's been.'

'Bien sur. But you know it's good to take a break, as you say to Mrs Fellows *always*! You are as bad as she is.'

A cloud had slid across the sun and the abrupt change in temperature was noticeable. Amanda gazed lazily at it and saw that it was just a small cloud and would soon be gone, as indeed it was, the sun once again radiant. But it was not to last. Another much larger cloud soon took it's place, and there were billowing banks of reinforcements building up close by. Sophie appeared just as Amanda was making up her mind to move.

'Ah, good timing, I was just thinking it's time to move inside. Good ride?'

'Lovely. But Hector shed a shoe along the lane on the way back. Seamus is away to ring the farrier. He said they probably both need to be done now anyway. Cold isn't it when the sun goes in?'

Gilles was already rising and Sophie grinned as he moaned about the 'fucking British weather,' handing his book to Amanda and taking his place as always behind her.

'I'll bring the lounger Gilles. I think it might rain.' Sophie didn't wait for a reply already beginning to fold it up. Gilles had set off wheeling Amanda toward the house, replying only to labour his complaint.

'Of course. It is going to rain. *Of course*!'

They entered via the ramp into the annexe the breeze already strengthening and a few large drops of rain were tapping on the laurel leaves.

Back in the house Sophie headed off to shower whilst Gilles assisted Amanda with the stair-lift, and to walk the short distance into their bedroom where she sat down at her desk. There were still a couple of hours till lunch, and she needed to get on.

Gilles lay on the bed and tried to find his page, Amanda half turned in her chair, looking at him.

'It's alright for some!'

'D'accord! It is the price of fame cheri, and of course the fortune that accompanies it!' He was referring to the celebrity and not insignificant earnings from Amanda's literary success, as well as glorying ruefully in his own lack of it. Gille's philosophical treatise on not dissimilar themes of living and dying had indeed been well received by the academic community, but it was a very low key 'success,' never going to compare with the fanfare and bulging coffers from the blockbuster novel.

She turned and opened her laptop. Outside the wind had risen and was gusting, the rain heavy forming tiny rivulets running down the panes. How suddenly the weather had changed. She didn't feel in the mood.

'Good job Sophie got her ride in early.'

'Yes.'

'I miss it. It's one of the things I miss most.

Gwyneth was the same. Except she told me she carried on well beyond when she should have stopped.'

Gilles put down the book:

'It's dangerous. You can easily fall off even if you are OK. What about Sebastian?'

Amanda still gazed out the window. She sighed.

'I know.'

All was quiet. Just the sound of rain sweeping against the window. Gilles marked his page and sat up. He knew there was more to come.

'Do you want to come here?'

'Yes.'

He helped Amanda to stand and walked her to the bed where she was able to sit and with an effort swing her legs up, whilst he stood by ready to assist. He lay next to her and gathered her up in his arms, kissing the top of her head when she was snuggled in.

'What's the matter?' He whispered.

'Oh, I don't know. Nothing really. I may not finish it. You know that? I'd *like* to finish it, but there may not be time.'

Gilles was quiet and gave her a squeeze. They both knew the facts. It was six months since Amanda had been diagnosed as suffering from motor neurone disease. Her days were numbered. A year? Two? Much less perhaps. The decline had been steady, but could accelerate quickly, and no remission; no going the other way. Amanda was not afraid. Indeed she had greeted the news with interest, as if it completed a hitherto incomplete picture, a synchronicity which made everything else make sense.

She had prevailed upon Gilles to promise to face it without avoidance or fear. He had drawn strength from hers, and was not going to avoid the realities they faced, whilst the fear in his own heart would be a matter for him.

'I don't want to leave it till it's too late. Maybe we should go before Christmas, to Switzerland, just to be safe? I can write there just the same. Perhaps you could ski?'

'Yes, perhaps. Comme tu veut. Did you speak to Sophie?'

'Yes. She wants to be with us . . . at the end.'

Gilles nodded his head, processing this new piece of information.

'OK. Good. C'est bon.'

They were quiet for a little while. Only the rain and the intermittent ping of e-mails appearing on Amanda's computer. At last she drew back a little and tilted up her head to look at him. She had long divined his struggle: the certainty that he would lose her, perhaps within months and certainly not years was painful, and his efforts to disguise his inner dread could not be hid from her. Her dear Gilles, whose path had led him unerringly to her and hers to him. She would be gone, the easier thing, her consciousness dispersed in the ether. He would be alone. She reached up and kissed him.

'Are you alright?'

'Of course; bien sur.'

'Sure?'

He smiled and she did too, making his fear dissolve for now at least, lifted by the warmth of their love; her certainty and courage buoyed him up like a lifejacket in the slow running sea of Amanda's waning life. He kissed her, lingering, tasting each other, the smiles lighting up again as their lips parted, eyes alive with mischief and with love.

'*Are. You. Sure*?' Amanda repeated once more, beaming happily now and jolting him playfully to emphasise each word.

'Yes, Amanda. I am sure.' He shrugged. 'It is our destiny.'

Printed in Great Britain
by Amazon

59857177R00215